LIZ ALLISON &
WENDY ETHERINGTON

"*No Holding Back* is a wonderful introduction to the racing
world and an even better romantic read."
—*Fresh Fiction*

"This book offers up a more detailed view of the racing world
than your usual offering about NASCAR. Fans are sure to love it
and newbies, like me, will find it fun and informative
with a terrific romance."
—Jeri Neal, *The Romance Readers Connection*

"It is a tribute to Liz Allison and Wendy Etherington
that despite not being a fan of NASCAR, I became quite
enthralled with this story. This goes to show that anyone
can read this book and love it. But NASCAR fans will
especially love the storyline and the characters."
—Heather Eileen, *Romance Junkies*

"The writing team of Liz Allison and Wendy Etherington has
produced an excellent novel in *No Holding Back.* Between the
roar of engines and the cheering crowd, two people discover
that nothing should stand in the way when love is the prize."
—*A Romance Review*

LIZ ALLISON &
WENDY ETHERINGTON
Risking Her Heart

HQN™

ISBN-13: 978-0-373-77319-0
ISBN-10: 0-373-77319-6

RISKING HER HEART

Dear Reader,

Are you ready for another hot lap with the Garrisons?

Even though it's been several months since you last spent time with our racing family, don't worry, you haven't missed a thing. *Risking Her Heart* picks up right where *No Holding Back* left off. If you're new to our fast-paced world, you'll get up to speed quickly.

So we come to the story of rich, gorgeous playboy Parker Huntington and practical, responsible Rachel Garrison. We liked exploring the idea of two people who seem to be complete opposites on the surface, but deep down are very much alike. Both are the leaders of their family. Both have a tendency to take on too much responsibility. And both fiercely guard their hearts.

It took quite a lot to get them to open up to each other, but we think you'll agree that the struggle was worth the love they found.

And to everyone who's e-mailed about the conclusion to our trilogy...yes, big brother Bryan will be the next to make that journey to happily-ever-after. (Well, if we can drag him away from his brooding, that is.)

We can be reached at www.lizallison.com or www.wendyetherington.com or P.O. Box 3016, Irmo, SC 29063.

Happy reading and racing!

Liz and Wendy

To Honey and Cody, our faithful,
four-legged writing companions.

Risking Her Heart

CHAPTER ONE

PARKER HUNTINGTON snagged two glasses of champagne from a passing waiter as he headed toward the stunning brunette dressed in a figure-hugging column of gold sparkles and satin.

She'd scooped up her long, dark hair into a twist at the back of her head, leaving her neck bare but for a few silky-looking tendrils brushing her shoulders. Her lips were pink and glossy; her skin glowed. She looked happy and relaxed, more than he'd ever seen her.

And tonight she'd belong to him.

His patience had come to an end—not that he'd ever had all that much to begin with. He was finished with letting her use her family or her work as excuses to dismiss or avoid him. He was tired of exchanging hot glances and having veiled conversations about the chemistry between them.

They were attracted to each other, and it was long past time to do something about it.

Weaving his way through the throngs of people, he told himself that surely, in such a public forum, she wouldn't outright ignore him.

Be cool, man. You seduce women as easily as you breathe. Why should this one be any different?

"Why indeed?" he whispered to himself as his heart went into a full gallop and Rachel Garrison turned toward him.

The bright smile on her face faded, became tight. Her light blue eyes frosted briefly, then cleared of any expression. She was trying so hard to convince him that he was a casual, sometimes annoying business acquaintance.

Or was she trying harder to convince herself?

Determined not to let her familiar reaction dissuade him, he handed her the glass of bubbly and smiled. "Good evening, Rachel." Anticipating a sarcastic comment, he added, "You look lovely."

She sipped from her glass and glanced around. "Thank you."

"I hear we're planning a wedding," he said, his gaze sliding to Cade and Isabel, who were standing a few feet away, wrapped in each other, seeming oblivious to the crowds of people around them and the fact that he was about to accept second place in the NASCAR Nationwide Series championship.

"Yeah. I hope he lets go of her long enough to give his speech."

Was he a masochist for so enjoying her dust-dry comebacks?

Staring at her profile and imagining sliding his finger down her satiny cheek, he shook his head. No, pleasure was the act that frequently came to mind around Rachel. "Well, aren't we bitter in the face of deep and abiding love."

"I'm not—" She sighed, then shook her head. "I'm thrilled for them. I've never seen Cade this happy. I'm just—"

"Cranky?"

She glanced at him, amusement flickering in her eyes. She was a smart woman, so she must appreciate intelligence in other people. Why hadn't she yet been wowed by his brain?

"I'm not cranky," she said. "Three-year-olds are cranky."

"Of course. Maybe you're just tired."

"No."

"Annoyed?" He grinned. "At me perhaps for anticipating your deep-seated need for witty conversation and refreshment, then generously providing both?"

Her smile broadened, then she shook her head. "Why do you always talk like you're trying to impress your 1930s Harvard economics professor?"

He toasted her with his glass. "Just one of those aggravating habits you could learn to love if you weren't always running the other direction every time you saw me."

She snorted in disbelief. "I don't run from you."

"I beg to differ, but I won't argue the point. You looked happy earlier."

"I *was* happy."

"Before you saw me."

She said nothing.

Ouch. "What is it about me that gets your back up so effortlessly?"

She narrowed her eyes. "Your fancy words and highbrow degree don't impress people. It pushes them away."

"And I was about to flash my mini diploma—the one I had laminated by the thousands to pass out as business cards." He raised his eyebrows. "Really, Rachel. That's the best you can do? You don't like me because of where I went to school?"

"Fine. If you really want to know. I think you're too arrogant, self-important, egotis—"

"Yes, I'm familiar with the meaning of arrogant." Frankly, he considered himself confident and very self-aware, not arrogant. Certainly not egotistical.

"You just might want to tone it down," she said. "Relax the proper manners a little." Her face flushed. "They make fun of you. The guys in the shop."

"Yes, I know."

"Like you're a modern-day Beau Brummell. Well, actually, I provided the Brummell part. They just know you don't fit in."

He nodded in acknowledgment. He'd always gotten along much better with women. They all wanted him for one thing or another. Except one.

He studied Rachel. Well, perhaps two. Though he was certain he could adjust her thinking, given time.

As for a camaraderie with guys—at least guys his own age—he struggled. He'd often been accused of being born out of his time, and the Brummell accusation was reasonably accurate. He *did* have an excellent fashion sense.

"My grandmother was a stickler for diction," he said. And it was a defense mechanism, a way of trying to make himself seem clever and sophisticated enough to belong to his family. "It's a habit I can't seem to break. Maybe I could let the guys wow me with their knowledge of engines and aerodynamics. My economics professor never got around to that particular discussion."

A genuine smile quivered on her lips. "As long as you let them do that while you buy them a beer."

He winced. "I prefer wine."

"Of course you do." She looked heavenward—for guidance or maybe patience, he wasn't sure. "As long as we're clearing the air, you might as well know that you, ah...*get my back up*—" She angled her head. "Like a cat, I guess?"

"There is a resemblance around the eyes..."

"Yeah? Then you might want to make sure you keep your distance, so you don't get scratched."

Fascinated by the heat in her eyes and anticipating the moment he turned it to desire, he leaned closer. "I'll keep that in mind."

"You annoy me because you nearly ruined my brother's career."

"I did that all by myself, did I? Wow, I must be pretty powerful."

"Don't be cute. You had him arrested."

"I believe the police did that."

"Because you pressed them to."

"My father—" He stopped when her scowl deepened and lines appeared on her forehead. He wanted to rub them away. He wanted her to smile at him again.

Dream on.

"I was going to say my father encouraged the police, but in your eyes we're one and the same, and since I did nothing to stop him, I'll set aside that defense. I've taken responsibility for my mistakes. Cade and I have made our peace. I could also point out that your brother hit me, not the other way around."

"You drove him to it—criticizing his driving, interfering with the team."

And making the mistake of sharing my attraction to you.

A variety of events had led to the demise of his and Cade's business partnership. But after a year and a half apart, they'd managed to work through their issues, sign a new deal for Cade to drive the Huntington Hotels car for the NASCAR Sprint Cup Series next year and somehow become friends along the way. Cade probably still wouldn't be wild about Parker pursuing his sister, but he hoped they could overcome that complication.

Since that's precisely what he intended to do.

"Perhaps I did," he said to Rachel. "But he's accepted my apology. Why can't you?"

"I don't—"

"How much longer do we have to wear these dang things?" Sam Benefield, Cade's crew chief, asked as he approached, tugging on his tie.

"It's once a year," the woman next to him, presumably his wife, said.

The woman on the other side of Sam looked as if she might be in her early twenties. His daughter? She rolled back her shoulders, obviously to better show off her cleavage, and gave Parker a dazzling smile.

"I'm Parker Huntington," he said, shaking each woman's hand in turn.

Sam gruffly apologized for not initiating the introductions, and Parker learned the women were indeed Sam's wife and daughter.

"We're all so excited about next year," his wife said. "With you being part of the team, we may even get Emily to a few races." She cast a teasing look at her daughter. "She's in school at UNC—hotel and restaurant management."

As Emily tossed back her hair, Parker smiled at her, though it was the casual one he reserved for daughters of business associates.

She was a lovely woman, with wheat-blond hair and soft brown eyes, and an obviously inviting smile. But while he certainly enjoyed all kinds of women, he had standards. And he drew a sharp, age-appropriate boundary line between himself and college students.

He reached into his jacket pocket for a business

card. "When you graduate, call my office. I'll be glad to set up some interviews for you."

"That would be wonderful," Emily said in a fake-sounding, throaty voice. "Thanks." She glanced at the card. "You live in New York?"

"I actually have two offices—one in New York and one in Charlotte."

"Charlotte?" Rachel asked, her eyes widening. "Since when?"

"Since this week. I have to keep an eye on my race team, don't I?"

She visibly relaxed her face—probably to keep from rolling her eyes at the prospect of having him in town. "It's not your team, and we're doing just fine. Thanks."

Was it such a surprise he was crazy about her?

"They're opening the doors to the ballroom," Sam noted as people moved around them and toward the main doors. He tugged on his wife's arm. "Let's get this over with."

Rachel patted Sam's shoulder. "At least you don't have to give a speech."

"Though you might want to prepare one for when we win the championship," Parker added, following them.

"I'm fine with second," Sam said.

Rachel laughed. "Yeah, right."

Once they were in the ballroom, they were separated, since Rachel and her family were sitting near the front, while Parker, who hadn't sponsored a race team for the past year, had to settle for a seat in the back.

The program rolled along slowly. Several times, Parker found himself running through his mental to-do list and his scheduled meetings for the following week. After Cade gave his speech and left the stage, Parker headed to the suite he and the executives at Go! Energy Drink had rented for the banquet weekend. Go! had been Cade's sponsor for the past year, and they'd agreed to come on board as an associate sponsor for next year's team.

With the media dispersed and the TV cameras turned off, the team members could relax and really let go in private. Parker was counting on the partying mood to affect Rachel, give him the opportunity to charm her, then to discreetly lead her to his suite and seduce her.

Laying out that plan so succinctly sounded slightly cold-blooded, he supposed, but then he didn't plan to be anything less than honest about his intentions. They would give in to their chemistry, have a weekend of fun, then move on. He wouldn't complicate her life. He didn't get *involved*. And from what Cade's fiancée, Isabel, had told him, Rachel didn't either. Men usually tried to use her for her business or racing connections.

She could certainly trust him in that area.

Plus, he didn't expect undying love or devotion and doubted Rachel did either. They were both busy people with very full lives of traveling and business.

Business which had become increasingly difficult when he found himself constantly staring across the table at Rachel's lips and thinking about kissing them rather than what they were saying.

Yes, it was best to get this attraction out of their systems.

With a glass of wine in his hand, he leaned in the balcony doorway and waited for her.

He doubted he'd have to linger for long. After hours of smiling politely, responding to media interviews and listening to endless streams of thanks and congratulations, everybody was usually ready for a drink or two.

She walked in with her father and older brother, Bryan, both former drivers, champions and now integral parts of Garrison Racing. Parker respected both men for their business sense, driving skills and leadership to their teams. Despite the occasional bouts of tension, the Garrisons were a close-knit family. They teased, supported and bickered with equal passion. When he'd first met them four years ago, a deep-seated need he hadn't been aware of to that point blossomed.

He'd found himself longing for their casual hugs and fierce dedication, not just to the racing business but to each other. He wanted their ease with their legacy in the industry. Their bond with their colleagues.

The formality and properness of his own family had seemed oddly out of place ever since.

After a moment or two of conversation, the Garrisons separated, with the guys heading to the bar and Rachel walking directly toward him.

He'd barely started to smile when she breezed by him.

"I need some air," she said.

Never one to miss taking advantage of a golden opportunity, he followed her. He said nothing as she wrapped her hands around the balcony railing and drew several deep breaths. He watched her, admiring her profile, the subtle curves of her body, grateful for the slight breeze that carried the scent of her sensual, Oriental-spiced perfume.

Even for December in central Florida it was warm. If they'd been standing on the balcony of his apartment in Manhattan, he'd have been able to offer her his tuxedo coat or wrap her in his arms for warmth.

Still, the weather had its advantages. He was able to notice the faint sheen of gold sparkles on her bare shoulders. The freckles on her nose she'd probably gotten during the boat trip around the resort yesterday.

She leaned her head back and stared up at the starstrewn sky. She was obviously troubled, and the realization put a kink in his seduction plan.

After several minutes, she turned toward him. "Did you stay for the whole endless thing?"

"I left after Cade's speech. I had to make sure the suite was ready."

"Lucky you. Half the time you can't get two

meaningful words out of a driver, crew chief or owner. I guess they save it all up for tonight." She rolled her neck, as if trying to loosen the tension.

He fought the urge to use his fingers to knead away her troubles.

"Is that some fancy wine?" she asked, her gaze moving to his glass.

"It's your standard-issue hotel Chardonnay."

"Are you being condescending because this isn't *your* hotel?"

"Naturally. Would you like some?"

"Let me taste yours first."

He handed her the glass. The idea of her lips pressing so close to where his had once been made his heart thump hard in response. Perhaps he could solve her troubles with a little TLC.

"It's pretty good," she said.

"It's yours."

"Thanks." She took a long drink.

"I can get you a bottle of whiskey if you think that would be quicker."

"Quicker?"

"To dull the pain of whatever's hurting you."

Her gaze shot to his. "I'm not in pain."

No longer able to resist the urge to touch her, he slid the back of his hand across her cheek. "Aren't you?"

She stared at him for three pulse-pounding moments, her electric-blue eyes warming, then, before he could pull her closer, she stepped back. "I'm fine."

He dropped his hand, curling it into a fist at his side briefly. He might be out of patience, but he wasn't out of moves. "If you say so," he said smoothly.

"I just need a break from racing. It's been a long season. Plus, Dad's gone crazy being a bachelor, and Mom was so obsessive and high-strung at Thanksgiving, we probably all drank more than we ate. We're all ready to bolt to Hawaii, which is where Cade suggested we spend the holidays."

Parker had heard about Barbara Garrison's Thanksgiving gala from Cade, of course, but Rachel had never shared personal details or feelings with him before.

Did he want *her to share personal details and feelings? Wouldn't that fall into the category of* involved?

"I told Cade all of you are welcome at my hotel on Maui." Where, amazingly, he'd be spending the holidays himself. He shook aside his concerns about getting in too deep with a relationship and considered that he and Rachel could extend their weekend of chemistry.

"Mom'll never go for it," she said. "She's in pain and trying to pull us close around her to heal herself. We can't leave her."

Spending a lot of time with the Garrisons over the last six months, he'd learned that Rachel tended to take on her family's burden. In that, they were alike. And the source of her troubled expression became obvious.

"You think she still loves him?" he asked, glancing into the room, where Mitch Garrison was no doubt flirting with some much younger woman.

She bit her lip. "Yeah."

"Does he love her?"

"I have no idea. He's moved out to the condo at the track and redecorated it like an Elvis-style bachelor pad. It's weird. Nobody has any idea if he's actually enjoying dating a bunch of girls younger than his kids, or if he's just trying to prove a point to Mom."

"She gave him an ultimatum, and he called her bluff. Now neither of them know how to go back."

Her gaze slid to his, obviously surprised he understood. "I think so." Still watching him, she sipped her wine. "I've been trying to get Bryan and Cade to understand that for more than two years." She paused. "It's possible, Parker Huntington, that I've misjudged you."

He tried to look shocked. "You think?"

"It's also possible the guys at the shop make fun of you because they're jealous of your success with women."

"My success?"

"Sam's daughter nearly tripped over her tongue, panting at you."

"She's hoping to start a career in my industry."

"She's hoping to tear off the buttons on your shirt. With her teeth."

"And I figured her interest was all business."

"You absolutely did not. Look at you." She toasted him with her glass. "You're smart, rich, gorgeous…"

He grinned when her face turned red. "You think I'm gorgeous?"

She rolled her eyes. "Oh, please. You know you are."

"But I annoy you."

"You're not my type. That doesn't mean I can't understand your appeal."

"Just not to you."

The friendliness in her eyes faded. "No, not to me."

"Because I'm arrogant, self-important, egotistical and nearly ruined your brother's career."

She looked slightly embarrassed. Or maybe the flush in her cheeks was from the wine. "That was rude of me. You didn't ruin his career, and he had a hand in his own troubles."

"I didn't realize you were still angry with me," he said quietly. "I understood from Cade that you were the one who encouraged him to apologize for hitting me. You were the one who told us to set aside the past and move on."

"I'm not angry with you."

"You just want to be."

She lifted her eyebrows. "And why would I want to be?"

"So you don't have to admit how wildly attracted you are to me."

"There's that endearing arrogance I've been missing for the last two hours of boring speeches."

He raised his own eyebrows. "You're going to deny the sparks between us? You always seemed like a direct woman. I never considered that you did much pretending."

"I'm not pretending." She set aside her glass and turned, leaning against the railing and looking up at the star-strewn sky. "Thanks for listening to me babble about my family problems."

She was in denial *and* she was changing the subject. *How interesting.*

"I'm glad you felt comfortable sharing them with me," he said.

"I don't think I intended to. It just all jumped out, probably because Mom wasn't here tonight." Her voice lowered. "She always used to be here."

"My parents are divorced, too. I know how it feels."

She glanced back at him, a half smile on her face. "Yeah? I always figured your parents for the refined, blue-blooded, married-for-life-and-the-family-name types."

He fought a chill. "They're not."

"Maybe one day we can actually sit down over coffee and share our life stories."

He'd prefer champagne, moonlight and an intimate dinner. He leaned against the railing next to her and slid his fingers across the back of her hand. "We could go up to my suite. It's private, and I actually have good wine."

She angled her head. "Are you coming on to me?"

If she had to ask, clearly he wasn't doing something right. And for the life of him, he couldn't figure out what. What was it about *her*, this particular woman, that both intrigued and frustrated him? Why did she make his hands tingle and his stomach do backflips? He wanted to find out, or find a way to extinguish the fire he harbored for her. "Yes," he said simply, certain she'd appreciate his directness.

"We work together."

"Why should that matter?"

"Because I don't get involved with people I work with."

"Who said anything about involved? I was thinking we'd spend the weekend together, possibly the holidays."

"A casual affair? How romantic." She shook her head and stepped back. "Not interested."

"I don't see anything casual about this at all, and it *will* be romantic." He closed the distance she'd made and cupped her cheek. He bowed his head, so his lips were inches from hers. "Come on, all these hotel rooms, and you don't want to find out if we're… compatible?"

Her gaze lowered to his lips.

He didn't dare breathe. She was nearly his. Another moment or two, and he'd be kissing her, as he'd fantasized for what seemed like endless months.

She stepped back. "No, I really don't."

"You're just going to stand there and deny you're attracted to me?"

"Yes."

What's wrong with me? he thought but didn't dare say.

He was frankly baffled that she didn't want him. He'd seen the heat in her eyes, felt the brief tremble when he'd touched her. Why was she claiming she didn't feel that?

There were plenty of other women who wanted him. Why not her?

"I'd like us to be friends," she said.

Friends? He nearly choked. That's what women said to pitiful loser guys they really wanted nothing to do with.

"I *did* tell Cade we should forget the past and make a fresh start," she continued. "It's time I take my own advice."

He tamped down the humiliation rushing through him. "Okay."

She moved away from the railing and him, looking like a golden goddess he could admire but never actually touch. "I should probably mingle. See you after the holidays?"

His fancy words for once escaping him, he nodded. "Sure."

"It was sweet of you to flirt with me," she said from the doorway.

Sweet? If she kept trying to make him feel better about rejecting him, he'd wind up jumping from the balcony. "I wasn't being sweet."

"A few days ago, I wouldn't have thought so

either. Still, you were." She waved, then disappeared into the crowd.

Sweet. Friends. Hell. Fine.

He strode back inside. He had better things to do than chase Rachel Garrison.

He had a company to run. He'd waited in the wings for far too long while his father made bad personal and business decisions. Even though he'd accepted his appointment to CEO of the family business with grace, he'd burned with the question *What took you so long?*

He wasn't waiting on her to realize how great they could be together. His mother hadn't wanted him either, and hadn't he gotten along fine without her?

CHAPTER TWO

"MR. HUNTINGTON'S on the phone."

Standing at the copier, Rachel waved but didn't turn toward her new office manager. "Tell him I'm in an important meeting."

"But you're standing right here," Carmen Gonzalez said.

"I'm having an important meeting with the copy machine."

"But—"

"I'm *busy.*"

Carmen muttered something in Spanish that sounded distinctly derogatory before she picked up the phone and gushed all over Parker Huntington.

As the copier spit out its stacks of paper and Carmen concluded her call, Rachel turned, shaking her head at her newest employee. The one, she couldn't help but admit, that had been hired with Huntington's sponsorship money. "I'm getting an English/Spanish dictionary first thing tomorrow," she said when Carmen hung up the phone.

Completely unashamed, Carmen smiled. *"Sí, señorita."*

In her mid-sixties, happily married for forty-plus years, with three sons—a doctor, a lawyer and a priest—Carmen felt completely at ease with her secure place in the universe.

It was incredibly annoying.

"We need to get the promo kits for Atlanta assembled today," Rachel said.

"Sí."

"And verify the meet-and-greet schedule, plus the fan-party details, for Bristol."

"Sí."

"And no more pro-Huntington comments."

Her dark brown eyes flashed with defiance. "He's so handsome, Miss Rachel. He'd be perfect for you. You're a woman who's alone and single and des—"

"I am *not* desperate." She was in a slump, dating-wise, no doubt due to the fact that she didn't want to go out with anybody involved in racing and those were the only people she knew. "And I'd have to fight off every bikini model on the East Coast to get to Parker."

"If you said the word, he'd run to your side and devote himself to you completely and forever."

"Carmen, if Satan himself showed up at our front door, but he looked like George Clooney, you'd invite him in for sangria."

"If *any* man showed up at your door, we should open champagne."

Rachel waited three, hard heartbeats before responding. "I could fire you, you know."

Carmen shrugged. "Then who'd answer the phones?"

Rachel snatched her copies from the machine, then stomped into her office, flicking the door closed behind her. After Cade's recent move to the NASCAR Sprint Cup Series, she'd shifted from the reception desk to her own office. The ability to shut the door was a luxury she was still getting used to.

Each team within Garrison Racing Incorporated had its own set of offices, supported by and semi controlled by the main GRI center. Since Cade's team now had a premier sponsor and a second-place finish for last season, they'd made some management changes to their arm of the business.

Rachel was concentrating on the overall business plan as well as dealing with Cade's appearance schedule, while her brother's fiancée handled the PR and marketing aspects. Carmen had been hired to answer the phones and do general office work.

Not to give relationship advice.

But Carmen had also become the mother hen to their little group. She fussed over all of them, making sure they ate and got where they needed to go on time. She nagged Cade much more sweetly and effectively than Rachel herself did. She screened calls with grace and a firm hand. She learned faces, names and phone numbers with ease.

And she did know her sangria.

Because of Carmen's guidance, Rachel finally had time to breathe. To actually plan rather than just react. To think and contemplate the future.

Even if Parker was a slick New York business-man, who was completely out of her down-home, North Carolina mentality, he was a brilliant one.

Their marketing campaigns were stellar. The race team was rockin' on all eight cylinders. The fact that he and Cade had overcome the past and become good friends was a classic feel-good story for the media.

But a lot of times over the last three months, she'd stared into space and thought about that night in Orlando, when Parker, breathtakingly gorgeous in his tuxedo, the breeze ruffling his black hair, his piercing green gaze focused intently on her face, had stood next to her on the hotel balcony and brushed the back of his hand over her cheek.

The warmth that rushed through her body each and every time she thought about that moment was aggravating and ridiculous, reminding her that she'd shamelessly lied about not being attracted to him.

Getting involved with a colleague was trouble. Not to mention Parker was a player like Cade. Well, Cade was actually a former player now.

Parker flirted with every female breathing. He didn't want to get to know her. He wasn't serious about a relationship. *I was thinking we'd spend the weekend together, possibly the holidays.*

Please.

She wasn't into meaningless hookups. She wanted a stable guy. One who wouldn't leave her after forty years of marriage for a series of women half his age the way her father had her mother.

And still that one touch, that moment of heat and interest in Parker's eyes, haunted her.

Her unwanted attraction to him had to fade.

Chemistry aside, she didn't date business associates. She kept her personal life, such as it was, away from racing. Every other part of her life involved her family and their racing business, so she was entitled to something for herself. After several bad relationships with members of other teams over the years, she'd decided to turn away from drivers, crew chiefs, owners, even the cute NASCAR official in Research and Development who'd sent her flowers for nearly half a season a couple of years ago.

At the time, Bryan's accident and the end of his racing career had recently cost him his marriage. Her parents' marriage had been falling apart, largely due to the intense racing schedule, and she didn't have the strength to pursue a relationship that seemed doomed at the start.

Because of these self-imposed rules, she'd severely limited her social prospects, since the only thing she did all day, talked about all day or focused on all day was racing. Which was why Carmen was bent on matchmaking her and Parker.

She flopped in her chair and stared at the ceiling.

While Parker was a great businessman and sponsor, he'd never lose that arrogant, bossy streak. And didn't he aggravate her like crazy with his ten-dollar words? Didn't his oozing sophistication make her feel like a complete hick? Didn't she have about as much chance as stock cars racing in the rain at keeping his attention?

After the last few months, she could say the answer to the last question was an unequivocal yes. Though he'd talked of chemistry and private suites back in December, after she'd turned him down, he'd walked away from her and every other woman in town had rushed into his arms.

She shook her head and swung around to her computer.

It was for the best. She wanted to get along with him, to trust him enough to help her forward the interests of Garrison Racing and propel her brother's career into the elite category of drivers in NASCAR. That was all happening on schedule.

Plus, they'd become sort-of friends. Since defusing the romantic tension, he'd loosened up, as she'd suggested he do. The last time she'd seen him, he was wearing worn jeans, had a close-cropped—and kinda sexy—goatee, had let his sleek hair grow chin length and shaggy and was sucking down beer with the boys.

Regardless of whether he was Harvard Boy or Scruffy Boy, having any sort of close relationship—even a temporary one—wasn't an option today any more than it had been back at the end of last season.

She pushed aside the issue of Parker and checked her e-mail. Mostly she had interview requests for Cade. They were only three races into the season, and he had finishes of third, second and sixth. They were officially the hottest team in racing.

She grinned as she set up two radio interviews for tomorrow afternoon. Reporters weren't questioning Cade's commitment or temperament, or wondering which sponsor he might take a swing at next. They wanted to talk about their success, their hopes to make the Chase for the NASCAR Sprint Cup, their championship prospects.

It was good to be back.

"Don't forget to call Mr. Huntington," Carmen said through the phone's intercom.

"Uh-huh," Rachel said absently. Couldn't she get the dang man out of her head for ten lousy minutes?

"Do you need me to dial the number?" Carmen asked.

Rachel glared at the phone. *"No."*

"Hey, Rach," Cade said as he opened her office door. "Am I clear tonight?"

"Yeah." What excellent timing her brother had. Being ridiculously in love had only brightened the mischief in blue eyes so like her own. His hair, a slightly darker shade of brown than hers, was curiously tousled, leading her to wonder just what kind of meeting he and Isabel had been involved in for the last two hours.

Yet another positive to gaining a sister-in-law.

Rachel didn't have to field calls from flirty women all day. Unlike Parker Huntington. *His* assistant was probably ready to jump off the nearest scoring tower.

"You've got two phone interviews for radio tomorrow," she said to Cade. "Then we head to Atlanta at five."

"Great." He glanced at his watch—a gift from Isabel and another one of her positive influences on him. "I'm heading out of here in a few minutes. I'm supposed to meet Parker for a beer at six."

She'd said nothing to her brother about the encounter with Parker on the hotel balcony. The moment had passed and mentioning it would only give momentum to the useless spurts of attraction she'd been feeling toward Parker ever since.

"Have fun," she said, turning back to her computer.

"You want to come?"

"No, thanks. I still have some work to do."

"You and Izzy both work too much."

"There's a lot of work to be done."

She heard him move toward her. "Come on. You need to get out. I know you don't like Parker, but we're going to Midtown Sundries. It'll be packed, probably with some great guys."

She glanced at him over her shoulder. "I like Parker fine, and I don't need you to set me up with any guy."

He winked at her. "That's not what I hear from Carmen."

"Carmen exaggerates."

"Yeah, but—"

"Miss Rachel, you have to do something about that cat."

Rachel's gaze flicked to Carmen, scowling and hovering in the doorway, then to the empty basket beside the bookcase. Shaking her head, she pushed back from her desk. "Where is he?"

"Break room," Carmen said. "*In* the snack basket."

"I'll get him," she said as she walked from the room.

Carmen followed her. "It's not sanitary."

"The snacks are in packages. He's not really touching them."

"Humph. Crushing them is more like."

"He just likes the rattling sound the paper makes."

Rachel strode toward the break room, stopping just inside the door. The floor was littered with chip, cracker and pretzel bags. Sitting in the dwindling basket of snacks on the counter next to the microwave was her large—okay, fat—orange Persian, Max. Though his smashed face was stamped with the breed's perpetual look of annoyance, he blinked his yellow eyes innocently.

"I thought we talked about this sort of behavior," Rachel said, crossing her arms over her chest.

"Um, Miss Rachel, he's a...well, he's a...cat," Carmen began uncertainly. "He can't understand you."

Rachel glared at Max. "Oh, he understands all right."

With great dignity Max lumbered to his feet, swished his tail, then dropped to the floor, crunching two bags of Doritos in the process.

"I thought cats were supposed to be light on their feet," Rachel said to his sashaying backside.

Max simply rubbed his back against the wall as he turned the corner in the hall before slinking his way toward her office.

Smiling, Rachel shook her head. She'd started bringing Max to work because she spent more time here than she did in her condo. While cats flourished without the burden of humans around for most of the time, it seemed neglectful to leave him at home when she could bring him to work. She often talked through her troubles out loud, and, in recent months, she was comforted that some other living thing was listening.

"Have you called Mr. Huntington?" Carmen asked sweetly.

"Do you nag your sons this much?" Rachel retorted as she followed her cat.

"No, they have the good sense to listen to me."

"That was a good one," Cade commented.

Rachel spared a glance over her shoulder. "Oh, shut up."

"If you need to talk to Parker, just come out with us tonight," Cade said as they headed to her office and Carmen went the opposite way back to her desk.

"Is Isabel coming?"

"We're hooking up later. Why?"

"'Cause when she's around I don't have to play bodyguard. She scares away all the overexcited fans."

"I'm popular. Is there something wrong with that?"

"Not according to the licensing department. I think they've hired temps to field all the incoming offers."

After making sure Max settled himself into his basket for an afternoon nap, she walked toward her desk and the pile of work that awaited.

Despite her resistance to Cade's invitation, she knew she could use some relaxing time. But she'd have to go home and change first. No way she was facing Parker and his varied collection of flirty swimsuit models in her wrinkled khaki pantsuit.

If she went out, she'd have an excuse not to go to her mother's house, where she'd have to hold her hand through another bout of tears and misery at being sixty and single. At Sundries, she could have a glass of wine, find out what Parker wanted, get Carmen off her back and remind herself that the hotel chief wasn't now, nor would ever be, her type all at the same time.

Or she could just head to the mall, yank out her credit card and use retail therapy to avoid her problems.

"I'd rather go shopping," she said as she dropped into her chair.

Cade shrugged. "Okay, whatever. Why don't you take Izzy, then you can still meet us later."

She stared at him. "Do *you* want to tranquilize her first, or should I?"

"She shops," he said defensively.

"She buys things. When she absolutely can't find any other way around it. Even then she does it all online."

He sank onto the edge of her desk, his gaze flicking to hers. "Yeah. Maybe. It's kind of weird for a girl, isn't it?"

"I'll say. Has she found her wedding dress yet?"

"No." He frowned. "You were supposed to work with her on that."

"And I'm getting nowhere." She paused, swallowing. "You don't think she's, uh…changed her mind about the wedding?"

"No," he said quickly. Too quickly. He sighed. "But she's not exactly wandering around the house with bridal magazines and making cooing sounds over veils either. Aren't women supposed to obsess about this stuff?"

"*Some* women." But she'd gotten to know her future sister-in-law pretty well over the last few months, and she knew that Isabel's background—poverty, despair, one parent in jail, the other who-knew-where—had formed a hard, solid wall around her heart. Her eventual adoption by her maternal uncle had started the healing process, but only Cade had managed to work his way completely through to her heart.

"She's probably just nervous," she said.

"Isabel? Get real."

"Some people get defensive when they're scared."

"Then she must be terrified."

Considering, Rachel leaned back in her chair. "She loves you. She'd do anything to please you. Maybe we could, well, *guilt* her into shopping for her gown. If we can actually wrangle her into one, I'm betting she'll burst into tears, then throw herself into the planning like a general on a march to protect worldwide freedom."

"That could work," Cade said slowly. "What about Mom? With Thanksgiving and Christmas out of the way, she needs a new project."

Rachel shook her head. "Talk about nagging, and you've already turned over the reception to her."

"I know, but it's our wedding, Rach," he said, and she saw sincere worry in his eyes. "The only one either of us will ever have. Hopefully."

They exchanged a long, silent look of sibling frustration, then dawning understanding.

"*Carmen,*" they said together.

"I THINK BEING surrounded by chicks all day is making me crazy."

Parker raised his eyebrows as he glanced across the table at Cade. "One of those chicks is your future wife."

"Yeah." He grinned. "Okay, so it's not all bad. But if I could get my future wife to actually *want* to plan our wedding…well, that would be good. And Carmen is like another mother, as if I needed another one of those. Then Rachel has been so weird lately."

Parker swallowed a mouthful of beer and nodded. He ignored his instinctive curiosity about Rachel and tried to visualize his drink as a blackberry-infused, peppery Merlot. Other than having to drink beer, his renewed enthusiasm for the dating scene, plus his mission to fit in better with the guys, be more easygoing, *look* more easygoing, was going great.

He grinned as he caught sight of his reflection in the mirror behind the bar. He looked...disreputable. Or so his grandmother had accused when he'd visited her a few days ago in New York.

Remembering her horrified expression, he silently thanked Cade again for encouraging him to re-embrace his motorcycle-racing, rebellious youth. It felt good to be different.

"And she's always bringing Max to work," Cade continued. "*He* causes way too many problems."

"Max?" he asked, abruptly tuning back in to Cade's rant. "Rachel's dating somebody?"

"No," Cade said, hunching over his beer bottle. "Max is her cat. You've seen him, haven't you? Big, fat, orange dude."

Parker shook his head and refused to acknowledge that he was glad Rachel was still unattached. He was certainly happier not dwelling on their attraction. "We haven't been formally introduced."

"He gets Carmen worked up," Cade continued,

presumably about the cat, "then she complains to Rachel, who gets aggravated."

"Does he?" Parker felt a sudden kinship with Max. He was personally familiar with Rachel and aggravation.

"Then she goes back to staring into space."

"Carmen or Rachel?"

"Rachel." He narrowed his eyes. "I had to push her hard to get her to come tonight."

"Rachel's coming?" Parker asked, taking care to be casual. He had a date later, so it hardly mattered, but he did need to talk to her about the Atlanta race promotions.

"Yeah." Cade's gaze met his with a narrow-eyed one of his own. "And don't get any ideas about looking at her the way you always do."

"How do I look at her?"

"Like you want to see her naked."

That had certainly been true in the past, but Parker had moved on. "I have plenty of female distractions," he said. "I don't need Rachel."

"True." The tension in Cade's face relaxed. "I'm trying to get her out more. She needs to do something besides bury herself at the office. I need to scope out a guy for her. Maybe you could give her pointers on finding one."

That's what *friends* did, didn't they? And while he'd resigned himself to that semihumiliating role in Rachel's life, he wasn't sure he'd dismissed his attraction to her so completely that he could offer dating advice.

And why was she staring into space? That certainly didn't sound like the GRI executive he knew, the one who could negotiate with Southern charm or lay out her demands without a flicker of expression that would reveal her goals or bottom line. The one who effortlessly managed her brother's life, or fit in comfortably and equally among tire changers, old and young drivers, business executives and fans.

"Problem is," Cade continued, "she's got this big issue with dating racing guys."

And sponsors. He cleared his throat. "Racing guys? Like drivers?"

"Like anybody who makes their living in NASCAR."

Since he'd heard this from the woman herself, he simply nodded. Still, he didn't make his living in racing, and she'd dismissed him with a glance and a few abrupt words.

"It's really limiting her dating pool," Cade added.

"And you're determined to scope out a guy for her…why exactly?"

Cade paused with his beer bottle halfway to his mouth. "'Cause she's staring into space. Have you been listening?"

"To every word."

"She's lonely."

Parker's heart leaped. And that was bad. He shouldn't be encouraged because she was troubled.

But the idea that she might regret turning him down was oddly cheering.

For months he'd made it his mission to pursue other women, to soothe his bruised ego, to assure himself that he was wanted. Cade might have screaming fans, but Parker knew he wasn't a pariah. He'd never lacked for friends, dates or bed partners. Some just wanted his money and power. Some wanted to play. Some were fun to look at. A few wanted the whole package.

He enjoyed them all. Now the one he'd longed for, but who'd cast him aside, was...lonely.

His brief moment of joy dissipated.

He wished isolation on no one.

"Okay, I'm here," Isabel said as she and Rachel approached their table. "But if she keeps looking at you like that, I'm going to yank out her overly frosted hair by the roots."

Grinning like an idiot, Cade pulled his fiancée down to share his bench seat. "Who, baby?"

"That chick at the bar," Isabel said, jabbing her finger toward the other side of the room.

Which one?

Parker swallowed the question, as there was a trio of blondes sitting at the bar, all whispering and pointing in their direction, and Isabel looked angry enough to spit nails.

Instead, Parker rose, gesturing for Rachel to share his side of the booth. She said nothing and moved by him, careful not to let any part of their bodies touch. But he had a moment to appreciate her slim-fitting pale blue sweater and faded jeans, her glossy and straight dark hair, her full, pink lips. A spicy aroma emanated from either her hair or skin, and he fought to recapture his resentment that she'd rejected him.

After forcing a polite smile, he returned to his seat. Staying cool, he shifted his gaze to Isabel. "Since when are you so impatient with fans?"

"Since I trip over them twice a day, and they're all after my man."

Cade laid his finger against Isabel's jaw and turned her angry face toward him. *"Your man?"*

"And don't you forget it."

"I won't." He kissed her lightly.

Parker sipped his beer. Watching the naked affection between Cade and Isabel was both lovely and uncomfortable. They had something deep and lasting he knew he could never have.

He settled his gaze on the waitress, who knew them as regulars, as she placed a glass of Chardonnay in front of Rachel and a bottle of beer in front of Isabel without asking for their order.

"You are a treasure," Rachel said, scooping up her glass.

"Drinks are on the house," the waitress said, her eyes dancing. "For the guys anyway."

Rachel rolled her eyes. "Naturally. You know these guys aren't a one-man show. This is a team sport. Right, Isabel?"

Isabel turned a dreamy, distant gaze on Rachel. "Huh?"

Rachel waved her hand. "Nothing. Have a beer. Focus on your man. I'll handle everything." She sipped her wine. "At least *somebody's* happy," she said as Isabel and Cade whispered to each other.

"You're not?" Parker asked.

Her gaze slid to him, roving his face, leaving him to wonder what she thought about him these days, what she thought about the change in his appearance. Or if she'd even noticed.

"The shoes I ordered from Nordstrom's to wear to the Atlanta race are on back order," she said.

"Ah." Over the last several months, he'd had an opportunity to get to know Rachel's shoe obsession up close and personal. They'd had dinner meetings at the mall with Cade and Isabel. She'd rushed home for shipments from an online shoe store. He'd even caught her off guard in her office one day with several boxes of new shoes surrounding her. She'd tried on various ones in front of the mirror, then she'd spent several minutes quizzing him about which ones he thought would go better with her new navy suit.

While he appreciated her fashion confidence in him, he struggled to shift from wanting to seduce her to being her friendly stylist.

"I'm their best customer," she went on, pouting a bit. "I want my shoes."

He refrained from telling her she had dozens of

other pairs to wear, because he had his own issues with dressing to perfection. "It's likely out of the local store's control."

"True." She waved the topic of shoes aside. "You called earlier. Did you want something?"

"Direct, as always. And here I thought we might have a pleasant conversation. Let's try. Shall we?" He waved his hand toward her when she remained silent. "Good evening, Rachel. You look lovely."

He'd said the exact words to her back in December. He wondered if she remembered.

She blinked. "You called earlier to tell me I look lovely?"

"No, this is the pleasant-conversation part."

"Ah." Grinning, she looked him over. "Well, you look…different."

"I was due for a change, don't you think?"

"I guess." She angled her head. "Does this have anything to do with me saying you didn't fit in with the guys?"

"Actually, it was Cade who suggested a new look."

She nodded, but he noticed a flash of surprise in her eyes.

Of course he realized she'd suggested he relax around the guys as well, but acknowledging that fact would put too much weight on their conversation back in December. Maybe it was simply pride, but he'd rather not recall every detail of her rejection.

Though he did—and often.

Why, he had no idea. They'd agreed to be *friends,* hadn't they? They were getting along better, working well together. He and Cade had reestablished their business affiliation and become friends.

He couldn't jeopardize his relationship with Cade and his business interests for a slight case of lust he hadn't fully shaken off.

Could he?

CHAPTER THREE

RACHEL SWALLOWED and felt a tug of desire deep in her stomach.

It was a familiar yet unwelcome sensation.

Heaven help her, the man looked better every day—even though it seemed impossible to improve perfection.

These days he wasn't just gorgeous. He was mysterious. Intriguing. Charming.

His silky-looking, chin-length black hair made her fingers tingle. His easy smile made her want to smile back. The effort he was obviously putting forth to bond with Cade and the rest of the team was endearing.

But she didn't want to consider him endearing. She wanted his friendship, his business expertise. That was all.

"Well, ah, you look…good," she said, hesitant to give him more than that.

"Nerves?" he asked. "From the woman who threatened to arrive—by helicopter—on the doorstep of the ball-cap company unless we received our shipment for our fan promotion this weekend?"

She bumped shoulders with him. "Hey, the helicopter threat was enough. I got my hats, didn't I?"

"You certainly did. And a couple of cases free as I recall."

"What about you last week in Vegas? I don't remember you smiling politely at your hotel staff when Cade and Isabel's room wasn't ready when they arrived."

"I see nothing wrong with demanding a certain level of competence from your employees."

"And having them shake inside their proper blue suits when the boss comes charging onto their doorstep."

He lifted his chin. "I don't charge."

"No, you stroll." She paused. "Arrogantly."

"And I thought we'd gotten past all that."

"We have, but you can't expect me to give up ragging you completely. It's part of the family motto."

"And I'm part of the family?"

Their partnership in making Cade a superstar had certainly bonded them, but she didn't let too many people inside the intimate circle of trust that involved her family.

"The extended part," she said finally.

The waitress plopped two frosted mugs of beer in the center of the table. "Compliments of—" she turned and pointed toward the blond trifecta at the bar "—your fans."

The blondes waved and smiled, the waitress

rushed off, and everybody at the table stared at the mugs as if they were bombs.

Given Isabel's current state of mind about women chasing *her man,* and intimately familiar with her hair-trigger temper, Rachel felt the need for levity. She cleared her throat. "I guess those aren't for us, Isabel."

Cade brushed Isabel's hair off her face. "It's just a fan thing, honey. No big deal."

Isabel's face flushed deep red. "I'm *tired* of fans. Did those chicks not read the newspaper announcing our engagement? I have a million things to do at the office, but instead I'm fending off overenthusiastic fans. I have to accept my love life is now up for public consumption, there's a camera in my face every weekend all weekend, *and* I have a wedding dress to buy." She fisted her hand in Cade's shirt. "Will I get to wear it, Cade? If the fans—the built, blond, beautiful fans—are always going to be around, will I even get to wear it?"

Rachel had never seen Isabel like this. It wasn't just anger in her eyes. It was fear.

And the panic seemed to be spreading, since Rachel couldn't think of a single thing to say. Cade and Isabel were meant for each other. They *belonged* together. Rachel had a lousy romance track record, as well as Bryan and her parents, so the couples who worked, who just…worked were more precious than gold.

She took a gulp of wine and wondered how soon she could get more.

"They're mine," Parker said, yanking both mugs toward him so abruptly, beer sloshed over the sides.

Rachel tried to swallow, but choked. "They are?" she managed to gasp. She caught the hope in Isabel's eyes and nodded, "Sure. Sure they are."

Parker laid his hand over her forearm. "Would you mind letting me out, Rachel? I should thank them."

"Oh, sure." She moved out of the booth, then watched him cross the room to the blond trio. She ignored the weird bottoming-out feeling in her stomach. Smart, she told herself. He was smart to distract Cade and Isabel. The beers weren't really for him. And he knew it.

Parker moved between two of the women. Smiling flirtatiously, he slid an arm around each of their shoulders.

Were the beers actually for him?

"Drinks for Parker," Cade said, hugging Isabel to his side. "Nothing to get upset about."

Rachel waited for Isabel to roll her eyes. Or claim she wasn't upset. Or tell Cade he had to be flat-out stupid to think she was buying that lame excuse.

She did none of those things.

She laid her head on Cade's shoulder, relief washing over her face as she said, "Okay."

If this was what love did to normal, sensible businesswomen, Rachel wanted no part in it. And lately it certainly seemed she had a sign posted on her back—*please give me plenty of concrete demonstrations of why relationships are way more trouble than they're worth.* The last guy she'd gone out with had spent most of the night telling her about various relatives and which driver they were devoted fans of, and how special it would be if he could get their autographs.

Then there was Bryan's divorce. Her parents' divorce. And, finally, Parker's racy, temporary goodtime proposal.

Which, even if she'd considered his proposition of a casual affair, she'd blown the opportunity months ago.

She refused to glance in his direction. He'd thought up an excuse for the drinks fast. As she'd realized many times recently, that brain of his wasn't completely wasted on meetings, balance sheets and throwing classy parties.

He'd headed off an argument between Cade and Isabel that could have gone south very quickly. He truly cared about the state of their relationship. He was Cade's friend, not just a colleague. She'd watched their relationship slowly build over the last six months and now she had proof.

What truly lay beneath the surface of this man she considered both charming and calculating? He was shallow, but still concerned for others. Competitive, but gracious.

Considering, she drummed her fingers against the table.

Maybe she was giving him too much credit for claiming those beers. Heck, he probably just wanted the women all to himself. Given his social schedule over the last few months, that was the reason she'd rank first.

Still, while she'd frozen, he'd saved the day.

She glanced up, prepared to get Isabel's opinion about Parker's actions, and winced. The affianced couple was so focused on each other, they likely had forgotten she was sitting across from them. She was clearly the third wheel in this party.

"Hey, I see somebody from Ry-Pat Racing I need to talk to. Catch you two later?"

Cade turned toward her, his eyes dreamy and unfocused. "Huh?"

Rachel tossed some money on the table, scooped up her glass of wine, then slid out of the booth. "Bye."

She walked across the room, casting only a passing glance at Parker and his blond beer benefactors, then strode out the door to the patio. All the tables were filled, and she recognized quite a few people from the NASCAR community.

The restaurant had opened the outside area by the lake and made it comfortable with portable heaters. Spring was on its way. There were days you could open your windows to a warming breeze. The mornings of waking to frosted grass were subsiding. Trees held buds that were beginning to crack and reveal the colorful flowers striving for the warm sun.

But winter hung on with a brisk day here and there, or, like tonight, a biting wind gusting intermittently across the lake.

"Well, well, Rachel Garrison and without the honor guard of the Garrison men."

Her standard glare for idiots firmly in place, Rachel turned to face Chance Baker. And her former sister-in-law, Nicole. Who was now Chance's girlfriend.

"Well, well, Chance Baker without his PR team. How will you ever formulate a coherent response without prompting?"

"I—" He glanced at Nicole, who looked equally blank.

Rachel wasn't sure if he was confused by the word *formulate, coherent* or *prompting.* Maybe it was all three.

"I have plenty of people around me," Chance said finally, defensively.

Rachel rose on her toes and peeked over Chance's shoulder—it wasn't hard, the guy barely pushed five foot six—as if looking for the people who surrounded, prompted and catered to the driver whose family had been rivals of hers for decades, dating all the way back to the time Chance's father had knocked her father out of the way in Daytona, denying him the opportunity to win that hallowed February race.

And though Rachel never thought of herself as a Miss Know-It-All, she'd never liked Nicole from the first moment her older brother had begun dating her. After the accident that had ended his racing career, Nicole had dumped him even as the "you can't race again" results were being processed, and had moved in with Chance less than a month later.

Though she knew she should be a better person, certainly a stronger, more evolved and empowered woman and business executive, Rachel reserved a special, hard place in her heart for both Chance and Nicole.

"I'd *so* love to stay and chat," Rachel said in a tone that indicated just the opposite, "but I have an important meeting to attend." Then she deliberately walked to the other side of the patio—alone—and leaned against the railing.

Idiots. Chance had found her without her family around her, so he was going to harass or intimidate her? What for? Had he actually been lying in wait for the right moment? She nearly laughed. Like he could intimidate her.

Think again, buddy. Why did she always have to find the idiots? She'd come to relax and finish some business with a sponsor.

Though running into a hot guy or two wouldn't have been exactly awful.

She had on brand-new jeans, a sweater that matched her eyes and snazzy platform wedges, and she'd hadn't been hit on yet.

"Give him a couple of days, he'll manage a comeback."

Rachel turned to face Jesse Harwood, an engineer with another race team. He certainly fit the hot requirement, and in a dark and dangerous way, but, based on her rule to not mix racing and dating, off limits. Maybe she should have clarified—hot, but not involved in racing. A tall order to fill, considering the entire county was bursting full of racing people.

"Hey, Jesse." She angled her head. "Who's making a comeback?"

Jesse leaned against the railing next to her, his direct dark brown gaze causing a lovely prickle of awareness in her body. "Chance Baker. He's thinking hard of a way to best you. Naturally, that'll take a while. Maybe weeks."

"Try never."

He toasted her with his beer bottle. "A more accurate prediction."

"How can you tell he's thinking?"

"He looks like he's in pain."

Rachel laughed. "Then let's leave him to it. How's your season going?"

"Long. Not making the Chase last year really revved the boss man up. He storms through the shop at least twice a day, barking on his cell phone and looking over our shoulders every chance he gets."

"He's under a lot of pressure," she said gently, thinking of Bryan and his temper when the GRI teams failed to meet expectations. "Millions of dollars and hundreds of jobs are at stake."

"Yeah." He nodded. "You'd know."

"It's a team sport, with a million moving parts, both human and mechanical. If a single component is off, it can throw *everything* off balance."

"No kidding."

"Try having your father, or your annoyingly stubborn older brother, looking over your shoulder."

He grinned and held up his hand. "No, thanks." He nodded at her glass. "You want another glass of wine?"

"I was actually about to go…"

"Come on. It's not every day I get to talk shop with a beautiful woman."

A drink wasn't *dating*, right? It was drinking. And talking. About work even. She nodded. "Wine and shoptalk it is."

"Is THIS SEAT taken?"

How lame could you get? Rachel turned toward Parker, noted the flirtatious smile on his lips and shook her head. "Do you put the moves on every woman with a pulse?"

"Of course not," he said as he slid onto the stool next to her. "Only about seventy-five percent."

She fought a smile. "I stand corrected. Before you ask, you can't buy me a drink."

"You reserve that privilege for chassis engineers from competing teams."

She raised her eyebrows. "Jealous?"

"Intensely."

He said it so casually she knew he was kidding. But he'd obviously noticed her and Jesse together. The man was a puzzle she was continually trying to piece together, break apart, then reassemble.

She raised her glass. "I've switched to water." She craned her neck to look around him. "What happened to your fan club?"

"Off to greener pastures. They wanted Cade, as you well know."

She knew. But she also wondered what those women thought was so wrong with Parker. True, he wasn't famous or a race car driver. As her gaze skimmed him, her pulse picked up speed. No, he was a different kind of fantasy.

"And I already have plans for tonight," he added.

Another swimsuit model, no doubt. She never realized there were so many in the Charlotte area. Propositioning her must have been a real downturn for him. Physically anyway.

With the subject of love lives settled, she addressed the topic she did want to talk about. "Why did you tell Isabel those beers were for you?"

"I was looking forward to the company of a beautiful woman. Or three." He grinned. "Why else?"

"Mmm. Scooping up Cade's leftovers?" While his smile fell away, hers broadened. "Interesting. I never figured you for that kind of guy."

"They weren't leftovers, as Cade hadn't sampled them."

"This is getting into a weird and disgusting area."

"I agree. Let's talk about something else."

"How about you answer my question—why did you lie to Isabel?"

"It's of no consequence. I just—"

"Don't try to con me, Huntington. I'm unconnable."

His bright green gaze searched hers. "Yes, I think we've already established that."

She waggled her fingers in a come-ahead gesture. "Let's hear it."

He shrugged. "She's obviously distracted and upset. She and Cade are devoted to each other, but they both work extremely long hours in a high-stress environment. That can take a toll on a relationship.

"She's used to her privacy. Maybe having her personal life as fodder for tabloids and Web chat sites is grating on her. Maybe the crush of fans and the demand for Cade's time is wearing her down. Or maybe it's the wedding itself causing the strain. Isabel is a practical, but independent, woman. Maybe she thinks they're rushing into marriage."

Rachel had thought all those same things herself many times over the last few weeks. It was odd to hear them said aloud. By a man, no less. And especially by somebody she never would have anticipated seeing so deeply into her brother's personal life.

"You start thinking like me," she said, "I may actually have to start liking you."

His eyes flashed with heat briefly, then the moment passed, leaving her to wonder if she'd imagined it. "You don't like me now? Aren't you *supposed* to like your friends?"

"I guess you are." She turned back to her water. They were *working* on being friends, she supposed.

He had a major role in her brother's life, in her family's business, but true trust and friendship was going to take a while. After years of disappointments and betrayals, she accepted few people into her inner circle.

There was some distance between them that he'd imposed as well. Understandably so. She'd no doubt damaged his ego, turning him down the night of the banquet. Very few women said no to him.

"Why did you call me earlier?" she asked, turning the conversation back to business.

"I've rented a suite for the Atlanta race, invited some key managers and executives from other sponsors. I thought you might want to drop by. Or at least have someplace to escape if it ra—"

Whirling, she laid her finger over his lips. "Surely you weren't about to say the R word. It's Atlanta. It's March. Are you crazy?"

"One of us certainly is," he said, his mouth moving against her fingertips and sending tingles dancing down her arm, so she moved her hand to her lap

"You'll jinx the whole weekend."

"You don't honestly believe—"

She stopped him with a glare. "I'll stop by the suite to escape the *bright, shining, springlike glare of the sun.* Thank you for the invitation. What gave you the idea to hook up the sponsors?"

"I did a cross-marketing analysis of all Cade's sponsors and realized we could benefit from each other's efforts if we got organized. Stay in Huntington Hotels, lease Escape Rent-A-Car, drink Go! and experience your most unforgettable vacation ever."

"Sounds like you've got it all worked out."

"The plan could use Isabel's touch, some of her innovation and insight. We also need to produce a cost-benefit analysis and determine how the financial burdens will be distributed."

"How do you plan to work that out?"

"The lead company will contribute the lion's share, but then it will have the highest profile in ads and media contact."

"I take it you're the lead company."

"Naturally. It was my idea."

"And you've already got the costs and rewards lined up in neat little spreadsheet columns."

He nodded. "Mostly. But I'd like Isabel's opinion."

"You'd like to distract her from the other complications in her life."

"I simply need her expertise."

"Why don't you want to admit you're doing something nice?"

He turned his head toward her. "Why are you trying so hard to convince yourself I have ulterior motives?"

She sighed. "We've been over this. To reiterate— I've spent most of my life guarding my family from users, from people with false motives, people who would sell us out to the media for the thrill of being in the know. If you haven't been in this business for three generations, then I'm suspicious."

"I've got three generations. Just not in racing."

She met his gaze for one, long, humming moment. "So you do."

"We work well together, Rachel."

"So far it's going fine."

"Are you ready, Parker?"

Rachel glanced over her shoulder to see a stunning redhead with lightly golden skin, a perfect body and doe-brown eyes standing behind Parker.

Parker rose, his tall, lean body coming to immediate attention, and Rachel fought a pang of what might be termed jealousy—*if* she were that petty and considered Parker anything but a sort-of friend. "Olivia, this is Rachel Garrison. Rachel, Olivia Lambert."

Rachel slid off her stool and exchanged greetings with the other woman, who, while polite, was clearly reserving her super charms for Parker.

"Sorry I'm late," she said. "My meeting with my agent ran long."

"Did you get the catalog?" Parker asked.

Olivia's smile widened—if that was possible. "The *cover.*"

"Congratulations." Parker hugged her, then kissed her cheek. "Olivia is a model," he explained to Rachel.

"And I got the cover of *Le Bain*—Paris's most popular swimsuit catalog."

And I'm dead on the money with Parker's chick parade. "How wonderful," Rachel said, tamping down her small-minded thoughts. Laying a generous tip on the bar for taking up space that might have gone to a customer who actually ordered something, she added, "Obviously, you two should celebrate. Alone."

"I can expect you in the suite, then?" Parker asked as she started to move off.

"Sure." She turned away, then, with a glance over her shoulder, she added, "Thanks for being kind to Isabel."

He inclined his head. "My pleasure."

As she strode to her car, she found herself replaying their conversation in her head.

It's of no consequence? Ridiculously, she was cheered that though he might have changed on the outside, he was still the same thesaurus-reading, smoking-jacket-and-pipe-required Parker.

And she did like him.

Even if that wasn't such a good thing.

CHAPTER FOUR

AT THE DIRECTION of the NASCAR official, Cade Garrison levered himself into his race car to wait for his qualifying run in Atlanta.

Though he should be focusing on his job, he'd rather think about his prospects for his poker game, scheduled for later that night. He visualized winning back the fifty bucks he'd lost to his teammate, Shawn Stayton, and finally beating Parker. At something other than racing.

His sponsor and friend knew business, was smooth as silk with women, had gained the confidence of the guys at the race shop and knew poker as well as any Vegas champ. With that computer-like brain of his, Cade suspected he counted cards, odds and anything else handy, but since most of his financial future was wrapped up with the guy, he didn't hold any of that against him.

Racing—on four wheels anyway, and much to Parker's frustration—was a different story.

Parker had balance and great reflexes, and he was handy on a motorcycle. Racing on the go-kart track at his family's farm, he did pretty well. But he'd never made the transition to stock cars.

It was a weakness that drove Parker crazy for some stupid reason.

Cade shook his head. Seriously, the guy had it all—money, smarts, women, respect, success. But he was never satisfied. He got the feeling Parker's father, who controlled his family's company before him, and his grandmother, who seemed to rule the family as a whole, ragged on him a lot.

Working with his own family and experiencing plenty of insecure moments with them that he'd never have with a regular boss, Cade could definitely relate.

"Hey, man, you in there?"

Cade glanced toward the open window and the team's car chief, Jamie Phelps, who also served as his safety director, making sure Cade got his helmet, neck restraint, gloves and the rest of the equipment on securely.

"I'm here," Cade said. "You actually think we have a prayer of getting a decent position?"

Jamie was a new addition to their crew this year. He was barely twenty-five and already a brilliant engineer. He and Sam, their crew chief, often butted heads, but working together had been the key to the team's early success.

"Should I look under the car for your positive outlook?" Jamie asked, angling his head.

"This car has a mind of its own, so be my guest. Maybe you'll find its sweet spot."

"We're working on the problems."

"How about another two-tenths of a lap?"

Jamie winced. "Ah, no. Not yet."

"But you have hope."

"Sure."

"And a positive outlook."

Jamie thrust Cade's helmet toward him. "Just press the gas pedal as hard as you can for as long as you can."

"Sure thing, Chief."

Grinning, Cade wiggled his head into the helmet, knowing Jamie hated to be thought of as in charge. He was a behind-the-scenes guy. He liked outwitting the competition through his computer simulations and was always surprised and annoyed when the cautions didn't fall within his planned window, or a competitor pulled a wild move on the track and threw off his projections.

When Jamie backed away, Isabel leaned through the window. "Have a good run."

"Yeah, sure. That'll be a mira—" Concerned by the paleness of her skin, he snagged her hand. "What's wrong?"

She forced a smile. "Nothing."

"There is."

Shaking her head instead of kissing his nose, which was their little ritual once he was in his helmet, she pulled her hand from his. "I'm just tired."

There was more, but he reluctantly let it go for

now. Over the last few weeks she was always tired. A shadow of sadness always lingered in her eyes.

When he'd told her the guys were coming by the motor home tonight for a poker game, she'd simply nodded. Usually, she at least rolled her eyes, or sarcastically asked if he wanted her to whip up some hors d'oeuvres or an exotic dancer for his male-bonding party.

The snacks would have been nice, but his Izzy wasn't much for cooking. And the only dancer he wanted to watch move exotically was her, which wasn't for his friends to share.

Today there'd been no comment at all. Just a nod. A distracted nod.

Something was wrong. And the possibilities of what that might be gave him a hollow ache in the pit of his stomach.

Before he could dig into his troubles too deeply, Jamie hooked the window net and patted the car's roof.

Time to go.

He pushed the car hard through his qualifying laps and wound up twentieth. Decent, but then there were seventeen more cars readying for their turn.

"How'd it feel?" Sam asked as Cade slid out of the car.

"Loose. On the edge of out of control."

"You picked up a tenth from practice."

"Holding on for dear life." He shook his head. "I can't do that for two hundred laps."

Sam braced his hands at his waist and looked frustrated enough to spit. "We'll figure it out. We gotta be missing something."

They headed toward the garage, and Cade gave his team the breakdown of the laps—what he'd felt turn by turn, moment by moment. They talked to the members of the other GRI teams and had come up with a basic plan for the next day's practice by the time Cade headed toward his motor home.

With his hand wrapped around the door latch, his concerns about Isabel flooded back.

Though they'd known each other for years, and dated secretly most of last season, they'd really only been together since December. They were getting married in the spring, yet their relationship was still new and uncertain in so many ways. He had no reservations, but the wedding plans had rattled Isabel for some reason.

Was it just the stress of dealing with a future mother-in-law obsessed with every petal of every flower arrangement and every sprig of parsley of every canapé? Were balancing her job and the wedding plans too much to handle? Was being thrown into the spotlight and into the family business overwhelming?

Or was it *him?* Was she having second thoughts about marrying him?

Heaven knew, he had little experience with committed relationships other than his family. And even them he didn't see eye to eye with all the time.

Before Isabel he'd enjoyed women, hung out with the guys and raced. He'd had a great but simple life.

Then he'd been tossed into an emotional tornado. He'd met a woman who was forbidden to him, but one he hadn't been capable of resisting. Now he was bound to a relationship he thrived on and had no intention of ever letting go of. But one that confused him at times.

There was still a sense of mystery and uncertainty that was exciting and unnerving. They knew each other, and yet they didn't. They got along, but still argued.

His and Isabel's journey was a path he walked every day, though he realized a big turn was just ahead. He loved her as he'd never really expected to love anyone. Somewhere, in the back of his mind, he'd dreamed of a relationship like the one his parents had shared in his childhood, but he hadn't realistically expected to find it. Then he had.

The family, the trust and legacy his parents and grandparents had started was a foundation he intended to build high and wide. And the fact that his parents had broken up didn't discourage him. It just made him more determined to make his marriage better. He and Isabel wouldn't let their careers take over their lives to the point that they didn't talk, or that their dreams and goals no longer matched. Or mattered.

But when your bride-to-be frowned more than she smiled...well, that couldn't be a good sign.

He pulled open the motor-home door, then eased inside.

And found Isabel hovering over the stove, stirring a pot of something that smelled like spaghetti sauce.

"It's not like his," she announced, glancing at him for a second before returning her stare to the pot.

"Whose?"

Clearly frustrated, she leaned back against the counter. "My father's."

Her father was actually her uncle, but Isabel hadn't known her birth father since she'd been turned over to foster care at age eleven and adopted by the gregarious John Bonamici. He was the only father she acknowledged. Legendary in the garage for his longtime devotion as a racing sponsor. And his expertise with anything Italian.

Cade cautiously approached the kitchen. "You're worried about the sauce?"

With a wooden spoon, she pointed at the pot. "Shouldn't I be?"

Oh, boy. The taste test.

Cade had zero experience as a husband, but he'd been learning on the fiancé fast track the last few months. And that look on Isabel's face, in the kitchen, meant she was pissed, disappointed or annoyed by the dish she'd made.

With a swift glance at her face, he decided today it was all three.

This was a tricky area. If the sauce was awful, was he supposed to say it was amazing, risk her knocking herself out to continually make something terrible for the next fifty years? And, if he went that way, he could also risk her uncle/father dropping by for a taste five years from now and saying it was an embarrassment to the family and the entire Italian community. Or should he risk her wrath, tears and disappointment if he said it wasn't quite up to par?

These are the worries and anxieties of a future husband. Why couldn't relationships simply be about great sex?

Sure enough, she dipped her spoon in the pot, then held it out toward him. "Taste it."

He approached her cautiously. "I'm not much of a gourmet. Maybe—"

"Taste it!"

Darting to her side, he accepted the spoonful of sauce. He'd eaten at her dad's house, and the man was a wizard with spaghetti and lasagna. Expecting to be disappointed, he frowned when the rich, slightly spicy sauce hit his tongue.

Her gaze burned into his. "See! See, it's not the same. It's not like his."

"No, it's not the same." He tasted another spoonful. "Different, but it's just as good."

"You're just saying that."

He set the spoon aside and pulled her into his arms. "I might be. But if you wore that black silk nightie later…" He grinned.

Eyes hot, she clutched his shirt in her fist. "Just as good?"

Ridiculously, her anger cheered him. Threats were better than tears. A strong woman like Isabel turning into a weeper was nerve-racking. "Rich and spicy. Lots of oregano, a nice touch."

"Maybe I doubled the oregano and forgot the basil. I was so nervous."

Cade suppressed a wince. Isabel didn't get nervous. If she was worried, she pushed through, and nobody who didn't know her well would ever guess she had a care in the world. "Whatever you did, you did it well. As always."

She released his shirt and wrapped her arms around his neck. "You just want to see the black nightie."

"I certainly do." He cupped her cheek and met her gaze. "But I want you to be happy more."

"I am." Snuggling closer, she laid her head against his shoulder. "I'm glad you like the sauce."

Cade held her against him, kissing her temple. He knew nothing was settled. He could still feel nerves vibrating from her body. But he hoped his support helped. He hoped she would cry less.

He hoped their love could survive their wedding.

RACHEL STRAIGHTENED her jacket as she stepped off the elevator and headed down the hall toward the suite Parker had reserved. As she approached the door, her stomach clenched.

Obviously, she was hungry. That was the only reasonable explanation.

Unless she was getting sick.

A cold/flu thing was going around the garage these days. Maybe she'd caught wind of those debilitating germs. She rolled her head, testing the tension in her neck and found it normal. She was fine.

Still, her stomach felt weird. Almost as if she was nervous.

She'd traversed pit roads, media centers and around every suite at every track where NASCAR sanctioned races. This weekend she'd tended to Garrison Racing business—meetings with executives, discussions with the team, fan appearances for Cade. She'd long ago stopped worrying about her daredevil brother and his other forty-two competitors strapped into 3400-pound race cars, and another business meeting or party certainly wasn't anything to be *worried* about.

Still, she wanted to represent the company and her family well.

She had on her favorite black pantsuit and had changed her comfy, wandering-around-the-garage flats for patent-leather stiletto pumps. She'd pulled out her ponytail holder and fluffed her hair. Hopefully, she looked like an executive, not a mechanic.

Ready to roll, she pushed aside the lingering weirdness in her stomach and walked through the suite's door.

Parker was the first person she saw.

And her stomach fluttered harder.

He was laughing with the CEO of Escape Rent-A-Car. With his new rebellious, scruffy style, he still managed to look elegant, charming and in control. How he did that was as disturbing as it was intriguing.

Her attraction to him was supposed to fade. It *had* to. His for her already had. And if she didn't get control of her quivering hormones, she was going to make doing business with him awkward. For which her brother would never forgive her.

Deciding she was being weak by lurking in the doorway, she walked straight toward him. "Parker, George, how are you?"

"Park here was just telling me about losing to Cade on the go-kart track earlier in the week."

"Yeah?" She worked up a teasing smile for the hotel executive. "Well, there's a reason Cade wears a uniform and Parker wears a suit."

George Kline, a florid-faced, heavyset guy, who looked more at home at an all-you-can-eat buffet than the boardroom, was actually one of the most respected and innovative sponsors in racing. "Park always wins the sponsor charity race." He patted his belly. "But then, that's only because I won't fit behind the steering wheel anymore."

George turned away to glance at the TV screen, which was silently broadcasting the cars as they began their pace laps.

Park? Rachel mouthed to Parker while George's back was turned.

Parker smiled and shrugged.

Rachel stared at him, surprised he accepted the nickname without question. He wasn't Park. How absurd. He was Parker Huntington the Third.

Of course he'd lost to Cade on the go-kart track—though, since Cade had been driving on that track, plus every other dirt and asphalt surface in three states since he was six, he did have a slight advantage.

When George turned back to them, and he and Parker launched again into the lap-by-lap discussion of the race, Rachel let her gaze slide over Parker, who wore, not a suit, but a rust-colored, button-up shirt and dark-washed jeans, both of which managed to look casual and expensive at the same time.

"I hold the track record there, you know," she said.

Good grief. The man and his I'm-adorable-and-casually-disheveled phase had also brought out her competitive worst. GRI employees didn't challenge sponsors—they paid the bills.

While the guys stared at her, she looked around, as if shocked her words had come from her own mouth. Awkwardly, she cleared her throat. "At the go-kart track. My record from when I was thirteen still stands."

"No kidding," George said, smiling slightly, but looking a bit confused.

"Rachel is the secret weapon at GRI," Parker said, his gaze connecting with hers.

That friendly, but still flirty, smile was one he was experienced at giving, and she found herself wishing it wasn't so meaningless. Didn't he want something more from his relationships than a series of superficial dates and fun-without-commitment weekends?

Coming quickly to her senses, she shook off the regret. What did it matter how Parker ran his love life?

"We could put you on the track," George said, jerking his thumb toward the 1.54-mile course just beyond the suite's window. "Brother and sister. I could work a great marketing campaign around—"

"Oh, no. *No.*" She swallowed, feeling her face heat, knowing she'd been too abrupt. What was *with* her today? "Go-karts are my adventurous limit."

Smiling slightly, Parker angled his head. "You think so?"

Rachel frowned. Was *everything* a come-on with him?

"Apparently not Park's," George said, clapping him on the shoulder. "He's a demon on dirt and two wheels."

"So I hear," she said, striving to focus on the conversation instead of on her questions and the current of energy that always seemed continually charged between her and Parker. "Though I can't picture him covered in mud and dust, jumping over hills and embankments."

"We all do crazy things in our younger days," George said. "I was an all-state tackle on my high-school football team, but I ain't gettin' hit for a living anymore."

"Unless you count your quarterly taxes," Parker said dryly.

George roared with laughter. "This guy, he just kills me."

Rachel couldn't help but smile in return. George might be loud and overly boisterous, but it was impossible not to get caught up in his enthusiasm. The idea that he and Parker obviously got along well seemed odd on the surface, but hadn't Parker spent the last few months proving he could fit in with anybody, anywhere?

"He's a gem, all right," she said, looking at Parker.

He toasted her with his water bottle.

"Speakin' of football," George said, "those Redskins are really…"

Rachel, whose whole life was consumed with one sport, had little interest in others. One of the downfalls of hanging out with guys most of the time was that they rarely wanted to discuss Christian Louboutin's latest shoe collection.

With her attention drifting, two people across the room, beyond George's shoulder, caught her eye. It was Isabel, talking to Amie, the fourth wife of the CEO of Go! and the most cheerfully annoying woman—girl, actually, since she was barely twenty— on the planet. Isabel had nearly slugged the goofy twit last month at Daytona. Those two together was not a good combination.

"Are you okay?" Parker asked.

An alluring scent wafted from him, and when she

jerked her gaze away from the potential disaster with Isabel, she noticed he'd leaned toward her. His deep green eyes were focused on her face.

Feeling a bit light-headed, she stepped back. "I'm fine."

"You're jumpy."

She fought to sound casual. "Am I? Too much coffee this morning, I guess." She nodded at George and shifted her gaze carefully away from Parker's. "I need to talk to Isabel. I'll see you guys later."

Glad for a sense of purpose beyond trying to figure out her brother's sponsor, she crossed the room, making a beeline for Isabel.

"...so I saw this great Chanel bag that I couldn't resist," Amie was saying, holding up a sleek red leather purse. "Atlanta absolutely has the greatest shopping, and, you know, T.K.—that's my husband—he takes me lots of great places, but, oh my goodness, the shopping is *fabulous* here."

"Hi!" Rachel said as she reached the two women. "How's your weekend going?"

"Oh, *hey,* Rachel," Amie said, flashing her bright white smile. "I was just telling Isabel about this great bag..."

Rachel let Amie's high-pitched voice fade into the background, while she glanced at Isabel, who looked as if her eyes might explode from her head at any moment. "How wonderful," she said, snagging the strap of Amie's bag. "The detail is amazing."

"Isn't it?"

As Amie launched into a detailed explanation of her new bag, Isabel backed away, nodding her thanks.

While Rachel realized she'd gotten her wish about somebody to discuss something besides sports, even she felt her attention wandering when Amie detailed the construction of the rivets on her latest pair of designer shoes.

Rachel's cell phone rang, saving her. She glanced at the screen, noting one of the GRI office numbers. "Sorry," she said to Amie, "I have to take this." She walked to an empty corner of the suite. "Rachel Garrison."

"Miss Rachel, we have a problem," Carmen said.

"What are you doing in the office? It's Sunday."

"I came in to double-check some figures. You know how we asked the accounting department to send over our expenditures for the month of February?"

"Yeah. We did that big Daytona promotion, and I wanted to see how the total costs fell out."

"I got the printouts Friday afternoon," she said hesitantly, "but they have several mistakes. Expenses we didn't incur. It's...odd. So, I came in to check the computer, thinking maybe there had been a mistake and the figures had been updated. The computer matches the printout."

"How much are the figures off?"

"Five thousand dollars."

Not exactly a decimal-point error, though she wasn't overly concerned. "It's probably just an oversight. Thanks for the update. I'll check it out in the morning."

"I don't like it, Miss Rachel," Carmen said, her tone ominous.

"We'll work it out. Go home. Enjoy your weekend."

Carmen promised she'd relax, and Rachel tried to push the problem out of her mind. It was too crowded in there already.

She wandered back to Isabel, who was still scowling, even though Amie was across the room, holding up her bag to a new set of admirers. "Maybe we can get a sponsorship out of the bag's designer," she said dryly to Isabel.

"We're certainly not going to make money on my spaghetti sauce."

"Your what?"

Isabel had that look on her face, the one Rachel had seen way too often over the last month. The worried look that was at odds with the confident, self-possessed woman she knew. "My marinara sauce. Cade said it was good, but I think he was just being nice." She furrowed her brow. "Or he was possibly just interested in sexy lingerie."

Rachel frowned. What marinara sauce had to do with lingerie she really didn't want to know.

"I'm going to be a terrible wife," Isabel added with a resigned sigh.

An accounting glitch and nervous office manager, a headache-inducing sponsor's wife, a shaggy-haired, lust-inducing sponsor and a family member's love-life crisis.

And the race hadn't even started.

Just another day in paradise.

CHAPTER FIVE

"You're going to be a great wife. And let's face it, girl, Cade isn't marrying you for your culinary skills."

"So why *is* he marrying me?"

Oh, boy. Way too loaded a question for Sunday afternoon in the sponsor suite. Delving into that subject—delivered in a desperate tone Rachel hadn't even realized Isabel possessed—was something for a night of chick movies, tears and too much ice cream.

"He has *millions* of fans," Isabel added. "How am I supposed to compete with that?"

"You're not supposed to. You're not a fan."

"Of course I am."

"You're not *only* a fan."

"I can't cook, and I don't care about or understand flowers, invitation fonts, color themes and catering menus." Isabel sighed. "Why is he marrying me at all?"

Rachel really wished she'd spotted a scowl or a hint of Isabel's normal determination. Sighing morosely wasn't something her future sister-in-law did. Frankly, it was a little scary. "Why is Cade marrying you? Hmm, let me think." She tapped her lips with her finger. "Could it be your sweet, malleable personality?"

Thankfully, Isabel frowned, so Rachel continued.

"Your tendency to wander around the house in lacy lingerie?"

The frown deepened. Ominous lines appeared between Isabel's brows.

"No?" Rachel angled her head. "Then it must be your honesty, your brilliant mind, your focus and determination, your complete and absolute support and love for him."

Isabel glanced at the floor. "I wasn't fishing for compliments."

"It's okay to need reassurance."

"I've relied on myself for a long time. I'm not used to all these people around."

"All the family members?" Rachel asked quietly.

Isabel's gaze jumped to hers. "It's not that you guys aren't great. You've welcomed me like I never thought anybody could. It's just…"

"There are so many of us."

"No, it's not that."

"We meddle."

Isabel closed her eyes and shook her head. "I'm saying this all wrong." Her laugh was self-deprecating. "Big shock." Finally, she opened her eyes. A vulnerability Rachel had never seen before suffused her face. "I don't trust easily."

Rachel nodded. She knew the feeling well.

"The only people I've ever trusted are the few members of my adopted family, and even with them I used to wonder when they'd realize I'm not like them, and send me away. And now you're all here, accepting me, bringing me into the circle. I wasn't ready for that. I keep wondering when I'll wake up from this dream. I'm not worried about how many family members there are, or that you like to meddle. You scare me because you're so close and solid. Where I feel like I'm walking a tightrope. Cade expects me to fit in, and I…don't."

It was oddly comforting to realize tough-as-nails Isabel had the same insecurities as the rest of the world. Rachel laid her hands on her shoulders. "You fit in fine."

"How? You don't even know me."

"You love Cade, and Cade loves you."

"So?"

"So."

Isabel waited, obviously for the rest of the reasons. When Rachel remained silent, her expression turned skeptical. "That's it?"

Rachel smiled. "That's it."

"But…" She paused and seemed to be searching for another argument to make. "What about the fans? What about their expectations?"

"Some will like you, some won't." Rachel shrugged. "You can't control that, and Cade won't care."

"What about the wedding plans? What if I make a mess of everything?"

"Flowers, invitation fonts, color themes and catering menus?" Rachel pursed her lips. "For flowers, go with basics—roses, carnations, lilies, maybe some ivy. Neither you nor Cade will notice or care, so that's just background noise."

"You're singing my song."

Considering the issue further, she leaned toward Isabel. "Or, even better, you could slip the florist fifty bucks, tell him you believe in his artistic vision and let him come up with something.

"Dump invitation fonts on Mom. It'll give her something important to decide that you couldn't care less about. For color themes, think of race cars. What colors go naturally together and which ones contrast? Then decide what you want—traditional or out there. That'll help you decide how to go.

"As for catering menus, I can handle that."

Isabel shook her head. "I'm not dumping stuff on you."

"Hey, I love food. Not that I'm a great cook, but I can certainly find someone who is." She thought of Parker and all his hotels. And culinary people. "Carmen has paprika, or maybe its jalapeños, in her blood. We got everything covered. Enjoy your engagement."

"I am."

Rachel raised her eyebrows.

Isabel's gaze darted away. "Okay, so maybe I'm letting it all get to me."

Rachel grinned. "You think?"

"But if you're willing to help, I'm not too proud to accept."

"Nobody does their job alone. You know how stressful race season is."

Isabel nodded. "All ten months of it."

"Exactly. So think of the wedding as a marketing campaign."

"How romantic."

My mother could do this better, Rachel thought. But since she wasn't in a romantic mood either, they had to work with what they had. Isabel and Cade's wedding would be beautiful, and, by damn, *hopeful,* if it killed them all.

"Marketing can be romantic, or at least sexy. And you need to put everything in perspective. The wedding is a party, a formal, important, meaningful party, but still that's all it is. The real work is the relationship—holding on through good times and bad, making each other a priority."

Isabel said nothing for a moment, then she straightened her shoulders. "You're right. I'm getting too worked up. The wedding is superfluous."

Fighting a wince, Rachel nodded. "Arrange for the guests to have a good time, get your man's ring on your finger and be happy nobody's rambling on about the next generation of Garrison drivers." *She'd* been given that speech a dozen times.

Some of the steel Rachel had come to expect with Isabel surfaced in her eyes. "Babies? You mean *babies?* We're barely engaged."

Rachel squeezed Isabel's hand. "I know. Focus on the wedding. Don't let the rest shake you."

"I'm freaking out."

"A little."

"I'm not setting my biological clock by the next race."

"That's a wise choice." The marketing director for Huntington Hotels waved frantically at her, so Rachel knew it was time to move on.

The life of a driver's economic support.

"And you're allowed to vent," she said to Isabel as she walked away. "You're family."

DISTRACTED BY the mouthwatering thought of finally getting to eat, and the food in question being shrimp and grits, Rachel bumped somebody's arm. "Oh, sorry. I—"

She froze, staring at the blond-haired, blue-eyed guy next to her.

Wow.

He had perfectly sculpted features, lightly tanned skin, broad shoulders and an *incredible* smile.

"It was worth it, darlin'," he said in a drawling Southern accent.

"I—" *Wow again.* "What was worth it?"

"You, bruising my arm."

"Oh, did I really? Sorry."

"You said that already." The blond god transferred his beer bottle to the hand holding his plate, then held out his free hand. "Damien Findley. I'm a friend of the Kline family."

Rachel shook his hand and felt a tingle of sensual awareness snake up her arm at the contact. "Rachel Garrison. I'm—"

"NASCAR royalty."

Though she was used to people knowing her family's name, her face heated anyway. "To some people, I guess. Do you work for Escape?"

"No, I'm a surgeon. I operated on George's mother a few years ago."

"Oh. Is she okay?"

"She's fine." He raised his eyebrows. "Maybe I should have mentioned I'm a *good* surgeon."

"I'll bet." Knowing her face was now beet red, Rachel managed an embarrassed nod. "Okay, well…" She started backing away. "I'll let you get back to your lunch."

He reached out and snagged her arm. "I'd rather you join me."

"Oh, well, I—" *Is that the fifteenth time you've said "well" or only the tenth?* "Sure."

He angled his head, as if confused by her less-than-enthusiastic response. And who could blame him? "You don't have anywhere else you'd rather be?"

She thought of Isabel in the middle of a break-down, Amie's endless description of her designer bag and Parker staring at her and making her knees wiggle inappropriately. Since her other choice was shrimp and grits and a hot doctor, her decision wasn't too difficult.

"No place at all," she said, then led the way toward two empty seats in the stadium-style rows in front of the huge window overlooking the track. Below them thousands of fans lurched to their feet as the field darted into three-wide racing. In the suite, the sound was muted, which never felt like a real race to Rachel. She liked the roar of the crowd and the engines. Still, the suite was for networking and business meetings, as much as watching the on-track action, and there was no way to talk outside the protective walls of the suite.

"I've never been to a race," Damien said as the cars rushed down the frontstretch and into the first turn. "How about sharing all the ins and outs?"

"No kidding? Where are you from?"

"One of the few born and raised here in Atlanta, but I was barely aware this track was here as a kid." He grinned. "I started playing doctor very young."

Her mouth suddenly dry, Rachel swallowed a bite of grits. "No kidding."

"You said that already."

She didn't doubt it. The man was beyond distracting. And she certainly needed a distraction right now. "Did I? Well, the basics of racing are, as you can imagine, basic. Build a car, drive it fast, cross the finish line first. But there are hundreds of variables in mechanics and strategy, dozens of different tracks, hundreds of people and millions of dollars that go into making that happen. Not to mention a nice dose of luck."

"And what's with this 'Chase' I've heard so much about?"

"The top twelve drivers after the first twenty-six races have their points reset, making it impossible for anyone but them to win the championship. Whoever's on top at the end of the season wins the big trophy, the big check and the coveted NASCAR Sprint Cup Series title."

"And how do you get points? For winning?"

Rachel drew a breath before she launched into the many aspects of points, positions, bonuses and all the rest. Damien might be a surgeon—a *good* surgeon—but she'd eat her fork, along with her grits, if his eyes didn't cross during her explanation.

He held up his hands halfway through. *"Enough."* He shook his head. "Racing isn't simple."

She patted his shoulder. "You'll get the hang of it." She paused. "After about a decade."

"I'm not so sure."

"NASCAR is always trying to stay one step ahead. Or one step sideways, depending on who you talk to."

"Maybe we should move to a simpler subject."

"Good idea. What kind of surgeon are you?"

"Neuro."

She coughed. "Neuro as in *brain?*"

"I do work on the brain, but I'm also trained in spinal and peripheral nervous system injuries and disorders. I've done quite a bit of work on police officers injured by gunshot wounds."

Rachel fought to clamp her jaw shut. Was there an operation for stunned idiocy? "You're a *brain* surgeon."

"Is that a problem?"

"No. No, of course not. You just don't *seem* like a brain surgeon."

"What are brain surgeons like?"

"Arrogant," she blurted out, though there was that cute guy on TV who was sweet and sensitive... Realizing she'd—again—stuck her foot squarely in her mouth, she said, "Oh, that was wrong. I don't really—"

"How many surgeons do you know?"

"Counting you?"

"Counting me."

Did Bryan's orthopedic surgeon count? "Ah, one, maybe two."

The expression in his pale blue eyes intensified. "Then maybe you should do your research on me."

Oh, boy.

He was handsome, charming, smart—*brain surgeon* smart, for heaven's sake—successful—if George's mother was anything to go by—and knew almost nothing about racing—extra nice, since that meant he wasn't obsessed with the sport like everyone else she knew. He was perfect. Weirdly perfect.

There *had* to be something wrong with him.

And then that something occurred to her. "Hey, if you don't follow racing, how did you know about my family?"

"Your family?"

"NASCAR royalty."

Damien leaned back in his chair and shrugged. "George's description. What does that mean exactly?"

"My family's been in stock-car racing a long time."

"And had great success?"

"Yes." Though the costs had been high. Her parents' marriage. Bryan's self-confidence and sense of purpose. The drive to win had even caused problems for Cade and Isabel. Would it continue to do so? Was it all worth it?

Maybe.

But not for her. She lived every day steeped in racing. Sometimes she felt she was drowning in it. She had to separate her work from her personal life. Somehow. "Cade, my younger brother, has a NASCAR Nationwide Series championship. My grandfather and older brother have one NASCAR Sprint Cup Series championship each. My father has two."

Damien smiled. "Royalty."

To say the least, she was uncomfortable with the terminology. "Family business."

"But a pretty interesting family business. My parents run an insurance office."

"That sounds blissfully normal to me."

He angled his body toward her, and she realized she hadn't watched a minute of the race, or made any connections with sponsors in the room since she'd seen him. He'd managed to distract her in a big way. "How long are you going to be in town?" he asked.

She glanced at her watch. "About three hours."

"When will you be back?"

"In October."

He laughed, and a ripple of pleasure skated up her spine. Leaning forward, he trailed his fingers across her hand. "Then I guess I'll have to find my way to you."

She pressed her lips together briefly. Here was the answer to finally burying her attraction to Parker, and possibly finding a social life outside of her job. "I can e-mail you a schedule. Maybe we can—"

"Rachel, can I talk to you?"

With a jolt of recognition at the voice, Rachel glanced over her shoulder at Parker. "Can it wait?"

He glanced at Damien, then held out his hand. "Not really."

As she grasped Parker's hand and rose, Damien stood along with her. Manners, plus looks and brains? Her mother would be pushing to plan a double wedding.

She quickly made the introductions between the two men, then excused herself to move into a corner and figure out what was so urgent that Parker needed to interrupt. "What's happened?"

"Nothing. I thought you needed saving."

"From who?"

Parker nodded in Damien's direction. "That guy. He seemed pretty aggressive to me."

She shook her head. "He's not. He's very sweet." This was a weird conversation to have with Parker, who she felt an attraction to when she shouldn't.

"I don't like the way he looks at you."

"*You* don't like?"

Parker shrugged, but his eyes were full of turbulent emotion. "Your father and brothers aren't here. It's my duty to protect you."

"Your *duty*?" She crossed her arms over her chest and glared at him. "You're kidding, right?"

He frowned. "No."

This was ridiculous. She didn't need protecting, and there was a small humiliation in being treated like a sister by the guy who'd consistently made her knees wobbly. "I'm fine. I'll see you later."

He grabbed her hand as she turned to leave. "There are a lot of guys who take advantage—"

She jerked her hand away. "You think I can't handle myself?"

He stared at her for ten humming seconds. "You can, of course. I'm sorry to have bothered you."

As he walked away, she rolled her shoulders and wished she could so easily roll off the tension between them, the confusion he produced in her. Their relationship was simple, after all. He'd propositioned her, she'd turned him down. He was currently dating half of North Carolina—and probably Manhattan, too. She was *trying* to date. They were professional friends. The intense looks they shared were simply residual…lust. Or curiosity. Or tension.

Or…lust.

He was a sophisticated, hot, interesting man. What woman *wouldn't* lust over him?

But feelings like those would cloud the business they needed to do. It would cloud everything. Maybe, if she found somebody to date, their attraction would finally be settled.

Wasn't that for the best?

Determined to put Parker out of her mind, she walked back to her seat next to Damien and made plans to see him again.

CHAPTER SIX

PARKER STARED philosophically into his beer mug. "She's going to see him again."

"Why do you care?" Cade asked, chalking his pool cue.

"I don't, of course." He met Cade's gaze. "Not in the way you mean."

They'd gathered in Cade's basement game room as they often did on Monday or Tuesday nights. Usually, their games were relaxing, a time to casually talk about the team, where their strengths and weaknesses lie. Tonight, Parker wasn't himself and wasn't focused on either the last race or the one coming up.

"You've got plenty of women to keep you busy," Cade said. "You're not still interested in my sister, are you?"

"Of course not."

"You asked her out, right? She said no. End of story."

Since he hadn't precisely *asked her out* and certainly didn't want to go into the details of what he *had* said to his driver's sister, Parker simply nodded.

Cade's eyes narrowed. "And I've already told you she's not interested in anybody involved in racing. You're involved in racing. We've got a contract."

"I'm aware of that." Parker set his beer aside and attempted his shot, which he missed. His concentration was seriously compromised tonight. "There was something off about that guy."

Cade shook his head as he lined up his own shot. "I'm gonna win the hundred you put on this game."

Still picturing that smiling hyena who'd clearly dazzled Rachel at the race the day before, Parker shrugged. "It's only money."

Cade straightened. "Now I *know* you're sick."

"He's a brain surgeon."

"Yeah, so the brain-surgeon guy is some kind of ultra chick fantasy, but Rachel isn't dazzled by that sort of thing. You've got big bucks. She didn't go for that, did she?"

Parker sent him a pointed stare. "I suppose she didn't. Thanks for reminding me."

"And Rachel's got brothers for protection. You don't think Bryan and I can handle this guy if he steps out of line?"

"Of course you could." Parker waved his hand, brushing the subject aside. He was only puzzled about why she'd chosen that doctor over him. His ego wasn't handling the rejection well.

"You sure there's not some other reason you don't like this guy?"

Parker noted the amusement in his friend's eyes. "You just love that she didn't want me, don't you?"

Grinning, Cade leaned on his cue. "Oh, yeah." He cocked his head. "Something comes too easy to you, you don't appreciate it. Take it from me."

"I appreciate plenty of women."

"Sure you do. You ever think that's the problem with you and Rachel?"

"There isn't a problem with me and Rachel. We're friends."

"Uh-huh." Cade looked doubtful. "Well, if a guy did want to be *more* than friends with her, he'd have to give up all his other *friends*."

Parker felt the blood drain from his face.

"Rachel doesn't date dozens of guys at once. She has *relationships*. Serious, long-term relationships. Not exactly your thing, huh, buddy?"

He was *capable* of a long-term relationship, he just chose not to have them. Too complicated, too time-consuming and too messy when they ended— or so he'd heard from his friends who'd been dumb enough to have them. Though Cade and Isabel were perfectly suited to each other. If true love and happily-ever-after still existed, they were the spokescouple.

"No," he said to Cade as he lined up his next shot. "Definitely not my thing."

He ignored the fear that whispered deep inside him, the small voice that told him nobody wanted him long term.

He missed the shot.

Cade lined up his shot, took it, then smiled when the five-ball fell softly into the pocket.

It was going to be a long night.

"If you want some good news," Cade said, "I'll tell you that the brain surgeon's going to have a hard time."

Finally, something positive. "Oh, really?"

"Our parents' divorce, Bryan's divorce. They messed Rachel up. I think that's where the *no-racing-guys* rule comes from. Two relationships down because of the crazy life we lead. It's what we do, you know? It's what we've always done. Why would racing break up Mom and Dad now? It's nuts."

"Maybe all the frustration over the years built up. The season is long. Hard on family life."

"So what're we supposed to do? Open a dry cleaners?"

Parker knew as well as anybody the perils of working with family. Dinners together became business meetings. Family members who couldn't perform the way a regular employee could had to be either fired or pushed away to some meaningless job. Control of the family and the business was a game for some and a heartache for others.

He thought of his cousin Patrick, who'd argued with his father about how the accounting department should be handled and had been pushed out of the company. Those actions had caused a rift that still hadn't healed. He thought of his grandmother, who was supposed to be focusing on her various charities and foundations, but instead interfered constantly in the company.

Emotions always ran high with families, and neither the racing nor hotel business was an easy road to start with. "I doubt the reasons for the divorces were that simple. And every industry has its own demands."

"Right." Cade shook his head. "Racing doesn't *cause* divorce."

"For your sake, I hope not."

"I'm a risk taker. Rachel isn't." The expression on his face softened, changing to serene contentment. "Isabel's the one for me. When a woman like her comes along and knocks you between the eyes, what else are you gonna do but grab onto her?"

You could run. Run hard and fast in the opposite direction.

Obviously noting Parker's stricken expression, Cade said, "Don't worry, buddy. It'll happen for you eventually."

Dear heaven, he hoped not.

Falling back into the rhythm of the game, they continued as if Rachel's name had never been brought up, for which Parker was grateful. He'd already spent too much time thinking about her. He needed to concentrate on his business. After being handed the reins of his family's company, half the business world was rooting for him to take the company to new heights, while the other half was salivating over the possibility of him destroying three generations of success.

In that regard, he understood Rachel's need to separate her personal life from the family business. Relationships were breaking apart all around her. The pressure was even affecting Cade and Isabel's relationship.

There was no doubt they'd work through their troubles, but at the moment, unfortunately, Cade's romantic life wasn't looking as content as he obviously hoped it would be. His future bride was currently beating the crap out of a boxer-style punching bag on the other side of the game room.

Parker glanced in her direction. "Does she do that often?"

"Nearly every night. I've replaced the bag twice."

Parker winced. "Have you asked her why she does it?"

"Hell no." He shrugged, clearly troubled and uncomfortable. "I expect it's something to do with the wedding."

"I thought weddings were supposed to be happy, fun, even special and meaningful."

Cade shook his head. "Boy, are *you* clueless."

After he predictably lost his hundred, he and Cade sat companionably on the sofa by the TV, while they watched the sports update and Cade sent occasional worried glances toward Isabel. "Do you think Rachel would ever relax her rule about not seeing anybody in racing?" Parker asked, the question popping out even though he'd promised himself to set the matter aside.

"Man, you never give up," Cade said.

"Just speculating." When Cade's skeptical stare remained, he added, "Rachel and I are friends. Maybe I could find someone compatible for her."

"Good luck with that. And think boring. The last guy she dated was an accountant."

"I'm an accountant."

"No, you're a financial whiz. Anyway, turns out this guy was an accountant, all right. But for a racing team. On his and Rachel's second date, he wanted to compare income statements, and she dumped him."

What was *wrong* with these men? You're having a dinner with a woman like Rachel, and you want to talk about *money?* Tacky. And stupid.

Oh, and you're loaded with brilliance, aren't you? You tried to maneuver Ms. Long-Term Relationship Rachel into bed after half a glass of wine. You didn't even take her to dinner first.

He bungled that, no doubt about it. If he had another opportunity—

No. They were both better off as things were.

Before Parker could—again—change the subject, Cade had crossed the room to talk to Isabel. When the two embraced, Parker quietly slipped from the room. In racing, romantic moments were rare, and those two deserved a couple of extra ones.

As he strode to his car, he admitted to himself that

he'd misled Cade. He certainly hadn't set aside his and Rachel's attraction to the point that he planned to run around researching dinner dates for her. But maybe he was reading the good doctor wrong. Maybe they could be happy together.

Somebody certainly should be.

"I DON'T UNDERSTAND these disbursements," Rachel said, staring at the printouts spread on her desk, the ones Carmen had called her about on Sunday. "They're not normal."

Max, lying in his basket instead of getting into trouble for once, blinked his golden eyes but didn't answer.

But then her gut didn't need an answer. After adding and re-adding the figures and questioning Carmen again, she had a bad feeling about what was going on. She didn't want to acknowledge her suspicions, what she saw in front of her face, no matter how improbable they seemed.

This didn't look like an oversight. It looked like somebody was stealing from her family.

Without further investigation, she couldn't be sure. And she certainly couldn't share her suspicions with her brothers, or her father, not until she was positive. They were drivers, not accountants. She needed help. To prove she was right. Or, even better, *wrong*.

Who could she trust? Who knew figures backward and forward? Who did she know who could discreetly weed through the tangle of expenses and get her the answers she needed?

You've already got the costs and rewards lined up in neat little spreadsheet columns.

Shaking her head, she leaned back in her chair. Going to him would keep the problem all in the family. Sort of anyway. He definitely wouldn't spill her ugly suspicions to anybody else, and he wouldn't want his own reputation tarnished by associating with a company in a financial crisis.

Were they in a financial crisis?

She simply didn't know. But she knew she had to find out.

"He knows what he's doing," she said aloud. "As he tells me twenty times a day."

Max yawned.

Rachel tapped her pencil on the desk. "You said it."

Biting her tongue, she ignored the warning signals about getting too personal with a man who'd once confessed an attraction to her. They'd settled that. She'd made it clear she wanted their relationship to be strictly professional. He'd accepted her decision. He'd moved on to bikini models. She'd accepted a date with a dreamy neurosurgeon.

Whatever leftover…heat there was between them would fade eventually. Right now, her family's business was more important than any personal discomfort.

Max rose and padded toward her desk, then

leaped on top. It always amazed her to watch his tubby body move with such ease and grace. When she was round in the middle with old age, she doubted she'd have the same abilities.

He nudged her pencil aside and plopped his long-haired body directly on top of the printouts, then lifted his neck for a scratch. Cats had it easy. Their lives were straightforward and uncomplicated.

Why did she feel as if her life grew more difficult by the minute? Why did she feel as if every time she climbed over one hurdle there was another one waiting?

Still, she picked up the phone and dialed.

HE SHOWED UP wearing an expensive-looking black suit, toting dinner and a bottle of wine.

"This isn't a date," Rachel pointed out as she held open the door to her condo, wondering when he'd abandoned the jeans, since his hair was still long and the goatee still present. The elegant clothes and rebellious grooming contrasted in an appealing, head-spinning way she knew she had to dismiss.

Parker, his green eyes gleaming, simply brushed by her and headed toward the kitchen. "We can't eat and work at the same time?"

Even though he'd never been in her place, he took off his suit coat, then made himself at home with an ease that had her fidgeting on the terra-cotta-colored ceramic tile. Her stomach fluttered as she watched him retrieve plates from the cherry cabinets she'd painstakingly picked out in the builders' showroom three years ago.

"How do you feel about baked ziti?" he asked as he opened one of the containers he'd brought.

"I'm not politically or morally opposed."

Grinning, he glanced at her. "I'm so relieved."

He stood there, looking at her for several long, humming seconds. The fluttering in her stomach started again—a feeling she should be getting used to around him by now. But she was supposed to be thinking about Damien. She had a date with him this weekend.

Damien, who was kind, smart, easygoing, funny and uncomplicated. Nothing like Parker. Well, Parker was smart, and it was kind of him to bring dinner, but the rest she wasn't so sure about. Except the complicated part. She was sure about him being complicated.

He finally looked away, and the moment, gratefully, passed.

Tucking the wine bottle beneath his arm, he carried the plates through the archway that led to the dining room. "Grab a couple of glasses, would you?"

Not wanting to spoil the comfortable atmosphere with the reminder that this was work, not romance, she retrieved the glasses and shooed Max off the counter when he jumped up to see what was happening. She'd need a hit of wine to prepare herself for admitting to Parker that she didn't have all the answers, and she needed his help to find them.

They settled at the dinette table beside the large

window along the condo's back wall. The sun had
nearly disappeared beyond the lake horizon, turning
the sky to a bruised purple and blue. She only had a
moment to appreciate the view, though, when Max
jumped into her chair and poked his squashed-
looking face near her plate of ziti.

"I take it that's Max," Parker said as she picked
up the tubby orange feline.

"That's him."

She held Max up a bit higher, so he and Parker
could check each other out.

Max blinked his yellow eyes, then yawned.
Parker raised his eyebrows.

"Sorry." She lowered Max to the floor. "Unless
you've got tuna in your pocket, he's not interested."

"How about ziti?"

"That would probably do it."

Parker uncorked the wine, and, being the connois-
seur he was, she found it an excellent fruity and
spicy complement to the ziti. He even put a small
plate of pasta on the floor for Max, who found it out-
standing and, after eating, twined himself lovingly
around Parker's ankles.

"Clearly, it's not only cartoon cats who eat pasta
and red sauce," Parker said.

Rachel cast an affectionately resigned look at her
chunky companion. "Clearly, he eats everything."

After exhausting the hot topics in racing, they
moved on to issues with their offices, including the
news that Parker's downtown Charlotte hotel had

recently been featured in *North Carolina Business* magazine.

"That's wonderful," she said. "Did you tell your father?"

"He knows. But then he's not thrilled I opened an office here in the first place."

"Why did you?"

"For the reasons I've said before—I wanted to be closer to the race shop." He sipped his wine. "I'll add that I also I need to make my own way with the company. Get out of New York and away from my family. Being here, near the sport where I'm spending the majority of my marketing dollars, seemed ideal." His lips quirked in a smile. "Though if Cade beats me on the go-kart track or at the pool table one more time, I may have to go back home because of sheer humiliation."

"Yeah? I hear you kick butt at the poker table." When he nodded, she added, "You can't be great at everything."

"Why not?"

Smiling, she shook her head ruefully. Same old arrogant Parker. In jeans or a suit, long hair or short. For some reason, though, she was charmed instead of annoyed. She knew he expected a great deal of himself and those around him. In a way, that made them similar.

When they moved on to the general news of the day, she found that the conversation flowed comfortably, as it had steadily done over the last few months.

Parker was smart, articulate and interesting. She could easily see how he kept the women enthralled, and she guessed his skill with numbers came in handy when managing them all.

But he wasn't only a superficial playboy. Thinking of the effort he'd put into both his relationship with Cade as well as all the guys at the shop, he'd, somehow, become part of their team. And for all her claims that she didn't let people into her inner circle easily, she was about to confide in him in a way she hadn't with anyone else.

From their tense-filled past to their self-conscious present, where she often felt their attraction spark to life at inconvenient moments, they'd formed an odd sort of bond. One that she kept waiting to feel wrong about.

"I should introduce you to my grandmother," he said as they carried the dishes to the kitchen.

"*Your* grandmother is a race fan?"

He laughed. "No. Definitely not. She's the matriarch. Like you."

"Are you nuts? I'm not a matriarch. My mother is."

He flicked a glance at her, then shrugged. "No, it's definitely you."

She crossed her arms over her chest. "Are you trying to tell me I need more moisturizer? Last time I looked, the lines on my face didn't warrant matriarch status."

"I didn't mean you're old. I meant you're the leader."

"I am *not*."

He slid the last plate into the dishwasher and turned to face her. "You say that like I've insulted you."

"I don't feel insulted, I'm just—"

Not worthy.

If she really thought about her family, and who ruled the roost, her mother was the emotional center. Ultimately, though, Rachel considered her paternal grandmother as the head of her family, even though she'd died when Rachel was in high school. Her grandmother had supported her grandfather in the early years of racing, when victories didn't mean big sponsorship dollars or TV time, it meant paying the electric bill—and sometimes not even that. Rachel had never made those kinds of sacrifices. Thanks to the drivers in her family, she'd never had to consider them.

But while she occasionally moaned about her lack of privacy, the constant and long hours at the track and no free weekends, she still managed to remember the people who'd provided for her.

However, a matriarch was an entirely different discussion. Though she ran Cade's office—and, let's face it, his *life*—she wasn't experienced or wise. She certainly didn't have all the answers, or know how to manage all the relationships and emotions that went into the family business. She had no technical idea what direction they should take to win races and championships. She could only manage the behind-the-scenes stuff.

And even that she was obviously failing at.

"Let's go out on the deck," she said, picking up her wineglass and pulling the printouts from the utility drawer where she'd stored them.

As she headed out of the kitchen, Parker followed her. He asked, sounding amused, "So you're avoiding the whole family-responsibility discussion?"

"Yep."

Once they'd settled on the deck, Rachel pushed his troubling observation about her and her family's leadership to the back of her mind and tried to think practically. She had no one else to talk with about this problem, and while she was taking a leap by sharing it with him, she knew it was the right thing, the only thing, to do.

She laid her hand over the printouts. "What I'm going to discuss with you stays between us. Agreed?"

His gaze flicked to the stack of papers in her lap, then to her face. "Agreed."

"Carmen found some discrepancies in the accounts for Garrison Racing over the weekend. I went over the figures today and couldn't find any explanation." She handed him the printouts. "I'd like you to look over them and give me your opinion."

He didn't look at the printouts. His gaze remained fixed to her. "I'm sure you have a whole team of accountants to run this by."

"I want to keep it quiet. I don't want my father or brothers to worry."

"And you're trusting me."

"I guess I am."

"Why?"

Sighing heavily, she rose, crossing to the balcony railing. "Why are you always so difficult?"

He followed, standing close. "One of those charming qualities you'd find endearing if you let yourself."

"Somehow, I doubt it."

Undaunted by her crabbiness, he asked again calmly, "Why are you trusting me?"

Why was she? An instinct, she supposed. She could rely on his business sense and discretion. And despite his chaotic love life, and the mercurial past he'd shared with her family, he was honest. He had a strict code of principles and loyalty that she admired and believed in.

"Because you won't blab," she said finally, "and you know financials. Now will you look at the figures?"

"Of course."

Without further comment, he returned to his chair and studied the printouts. Rachel stayed at the railing and watched the moon peek from behind the clouds. When the phone rang, she cast a brief glance at Parker, who was still focused on the papers she'd given him, so she headed into the condo.

"Hello?" she asked as she picked up the receiver.

"Hey, Rachel, it's Damien."

A blush washed over her. Sexy doctors had that effect apparently. "Hey."

"Are we still on for dinner this weekend?"

"Sure." She paused, thinking of the trust she'd given Parker and all that implied, as well as the logistical complications of any non–team member getting to a race. "You're really coming to Bristol?"

"We are talking about the Bristol in northeast Tennessee and not England, right?"

"Yeah." Leaning back against the counter, she laughed. "But Bristol is the undiscovered Monte Carlo of the South."

"Anybody that can squeeze a hundred and sixty thousand people around a half-mile track is a magician *and* a gambler."

"You've been studying."

"If I'm going to romance NASCAR royalty, I figured I'd better be prepared."

Her heart thudded. "You're going to romance me?"

"Yep."

She pressed her lips together to fight back a smile. "So, I'll see you Friday?"

"Unless I get lost somewhere along I-40."

"Pull over and call me. I'll send a helicopter."

He laughed. "That's a pretty good backup plan."

Rachel smiled. He was so easy and uncomplicated, charming and fun. "Just call my cell phone."

"I will. I—" Background commotion buzzed through the phone. "I'm due in surgery. 'Night, Rachel."

"Good night."

She laid the phone in its cradle. Wow, maybe he should transfer to cardiac surgery. He certainly made her heart race.

Walking toward the deck, she considered that she had two men in her life who'd knocked her off balance. Parker disturbed her—and not always in a good way. Damien interested her—so far, *all* in a good way. Was there any doubt about which man she should be going out with and which one she should be avoiding?

Plus, Parker had a *harem*. She was entitled to her own dates.

"You have a problem," Parker said when she sat beside him.

"Oh, goody. Just what I was hoping for."

"Look here." He pointed to a line of figures. "This expense to Asphalt Marketing. It's steadily gone up by a thousand dollars over the last few months."

"We pay them a standard fee to maintain the Web sites. There's no reason for that big of an increase."

"There are also quite a few increased disbursements for the printing company."

"Oh, hell."

"You're going to need to talk to your CFO and your bank."

"I'd like to keep it quiet."

His eyes direct and unemotional, he handed her the printouts. "Somebody's taken fifteen thousand dollars from you, and that's only on my first glance. You figure they deserve their privacy?"

"Fifteen." Her heart jumped to her throat. "I only

saw five." She groaned, pressing her fingers to her temples. "We're running for a championship. I don't want this to be a distraction."

"You're always running for a championship, and it will certainly be a distraction if the team needs to buy screwdrivers, and they can't because the account is overdrawn."

"That wouldn't—" She stopped. *Anything* could happen. The situation had gone from concerning to scary in the last ten minutes. "I'd like to keep it quiet," she repeated.

"Hence the reason you came to me."

"Mmm. *Hence.*"

"That's a dig, isn't it?"

"Yes."

"But isn't it nice to have a sponsor who can speak so eloquently to the press?"

"It's nice to have a sponsor whose checks clear."

He angled his head, which drew her attention to a wavy strand of black hair that slid across his sculpted cheek. She wanted to brush it back behind his ear. She wanted to touch him in a way that wasn't professional or casual. But that was probably because she longed to throw herself into anybody's arms, if only to escape the reality of what was happening to her family's lifeblood.

"Do you sit around at night and think of ways to put me in my place?" he asked.

"Oh, sure. It's my secret obsession. Can we get back to my financial crisis now?"

He nodded. "You need to find out who's taking money from the company as soon as possible."

"And why."

He angled his head and sipped from his wineglass. "Does it really matter why?"

"Yes, it does. Everybody who works for us is extended family. Wouldn't you care why somebody was so desperate?"

"Sure I care, but Huntington Hotels employs thousands of people. I can be sympathetic, but I can't risk my business on someone who's stealing." He laid his hand over hers and squeezed. "And that's what they're doing—stealing."

"I guess. It makes my stomach hurt to think that someone is betraying our trust. Maybe this person's mother is sick, maybe their child needs a lifesaving operation."

"If your employees are extended family, then wouldn't you know who was in trouble already?"

Why did the man continually challenge her? Why did big business have to be so cold? Being part of big-time racing, she certainly understood profits were the bottom line, but couldn't you make money and still have a heart? "Maybe. Maybe they're embarrassed."

"Well, your embezzler—"

She winced. "Do we have to use that word?"

"Yes." He stood, raking his hand through his hair in frustration. "That's what's happening, Rachel. Face it."

She glanced up at him, the hard expression on his face. She'd forgotten how tough he could be. This was a man who'd risen to the top of his profession because he made wise, as well as difficult, decisions. She found herself wondering about him and the choices he'd made for his own family's business. He'd gone against his father and opened an office here, but had he faced a crisis like the one she did now? How had he handled it?

With decisiveness, style and grace, she had no doubt.

"Your thief is bold—or not too bright," he continued. "He or she is taking large sums of money and not hiding it very well. And while I can be sympathetic about an employee's problems, it's a long step from personal financial crisis to stealing thousands of dollars from your employer."

"Exactly. Something big must have pushed this person over the edge."

"They're *stealing* from you." His eyes darkened. "Find them, *fire* them."

She lifted her chin. "I want to know why."

He turned away for a moment, bracing his hands against the balcony railing, then he looked at her over his shoulder. "Your compassion is one of your most amazing qualities."

"I…" She paused and met his gaze. "Amazing qualities?"

"Only as a professional businesswoman, of course," he added, his eyes unreadable. "And my professional opinion is that you call every person from accounting and licensing—which is where the money is being funneled out of—into your office. Question them, find out who's responsible, then fire them. Proving your case in court could cost you considerably more than fifteen thousand dollars, so you'll have to decide if you want to prosecute them when you'll likely never get back the money they stole in the first place."

"Oh, yeah. That's a great plan." She shook her head. "I'm not in charge of GRI. I can't call anybody into my office."

"So have Bryan do it."

"To do that, I'd have to tell him."

He crossed his arms over his chest. "You can't keep this from him. He has a right to know."

"I'm keeping it quiet until I find out what's going on."

"One of your employees is *stealing* money from your family. That's what's going on. Don't you think the president of the family business should be aware of the situation?"

"Bryan has too much to deal with now. I won't add to his burden."

Clearly frustrated, he slid his hands in his pants pockets. "You are an incredibly stubborn woman."

"You're just *now* figuring that out?"

"So how do you propose to solve the problem?"

"We're going to find out what's going on. Quietly."

"*We?* As in you and I?"

"Sure. You and me. In secret." Her gaze searched his, needing assurance, and somebody, for once, to share the weight of responsibility. "Do we have a deal?"

CHAPTER SEVEN

PARKER FOUGHT to ignore the leaping sensation in his stomach.

Work with Rachel on an important, secret project that, if he helped solve to her satisfaction, would endear him to her forever? Work with her on a secret project that would involve them spending long hours together?

Naturally, he should help. That's what friends did, right? What former hot-for-each-other people did, he wasn't sure, but they probably helped each other, too.

And yet part of him wanted to run the other way.

Even as the impulse shot through him, he shoved it away. Last night's deep discussion with Cade about marriage, divorce, Rachel and long-term relationships had simply spooked him.

"Let's see…" he began, furrowing his brow in mock concentration, "An indeterminate number of private, secret meetings with you or—"

"Not private," she said, watching him through those cool blue eyes that rarely lost their wariness. "Secret."

"How can they be secret if they're not private?" he asked reasonably.

"I just want it to be clear. These are business meetings."

There was nothing businesslike about his smile. "What else would they be?"

"With you, there's no telling."

"Is that your kind way of calling me devious?"

She nodded. "I guess it is."

"And yet my deviousness is about to come in handy for you."

"I guess it is," she said on a resigned sigh.

He moved slowly toward her, reflecting for the millionth time on how striking she was. There was something in her eyes, in her strength and spirit that drew him closer, as no one else ever had. He admired her struggle to hold her family and their business together no matter what it cost her.

And there were moments, like now, when her full effect washed over him, all at once like a wave, leaving him to wonder if he was fooling himself into believing he could set aside their attraction by simply wishing it so.

"Perhaps I'm so devious that *I* stole the money, hoping you'd come to me for help, and then I would get to spend many secret hours in your company."

"You're that cunning, are you?" she said quietly.

"I am. And what would you do if I asked for payment for my services?

"You want money?"

"I have money." His gaze slid to her mouth. "I was thinking something more...personal would satisfy."

She licked her lips, and he nearly groaned. "You just agreed that these meetings would be business."

Did she want them to be more? The look in her eyes and the trembling in his hands told him that though they'd agreed to set aside their attraction, neither of them plainly had. She was about to go out with that smiling surgeon; he was dating...well, vigorously.

Were they kidding themselves?

"So I did," he said finally, stepping back. "I'm at your service," he added, his tone brisk. "I'll need a list of all the people in accounting and licensing who have access to the bank accounts."

"I can get that."

They walked back into the condo, and, after grabbing his suit coat, he headed toward the door. His heart was racing as fast as his thoughts. "I'd appreciate you e-mailing me the information about the employees. I leave for New York in the morning."

"But you'll be at Bristol, right?"

He glanced at her over his shoulder and made sure his smile was mildly teasing. The intense moments on the deck were better left behind. "Miss me already, do you?"

She scowled. "The fan-club event on Friday night. You're *supposed* to be in charge."

"And you have a date, so I expect you'll have other priorities."

"How did you know…"

"The good doctor was very interested in you. I can't imagine he'd wait long to see you again. Wasn't that him who called earlier?"

She said nothing for a long moment, her gaze searching his. She'd let her guard down long enough to be curious. "You're spooky sometimes."

He reached out and stroked his finger across her jaw. "Just observant." Finding that he wanted to continue touching her, he slid his hand in his pocket. "Like now, you're wondering whether you should let me kiss you good-night."

"But I—"

"Let me solve that little problem for you—*along* with secretly handling your financial crisis. I think it's best if we simply indulge in a brief hug." Before she could protest, he snagged her by the waist and pulled her against him. The arousing scent of her perfume drifted toward him, the curvy lines of her body molded to his for just a second, then he released her and stepped back.

"We'll meet Saturday morning, in the hauler?" he asked, fighting to stay casual, though his body was humming.

Looking somewhat stunned, she nodded.

"I'll see you then," he said before striding quickly away. He was tempted to break into a run, but, thankfully, the Huntington arrogance she so often accused him of saved him.

At least until he got to the parking lot.

WEDNESDAY MORNING, Parker boarded his jet and flew to New York. At the airport, the limo driver took him into the city and Huntington Hotels's central office in Manhattan.

Back to business. Normal business.

He was an extremely powerful and wealthy executive. *She* was simply a woman.

A powerful, wealthy executive woman, to be certain. But he didn't fantasize about acquiring her company and her money, so, basically, Rachel was simply a woman.

One he couldn't forget.

Despite their best efforts, the attraction lingered. Would it always be there? Would she *always* distract him past reason? Was this some sort of revenge by Cupid? He'd always gotten what he wanted concerning women. Well, nearly always. His mother's rejection didn't count in the romantic scenario.

And while last night he was certain Rachel had felt the sparks he did, today he had his doubts. Did she think he was an ass for coming on to her? Had she asked for his help because she liked him, because she was attracted to him or because she needed him?

Mostly likely she needed his financial skills. Rachel was a direct woman. If she *wanted* him, then he had the feeling she wouldn't be subtle about it.

Still, he wondered if he should confront her about their attraction. Their talk in December hadn't gone well, and going down that road again seemed less than wise.

He certainly hadn't changed his mind about one thing—if she had accepted his weekend-of-fun offer back in December, he wouldn't be suffering now. The attraction would have burned out. He'd have truly moved on.

Thankfully, his cell phone rang, pulling him away from his personal issues.

One of his district managers had recently gone on maternity leave, and the assistant taking over for her had apparently misplaced the definition of guest services and insulted a valued client.

He was still trying to deal with that mess as he strode into his office. Used to the constant flow of compliments and complaints, his longtime assistant helped him out of his suit coat, brought him coffee and patted his shoulder in support without a word.

The next few days weren't much better.

Convention sales were down forty-five percent in Los Angeles, Dallas and Frankfurt. The banquet facilities in both Miami and Chicago needed major renovations.

Plus, his father and grandmother—deep into their constant campaign to question his every move— weren't happy about his decision to team with a celebrity TV chef to take over restaurant space in their premier New York and St. Louis hotels. They felt the renovation costs were too high; he knew the rewards in both publicity and their guests' palates would be well worth the money.

He'd won the argument, but not without a great deal of ridiculous posturing by his family. They'd given him the job. Why wouldn't they let him do it?

"You should be *here*," Henrietta Rafemore Huntington said, peering ominously at him from across her priceless antique desk on Friday afternoon. "Not running off to play with those silly little cars."

In the library of his grandmother's elegant Manhattan home, Parker sat on a Chippendale chair covered with white brocade silk and wished for all the world to be in Bristol, Tennessee, peering under the hood of a brightly painted race car. "Those *silly little cars* generate billions of dollars in business," he said, fighting to contain his temper.

"So pass this project off to a marketing manager."

"I prefer to handle it myself."

His grandmother cut her gaze toward him. "You shouldn't be. You should be here."

"So you've said." Tired of the endless challenge and arguments, Parker rose. "Is there anything else?"

He was halfway across the room before her demanding voice stopped him. "What's changed you? Is it some woman?"

Yes. Isn't it always?

The females in his life either cared too much, interfering and trying to control him, or, like his mother, didn't care at all. The rest of them—the

lovely, the smart, the eager and the grasping—satisfied and frustrated him over and over.

"Women are a weakness with the men in this
family," she added.

Facing the solid cherry French doors, he nodded.
"I've always thought that as well. But sometimes I
wonder if they shouldn't be a source of strength." He
paused, then added, "I need to make my own way,
Henrietta." Never had he affectionately called his
grandmother by any variation of that name. "You
and Dad agreed to let me. I appreciate your legacy
and generosity, but this is *my* time." By his side, he
curled his hand into a fist and turned toward her. "I
sincerely appreciate your advice."

"But you don't take it."

"I do. I implemented your mentoring program
for the managers, which has proven to be extremely
valuable. I will continue to listen to your sugges-
tions. I respect my family."

He turned away again and had his hand on the
doorknob, the avenue to clean air and escape from
conflict, when she spoke again.

"Your hair's too long."

Laughing suddenly, he glanced at her. "You'll
have to do better than that, old girl."

She paled. "I'm not old."

"No, you'll never be old. I didn't mean it as an
insult. George Stanhope, the English owner of
Stanhope Galleries, calls his grandmother that as a
sign of affection and strength. It seemed fitting."

"George Stanhope's hair is properly cropped."

His heart contracted, then seemed to shrink. "I imagine it is. Though his father is still unsatisfied with his performance as CEO of the family business. Perhaps you could recruit him."

Without waiting for her response, and surprised at the bitterness flowing through him, Parker accepted his coat from his grandmother's butler, then stepped outside into the frigid air.

The assault to his body was welcome. The easy affection of the Garrison family seemed so far away.

He climbed into his limo and felt more alone than he ever had in his life. He didn't want to rip his family apart, but he didn't want to be a slave to them either. How could he get through to them? How would he ever be good enough?

As he flew from New York to Bristol, he focused on the fact that the people at the track would value his opinion and dedication. And Rachel would understand the pressure he was under. He knew he shouldn't rely on her, but he recognized that she'd relied on him.

Her family was the most important part of her life, and she wouldn't trust just anybody with their financial security. There was nobody in his life he wanted to talk about his family with but her. Did that bond them, or just make him crazy?

As the plane touched down at Tri-Cities Airport, he turned his attention to something he could actually control—the meet-and-greet party he was due to attend at the track. Cade's fan club had asked

Huntington Hotels to sponsor an event where they could mingle with their favorite driver, get autographs and have him answer their questions. Since fans were the lifeblood of the sport, and Parker knew he still needed to win many of them over after the year and a half of separation he and Cade had gone through, he'd agreed to foot the food-and-drink bill for fifty guests that were selected by a fan-club lottery drawing.

It was a time to schmooze, not lust after his driver's sister.

Maybe he could add that as a side benefit.

He arrived at the track twenty minutes before the party. Even though he'd been in constant communication over the last week with his PR rep, Emily Proctor, he knew the boss's touch was always vital. He'd like to see the buffet and bar area for himself. He wanted to be sure the stage was set with a working microphone, plenty of chairs and the Huntington Hotels bannered logo hung straight. He wanted to see the faces of Cade's fans. Their excitement reminded him why he continued to crave the thrills, competition and dedication that was the heart of NASCAR.

He strode into the tent set up just outside Turn Two and quickly found Emily, who was standing on the stage, adjusting the microphones.

"M-Mr. H-Huntington," she said, her pale brown gaze jumping to his as her voice rose and fell in a nervous flutter.

Emily was new to the company this year. She was young, but smart and efficient. He'd hoped familiarity would help her get over her anxiety around him. There were people he enjoyed intimidating, but she certainly wasn't one of them. "It looks like you have everything under control. Is there anything I can do to help?"

"I—" She quickly shook her head, her eyes wide with worry, her straight, dark hair brushing her shoulders. "No. No, sir."

"Emily, I'm not here to hover over your shoulder. I'm here to help. There's no need to be nervous."

"But you're the boss. I mean *really* the boss." She nodded at the banner, which was hanging—in a perfectly straight line—behind them. "Your name's on the marquee."

He so loved her naked honesty. "True. But you've earned your place here as well."

She blinked. "Thank you, sir."

"You're welcome. Are all the gift bags assembled?"

She pointed to a table on the left side of the tent, just inside the entrance, where two smiling, attractive girls stood, wearing uniforms similar to the one Cade and his team wore every race day. "Everyone's name is on a bag, which contains the track-survival kit of sunscreen, earplugs, visor and snacks, all branded with our logo. We also slipped in copies of Cade's hero card and a permanent marker so that the fans would have something to hand him in the autograph session."

"That's an excellent idea," he said, genuinely impressed.

She blushed. "Thanks. I'll be standing next to him during the mingling part of the party, but I thought it would be a nice way for the fans to break the ice with him. So many people are dazzled and nervous when meeting a driver for the first time."

"Yes, they are." Though he considered Cade a friend and had been dazzled by few people in his life, he'd seen an adoring expression too often on a race fan's face not to appreciate their position. "We have power to the microphones?"

"We tested them earlier, and they're ready to go."

"Security is in place?"

"At every corner of the tent."

"Cade is here?"

"Isabel is bringing him. I talked to her a few minutes ago. Their ETA is ten minutes."

"The fans are here. I saw them outside as I came in."

"They're giddy, sir."

He raised his eyebrows at the old-fashioned word. "Seriously? *Giddy?*"

She blushed again. "Well, I mean—"

"You've been hanging out with me way too much, Emily." He patted her shoulder. "It'll pass. Hopefully."

"Actually, *giddy* is a pretty accurate description."

Parker tensed, knowing the owner of that voice. He turned, forcing a casually professional expression on his face.

Which failed miserably when he found not only Rachel, but that damn neurosurgeon, standing behind him.

Somehow, despite his teeth-grinding, he managed to make the necessary introduction of Emily, then searched deep and long for his ingrained manners as Rachel did the same with Superdoc Damien Findley, whose teeth were definitely just a little too perfect, and who laid his hand on Rachel's back twelve times in the space of three minutes. Either Emily sensed the tension between him and Rachel, or she was simply conscientious, but she moved away to check on last-minute details, leaving him with the two lovebirds.

Faced with Rachel on a date, an irrational, elemental sense of jealousy invaded him.

There was no doubt that Rachel Garrison was too much for him. Too much commitment, too much conflict. Yet he couldn't help longing for her, wondering if there could be something more between them than his usual, brief relationships. But putting his heart out there, to be stomped and mangled the way his mother had damaged his so long ago seemed stupid.

And he wasn't a stupid man.

Reminding himself of those simple things was difficult, but necessary. "I appreciate you two taking time out of your busy weekend schedule to come to the party," he said with forced politeness.

Rachel gave Parker an odd look, as if she somehow sensed his annoyance, but Damien smiled broadly. "Rachel's giving me a true behind-the-scenes look at NASCAR, so we figured this was a great place to start."

"Indeed it is," Parker managed to say. And even half civilly.

"We should probably move off the stage, though," Rachel said, her gaze flicking between the two men. "The fans will be here any moment. Damien, would you like a beer or something?"

He met her gaze and smiled. "Love one."

Parker nodded. "Excellent. Let's head to the bar."

He'd rather have downed a shot of tequila, or knocked himself over the head with a hammer, but he wrapped his hand around a bottle of water with a surprisingly steady hand. Maybe jealousy could be beneficial. Drivers managed their emotions, even using memories of times they'd been wronged, to win races worth millions of dollars. He'd once raced motorcycles to manage his energy and frustration, but he'd never been less than charming and polite with the women he was attracted to.

But now, just at this moment, he didn't want to smile and pretend he felt nothing while he watched Rachel give all her attention to another man. He wanted to snatch her away, to pull her to his side and *demand* she acknowledge their chemistry.

His saner side reminded him Rachel wasn't a trophy to be hoisted.

"Wine and racing?" Damien asked, after taking a

drink from his beer and nodding at the selection of wine bottles sitting on the bar.

Rachel had also gotten a beer, though Parker knew she preferred wine. Did the fancy doctor know that?

"Believe it or not, there are even winery sponsors," Parker said. "Though beer or soda is preferable to most fans in the stands. The tastes are changing, though, just as the fans are."

Parker smiled as Rachel scowled. At least he'd dragged her attention from her "date." Old-school fan versus new-school fan was a constant debate in NASCAR. He and Rachel were the very embodiment of the argument. Her family had been steeped in racing for generations; he was a corporate newbie. To him, both sides were powerful. "Because a guy wears a collared shirt instead of a T-shirt doesn't make him a less devoted fan."

"Some of these people haven't been around long enough to understand the history of the sport."

"The excitement may capture their attention at the moment, but they'll get the history in time. Be patient."

She shook her head. "Not in my genes."

He toasted her. "No, I guess not." But that single-mindedness was part of the reason he found her so fascinating, so he couldn't fault her.

She had amazing drive and focus. She was fiery and opinionated in a world where—except for his family—he was surrounded by yes-men and -women.

Her never-give-up attitude and devotion to her family was inspiring. Her ability to distinguish herself among her successful, famous siblings reminded him to continue to fight for his own views involving his family's business. Her struggle to come to terms with her parents' divorce echoed his own.

"Rachel tells me this track is one of the most exciting on the circuit," the doctor said, glancing around as if expecting a car to come whizzing by any second.

"It certainly is, but to what degree seems to depend on whether you talk to the drivers, media or fans," Parker said.

"At least it's not a one-groove track anymore," Rachel said.

Parker winked at her. "That's the driver's view. Some people still miss the beating and banging."

"It'll be interesting to see how this race shakes out and continues to fuel the debate."

"Either way, from the fan's side, it's an amazing spectacle." Noting Damien's blank look, Parker struggled with enlightening him. If the guy wanted to follow racing, he was going to have to learn to move fast. But hadn't he been the advocate for the new fan? Finally, he explained, "Last spring, they repaved the track here, so in the race last August the drivers could pass more easily and without bumping their competitors out of the way to do it."

"I thought the idea was to *not* hit the other cars," he said.

Rachel smiled glowingly at him. "It certainly is.

Especially if you're either the person who fixes the bent-up cars, or you pay the bills for those repairs."

"You do hit the other cars on purpose sometimes," Parker pointed out. "Bump drafting."

Rachel took pity on Damien's confusion this time and explained the concept of bumping the car in front of you to shoot both of you past a row of cars beside you.

Parker had to acknowledge the other man's attentiveness and intelligent questions. He was educated and had a job outside of racing. He was a *healer* of all things. He was obviously entranced with Rachel—though Parker still thought there was something smarmy about that perfect smile. He was from the South, so he talked like her. He didn't have a trace of arrogance that Parker could see—though personally, he'd want his surgeon to be more confident instead of gazing around at everything like a kid at a carnival.

Well, hell, he's perfect for her.

"Parker?" Rachel asked in an annoyed tone, making him think she'd called his name a couple of times already. "What do you hear about—"

Claps and shouts erupted outside the tent. A low buzz of conversation followed, drawing Parker's attention to the area near the stage. Cade strode in and shook hands with the security guard, then Emily in turn. Isabel walked by his side, acting more like herself than she had earlier in the week. Her narrow-eyed gaze swept the tent, as if making sure all the details they'd decided on were in place. Then she greeted Emily. She smiled and nodded as if pleased with what she saw. Emily beamed in return.

Parker was relieved Isabel, his brilliant partner in the marketing efforts regarding Cade, wasn't fawning over her fiancé or moving behind him as if intimidated. Or, worse, looking as if she was about to attack any female who gave Cade so much as a friendly smile.

A few months ago, he'd never have believed impossible-to-intimidate-Isabel—Scary Isabel to some who'd worked with her—would be so affected by the spotlight. But the fussy wedding preparations and the gossipy comments from fans and a small segment of the media about her "landing" NASCAR's most eligible bachelor had worn on her.

"That must be Cade," Damien said.

Rachel, her gaze following her brother with both affection and exasperation, rolled her shoulders. "That's him, all right."

Damien grinned. "You promised me an introduction."

"So I did," Rachel said, then her gaze slid to Parker's. "Can I talk to you alone for a minute?"

Wondering if she already had an update on the embezzlement situation, Parker nodded. "Of course."

Once they'd retreated to a relatively private corner of the tent a few feet away, she pointed at the concrete floor. "Notice my shoes?"

Now realizing where this was going, but determined to be modest—even if it killed him—Parker glanced down. "They're black. And shiny."

"You're not fooling me for a second." She stepped closer, her voice low. "Who do you know at Nordstrom's?"

He offered her a dignified smile. "I know a great many people in a great many places."

"Oh, yeah?" She crossed her arms over her chest. "The shoes I'd ordered, the ones that were on back order until the next millennium, the ones I told *you* about last week, appeared at my hotel, in a *fruit* basket." She angled her head. "Any thoughts? Comments?"

"Maybe the fruit people and the shoe people crossed paths in the elevator."

"I don't think so."

"Perhaps a secret admirer snuck into your room and placed the shoes in the basket. I would check on that sort of deviant, though charming, behavior."

She jabbed her finger at the center of his chest. "You got me these shoes."

He'd hoped she'd appreciate his efforts at being helpful and friend-like, not attempt to stab him. "I admit nothing."

She leaned forward suddenly, smiling, her lips brushing his cheek. "You should. It was very sweet. Thank you."

Sweet again. He fought a wince. Not the description he normally received from women he wanted... well, from a woman he *formerly* wanted in his bed.

Still, he knew she meant it as a compliment and that warmed him. "You're welcome," he said. "I'm here to serve."

"Mr. Huntington?" Emily said hesitantly as she approached, dragging his attention abruptly back to business. "We're ready. Should we let the fans in?"

His cheek still warm from Rachel's lips, he smiled. "By all means, let the party begin."

"HE'S SO AMAZING."

Parker nodded at the besotted fan next to him. "Isn't he, though?"

"So busy, but he always takes time for us fans."

"Sainthood can't be far away."

The fan, dressed from her ball cap to her tennis shoes in red-and-white Cade Garrison apparel, dragged her gaze from Cade, signing autographs across the tent, to glare at Parker. "Are you tryin' to be funny?"

"No, certainly not," Parker said quickly. He'd obviously let his sarcasm get to him. But after two solid hours of witnessing coos, sighs, shouts, screams and even one fainting over Cade, he was exhausted. "He's my driver, too, after all."

She waggled her finger at him. "And a good thing, too. I boycotted your hotels all last year after you dropped Cade. I even made Charlie—that's my husband—drive twenty miles out of the way on our vacation last spring. Charlie!" she called to a man standing in line at the bar.

Once Charlie had his beer, then trotted over to them, Parker had no doubt he was—again—about to be railed at by Cade superfans for his judgment mistake and not standing by Cade after their... disagreement. He lost track of the number of times he'd apologized while being glared at by men, women and children of every age imaginable.

Honestly, it was getting a little old.

And coupled with his annoyance at himself for constantly giving in to the urge to watch Rachel and her date move among the crowd while they laughed, chatted and *touched*, Parker was pretty much partied out.

"Charlie, didn't I make you drive twenty miles out of the way to avoid Huntington Hotels last spring?"

"You sure did."

"But then I canceled the ban when you decided to sponsor Cade again."

"And I'm immensely grateful," Parker said.

The fan narrowed her eyes. "You talk funny."

"So I hear."

When Charlie and his boycotting wife drifted away, Parker headed toward Cade. Glancing at his watch, he noted that the time allotted for the party had passed thirty minutes ago. If he didn't get Cade moving along, he knew the fans would hang around for the rest of the night. But after the Q&A session, they'd assured each attendee they'd get their hero card signed by Cade if they wanted, and there was no way Parker was going to let that promise go unful-filled.

He'd wind up hung by his designer tie.

"How many more?" Parker asked Emily, who stood behind Cade.

She glanced at the line. "This is the last group. Looks like about ten."

"When the last one has his autograph, we'll get Cade to the stage and let him say a few last words, then we need to move quickly to escort him to his motor home."

"The golf cart is outside the back entrance."

"Excellent. Just remember, Cade may want to drive."

"Really?" she asked in surprise.

"It's a driver's issue with control. Offer to drive his rental car sometime. You'll see. Anyway," he went on, "if he'll let you drive the cart, head straight for the drivers' lot. I'll make sure everything gets broken down here."

"Yes, sir."

"You can call me Parker."

Emily nodded, her gaze hesitant. "Yes, sir."

He would apparently have to be patient about Emily as well. Was he really such an intimidating guy? "Have things gone well with the autograph-ing?"

"Sure." She grinned widely. "He's so terrific with the fans."

Yet another reason he should have tried a little

damn harder to ride that motorcycle or, better yet, learned to race on four wheels. Emily feared him, while she clearly worshiped Cade. He supposed he could manage his employees by pressure and coercion—it had certainly worked for his father—but he'd rather not go that route.

Within a few minutes, the autographs were finished, Cade had said his onstage goodbye and Parker and Emily were escorting him to his golf cart, where Isabel joined them. Naturally, Cade did want to drive.

As Parker was about to send them off, though, Cade grabbed his arm. "Who's that blond dude with Rachel?"

"The brain surgeon." When Cade continued to look blank, Parker added, "I told you about him on Monday."

"Right." Cade frowned. "I don't like him. Did you see his teeth?"

Ah, a kindred soul. Maybe Dr. Perfect didn't have everything after all.

CHAPTER EIGHT

THE GROUND RUMBLED violently beneath Rachel's feet, the result of forty-three powerful stock cars roaring around the high-banked track at Bristol.

She never lost her craving for that sound, the smell of rubber and gas, the sheer spectacle of speed, light and blur of colors. The fans stood in their seats, nearly screaming as loud as the engines, the exhilaration on their faces easy to see. The crews hovered on the inside of the pit wall, where she stood as well, her heart slamming against her ribs, somehow, even after all these years, still amazed and awed that this was her life.

For all she complained about racing, the obsession to win, the sacrifices her family had made and continued to make, she knew she would always need this moment. The green flag waved the start of another race, one that held the promise of victory for one, and disappointment to everybody else.

That hope and struggle was in her blood.

And, maybe, despite the pain it had caused, she had to learn to accept her role in the history and the future.

At Bristol, the lap times were about fourteen seconds, so conversation was nearly impossible unless you spoke by radio. Text messaging was also popular. The overwhelming noise, however, didn't stop Damien from trying to shout questions in her ear. Curiosity must be a doctor's strength and weakness.

She tried to answer them, but half the time she didn't understand him and finally settled for grabbing a spare pair of headphones, fitting them over his ears and telling him—via a pad of paper—to simply watch, listen and enjoy. It was cute, really, that he wanted to learn so much, so quickly, but she'd spent her entire life around the sport. There was no way to impart that knowledge in a few hours.

As she watched him absorb the chaos of sensations around him, she found herself wishing there were more sensations from *her* about him.

He was smart, handsome and kind. He had a great smile and had a lovely habit of leaning toward her when she spoke, as if the words she said were of valued interest to him. But when he touched her, she felt no more than mild interest.

Didn't a girl want fireworks?

The heat between her brother and Isabel was palpable every minute they were together. They were so into each other, she'd had to snap her fingers in front of their faces countless times to get their attention.

Her BlackBerry vibrated in her pocket, dragging her attention from her personal issues back to business. She pulled it out and glanced at the screen, finding a message from Parker, who was entertaining clients in a suite high above the speedway.

Car looks good. How are things down there?

Smiling, she answered him. Loud. Crazy. The usual.

Miss it. Too quiet up here came the reply.

She couldn't explain the pleasurable flutter in her stomach at the idea that he was looking down on her and wondering what she was doing and thinking. It reminded her of the sensual interest she sometimes caught in his eyes when he looked at her. The attraction between them was supposed to be settled, but was it possible their interest in each other was only lying dormant, waiting for a moment to pop to the surface?

A moment, like when you're on a date and supposed to be thinking about your date?

Gotta go, she said in her text message back to Parker, then shoved her BlackBerry in her pocket.

Trouble in Turn Two brought out the caution, and Cade's team prepared for their first pit stop. She pulled Damien away from the wall and off to the side of the war wagon, which held all the equipment and where her brother's crew chief, Sam, sat several feet above the pit box. From there, Sam could direct his team's critical servicing to the car.

The moment Cade's No. 56 red-and-white Chevy pulled into the pits, the over-the-wall crew dived into action, changing tires, making adjustments and fueling the car. TV cameramen and commentators went into overdrive just as the pit crew did. Everyone else around the pit stall froze, fascinated by the frenzied ballet and striving not to get in the way.

Staring at her brother's profile, which she could discern through the car's window net, she thought about the press conference a few weeks before Daytona, when Cade and Parker had unveiled his new car. It was mostly white, naturally decorated with the red-and-gold Huntington Hotels logo on the hood, but he and Parker had also decided to add red lightning bolts from the doors across the front quarter panels, ending where the headlights would be on a normal car.

Even Rachel, who generally didn't care about how the cars were painted, provided they all had the traditional bright red Garrison hue somewhere, had to admit the psychological painting of lightning-hot speed was sharp.

Cade tore out onto the track less than fifteen seconds later. The field collected behind the pace car, with Cade in fourth. They went green three laps later, the engines roaring into Turn One like a tornado of sound and speed.

"Trouble, Turn Four!"

Rachel craned her neck to her right and saw a wave of cars rushing toward the start/finish line. Cade wasn't among them. He was spinning in a cloud of smoke in the turn.

"Damn!" she heard Sam say through her headset.

No matter how many times she saw a wreck during a race, she held her breath for a second or two. She knew the drivers were certainly safer than any regular driver on any interstate in the country, but there was a moment, when the smoke clouded her vision and the cars seemed to spin in slow motion, that she had to fight back pulse-pounding fear.

Her daredevil father and brothers weren't worried about getting hurt; they worried about damaging their car and championship dreams. They lived for adrenaline.

But for those who stood on the sidelines, there would always be moments like these.

Cade's car was smoking and crumpled against the outside retaining wall and SAFER barrier. Two others slid down the banking toward the infield, neither of them looking too racy.

"I think we're done," she heard Cade say through the headset a moment before the window net dropped.

"Wait for the safety crews," Sam said.

With the caution flag flying, the track safety truck pulled alongside Cade's race car seconds later. He climbed out through the window, accompanied by a rousing cheer from the crowd in the stands.

As her brother rode in the ambulance for the mandatory ride to the infield medical center, Rachel unclenched the fist she hadn't even been aware she was holding. It was because of Bryan's highway accident that she was on edge about every bump and scrape any of them took. For so long they'd seemed invincible. Racing royalty. Tragedy couldn't touch them.

But it had.

They were mortal. They hurt and suffered along with everybody else.

Isabel leaped off the war wagon next to her, jolting Rachel out of her reflection. Together and silently they grasped hands and moved quickly toward the care center.

Rachel had forgotten all about Damien until he jogged up alongside them. He mouthed the word *what?* and lifted his shoulders.

She grabbed his arm and kept moving, hoping he'd come along without question, since she couldn't spare the time for explanations. She knew Isabel wouldn't be completely at ease until she'd seen and touched Cade for herself.

When they reached the gate that led to the track's medical building, the press was already crowded around. The guard recognized Isabel and let her, Rachel and Damien through without a word. They jerked off their headsets as they approached the door.

Inside, away from the confusion and noise, Isabel had one question. "Where is he?"

One of the track EMT workers pointed down a short hallway. "Back there."

Rachel let go of Isabel's hand so she could go to Cade, then she leaned back against the cool, concrete wall, closing her eyes and ordering her heart to slow its erratic beating.

"Do you want me to check on him?" Damien asked.

She kept her eyes closed and shook her head. "I'm sure he's fine." Though why she felt nauseous, she couldn't explain.

Damien, bless him, said nothing more. He leaned next to her and grasped her hand.

He's fine, she said to herself for the thousandth time. He'd walked away waving at the crowd. SAFER barriers, safer cars and support equipment were all on his side. The anxiety she felt was irrational. NASCAR and the tracks did everything humanly possible to keep their drivers safe.

If only Bryan had wrecked on the track instead of the highway...

Still, the kernel of worry churning in her stomach wouldn't calm. She'd feel better when she could see her brother for herself.

She heard the outside door open and blinked. Parker appeared in the opening. His intense, green gaze darted around the small, stark room until it found hers.

Seconds later, without remembering moving toward him or him toward her, she was in his arms.

His familiar scent filled her nose, and the hard wall of his broad chest seemed like an ideal place to spend the next decade or so. She clutched his pristine white shirt, knowing she was probably ruining it, but knowing he wouldn't care.

"Where's Bryan and Daddy?"

He laid his hand at the back of her head. "In the suite. I told them I'd come."

Neither of them could be dragged to the doctor, so that news wasn't surprising, but she was ridiculously grateful Parker had been the one to come. She would have had to be too strong in front of her family.

"Are you sure you don't want me to go back and check on him?"

Hearing Damien's voice, Rachel lifted her head from Parker's chest. Suddenly, she was embarrassed. Her date was standing by as she threw herself into another man's arms, and she was completely over-reacting to her brother's accident. Cade was fine.

She glanced up at Parker for a moment. He seemed as surprised as she was to find themselves intertwined.

Embarrassed, she cleared her throat and stepped out of Parker's embrace. "No, but thank you," she said to Damien.

At the same moment she suddenly remembered who Damien was and what he did. Why was she throwing herself at Parker for help? Damien was a surgeon. If there was a medical issue, then *he* was the one she should be turning to.

She stood next to him, grasping his hand. "If the track doctor thinks Cade has a concussion, I may have you look at him tomorrow."

He nodded solemnly. "I'd be glad to."

"What's with the welcoming committee?"

Rachel turned at the sound of her brother's voice. She didn't move as he walked toward them, his charming, easy smile familiar on his handsome face. Watching him, her heart finally settled down in the proper place in her chest, and she couldn't find the words to say she was grateful to see him without sounding like an idiot.

Besides, one glance at Isabel's face told her he'd been fussed over plenty anyway.

"You tore up a perfectly good race car, you know," Parker said, coming to her rescue with his good-humored sarcasm.

Cade seemed to be glad nobody was going to make a big deal. "Take it out of my paycheck."

"I'll send Bryan a memo about it, buddy. Don't worry." Smiling, Parker backed away. "I'm off to make us all our next fortune."

"You'll update Bryan and Daddy?" Rachel said.

His gaze slid to her briefly, and she was again embarrassed by throwing herself at him. Too many women did so.

At least he was too classy to mention it. "Of course." He bowed. "Your wish, my dear Rachel, is my command."

"Plain crazy," Cade commented when Parker was gone.

"And fast," Isabel said. "That's a hell of a trip from the suites down here."

"I guess we're packing up and heading home," Rachel said.

"We'll never get Daddy away from the track till the end of the race," Cade said. "We might as well head up to the suite. I can have a beer for once."

Isabel swatted him playfully on the arm. "After you check in with Sam and the rest of the team."

As they started out the door, into the waiting arms of the media, Cade turned his head, looking over his shoulder at Rachel. "Thanks for coming to see about me, sis."

"A thrill a minute," she said, finally finding her smile. "This family is a thrill a minute."

"SHE HAS TO KEEP this fitting appointment, Miss Rachel," Carmen said, tapping her foot as she stood stubbornly in the doorway of Rachel's office.

"I'm supposed to kidnap her?" she asked, sending her office manager an annoyed glare from across her paperwork-strewn desk.

The last few weeks had been crazy. Between balancing her personal life—which, thanks to Damien, she actually had now—dealing with Cade's schedule and sponsor commitments, and with the added stress of investigating all the employees on Parker's suspect list, she was at the end of her rope.

Isabel's issues over her wedding gown were way down on the list of aggravations at the moment.

"The wedding is an important event for your family."

"This *business* is an important event for my family, and I have a vital part in running it."

"We're going to have manicures and lunch," Carmen said. "A nice girls lunch, then we'll go to the dressmaker's for the fitting."

"We can have a manicurist come here and order in lunch."

"Is that supposed to be a bribe? My son, Father Gonzalez, wouldn't be pleased with me if I accepted such an obvious effort to influence my commitment to the holy state of matrimony." She paused, smiling in a way that could almost be termed...angelic. "After all, this is your precious baby brother's wedding."

Rachel drummed her pen against a stack of paper three inches thick. The woman could give her mother lessons in guilt. And that was saying something, since lately she'd stopped crying over her broken marriage and forcing Rachel to thumb through old photo albums and childhood movies, lamenting the loss of their once close-knit family. The last few weeks she'd been so upbeat over finally dumping her *loser* husband, Rachel was ready to scream over the whiplash reactions.

Why was she dating at all? Dating led to caring, which led to years of devotion, followed by crying, anger, betrayal and loneliness.

She could be single and alone.

Still, the fact that she *had* been putting in too many hours and neglecting her family commitments—aka avoiding Cheery Mom/Sad Mom—only made Carmen's obvious ploy even more effective. *Precious baby brother.* Good grief. But with divorce fresh in her mind, was anything more important than making sure Cade and Isabel got off to a positive start?

"You promised to help," Carmen said, her bottom lip pooching out like a two-year-old's.

And, just like the parent of a two-year-old when faced with sad, dark brown eyes and the possibility of a broken commitment, Rachel folded faster than a poker player without a pair. "Fine. Lunch and manicures next week. Can you call the bridal shop and arrange the fitting then?"

"The fitting is today. Two o'clock." Carmen glanced at her watch. "Which gives you enough time to wrap up what you're doing so we can take the afternoon off. We'll have lunch at Cardoni's at twelve-thirty, which will fit in perfectly after your meeting with Mr. Huntington, then we'll have manicures and meet the seamstress at L'Elégante afterward." She started to turn away, then smiled over her shoulder. "And your mother is coming."

Rachel's jaw dropped. She wasn't sure which part of that unapproved plan she should jump on first. "What about Isabel?" She couldn't imagine her future sister-in-law, who couldn't find the mall without a GPS, agreeing to a day of girlie beauty.

"She's coming."

"How did you convince her?"

Carmen lifted her chin. "I told Miss Isabel you had to meet with her on an urgent business matter."

Rachel rounded her desk and started toward the door. "What urgent business matter? Carmen, you can't—"

Carmen's dark-eyed gaze drilled into hers. "It's her wedding."

The woman had a way about her that was part bully, part saint. And Rachel fell into line when faced with her office manager's plans every time. Mostly because they made sense. And her kindness and compassion were boundless. So, yet again, she was caving. But if Carmen's plans ever turned out badly…

"Fine," Rachel said, heading back to her desk. "Twelve-thirty."

Over the next several minutes, Rachel tried to put the upcoming afternoon out of her mind. Actually, she enjoyed pampering herself with lunch and manicures. She simply hadn't made time lately. But the idea that they were going to ambush Isabel didn't sit well with her. She and Isabel were more than future in-laws, they were friends.

Pasta. Isabel liked pasta, and she loved Cardoni's new chef. Maybe she'd eat and not be so concerned about a manicure and a pin-wielding seamstress. Maybe Carmen could guilt *her* into doing something for once. Maybe, just maybe, they could all escape the afternoon without bodily harm.

But she wasn't counting on it.

As twelve o'clock approached, she couldn't delay any longer and headed to Isabel's office. This was her wedding gown fitting. Surely she could be reasoned with to keep *that* appointment.

"Ah, Isabel?" Rachel said, pausing in the doorway. "Can I talk to you?"

"Not if it's about shopping." The fierce scowl on her face would terrify most people, but Rachel wasn't going to be dissuaded. While she was working on a secret investigation of her family business, worrying about missing funds and larcenous employees, her brother and his future bride were supposed to be gazing into each other's eyes and looking forward to their life of blissful love and happiness.

And they were going to do that if Rachel had to paint smiles on their faces and handcuff them to the altar. *Somebody* had to live happily ever after.

This family is due, dammit.

"You think I don't know you people are ambushing me?" Isabel continued, her dark brown eyes fierce with annoyance. "Think again. That woman from L'Elégante e-mailed me this morning, reminding me of my two o'clock appointment."

Rachel flung her hands up dramatically as she crossed the office floor. "Oh, well, the jig is up, I guess. Our grand plan to maim and torture you is busted."

Isabel simply glared up at her. "I'm not a shopper."

"Good." Rachel plopped into the chair in front of her desk. "We're not shopping. You've already *bought* the dress, after all. It might as well fit."

"Go away, Rachel."

"We're also having lunch and getting manicures."

"No, we're not."

"You know as well as I do that nobody's going to get any work done around here until you go. Carmen's determined to plan this wedding down to the last grain of rice thrown."

"So's your mother."

Rachel leaned forward, propping her hand on her chin. "And don't think I'm not going to suffer with her coming along on this outing. She'll drill me with questions about Damien."

Isabel's gaze met hers briefly. "I thought things were going fine with him."

"They are, but *fine* isn't good enough for Mom. She wants *details*. I'm not sharing details with my mother, especially a mother who smiles like a Halloween pumpkin, all frozen and forced. It's freaky and disturbing." She shook away the mental picture. "I thought you turned over the invitations to her to keep her busy."

Isabel leaned back in her chair. "I did, but apparently that wasn't enough. She wants to know if we want disposable cameras on the tables so that guests can take pictures during the reception. She wants to know if the groomsmen's corsages should have baby's breath.

"Why the hell would I want or need a baby breathing on a corsage? Is that some superstition? Does it have to be a *specific* baby? Where are we going to find this baby? It's—"

Astonished, unable to hold back, Rachel started laughing.

"Okay, you're not helping," Isabel said, her eyes narrowed as she tapped a pen on her desk calendar.

"Baby's breath is a flower," Rachel managed to say between giggles.

"Get out."

"It is. Haven't you ever worn a corsage?"

"No. They're stupid and probably itchy."

"Itchy, yes, but I don't think they're stupid. They're traditional and lovely when done right. And try not to stress over Mom and her organizing. It's her way of getting to know you, of trying to bond. She lives for this stuff—family gatherings and planning parties."

Her mom needed something to do besides her charity work, interfering in her kids' lives and finding new and inventive ways of pretending she didn't care about the end of her marriage. Besides, she had a great sense of style, she organized to the point of obsession. Come to think of it, Rachel needed to team up her and Parker ASAP.

"But I'm lousy at that stuff," Isabel said, bringing Rachel back to the problem of the moment. "Didn't I tell you I'm going to be a lousy wife?"

"You're not," she said briskly, knowing from experience that Isabel didn't like to be coddled. "You'll have fun today. It's just a little nail polish. And if you're good, I'll buy you some shoes destined to drive men wild."

"Men don't care about shoes."

Rachel raised her eyebrows. "They do if that's the only thing you wear."

She could have sworn her supposedly hardened future sister-in-law blushed.

Rising, she headed toward the door. "Yes to cameras and baby's breath. And for heaven's sake, call me when you get stuck. I'm here for you."

"I'm not good at asking for help."

Rachel smiled. "I know, but try."

Over time, she knew Isabel's wariness toward the family and all the implications of joining them would fade. Rachel herself knew about being slow to trust. Maybe not to the extremes Isabel had suffered through her abusive childhood, but she'd lost count of the number of guys who'd tried romancing her in an effort to get to her father and brothers. The ones who sweetly brought her flowers and pretended to like the same movies and music she did, only to suddenly, miraculously, express an interest in racing cars two months into their relationship.

She'd never found a man she could fully, wholly trust, but Isabel had. She'd found "The One."

In the doorway, Rachel turned. "Marrying the man of your dreams shouldn't be so difficult," she said gently.

"It's not." And finally Isabel smiled. "That part is pretty amazing actually."

Back in her office, Rachel returned a few more

phone calls, then fixed her makeup and put on her black pumps to match her suit.

The pumps Parker had gotten for her.

Smiling, she headed out of the office to her meeting with him, assuring Carmen she'd meet them at the restaurant promptly at twelve-thirty.

His friendship, which had begun with sponsorship and had extended to her collaborating with him on the embezzlement investigation, had become an interesting, sometimes unsettling force in her life.

His professional advice on the ins and outs of financials had made her much more comfortable in her decisions. Though she was keeping a secret from her family, she was doing so to save them all a lot of heartache. On a personal note, he was honest and challenging. Supportive and sensual. Charming and mysterious.

She wanted to know more about him, and at the same time, worried that getting too close was dangerous to her peace of mind.

Still, the confidence she had in his business sense made it easier for them to work together on the various PR campaigns for Cade, knowing things would get done and done well. She was so used to taking care of everybody, it was nice to have somebody *she* could lean on.

His list of possible embezzlers was another thing entirely.

They included the GRI accounting department manager, his secretary and two employees in the licensing department, which is where the missing money had been traced back to.

Rick Peters, their accounting manager, had worked faithfully for them for six years, and while his secretary was fairly new, she'd joined the company on Rick's personal recommendation. Mark and Jim in licensing were conscientious and bright. They had superior references, and all the sponsors loved them. Including Parker.

She couldn't picture any of those people stealing so much as a paper clip, but Parker had assured her that the paper trail didn't lie.

She parked in the garage below the Huntington, where she'd meet the girls for lunch, conveniently located next door to the downtown Charlotte office Parker had opened back in February, so he could keep a handle on his massive hotel business without flying to New York every other day and still spend time with Cade and his team at the shop.

Which they loved because he brought elaborate lunches made by the amazing Italian chef he'd recently hired for Cardoni's, the premier restaurant in his hotel.

His assistant showed her into his office immediately, and as Rachel stepped inside, he rose from behind his massive antique mahogany desk and walked toward her.

She saw him so often now in jeans and T-shirts, she'd forgotten what a presence he could be, decked out in his four-thousand-dollar suits, looking charming, wealthy and gorgeous. When he kissed her cheek, lightly, as he always did, she felt a flutter of pleasure move through her body and the urge to lean into him, to inhale the spicy, alluring scent of his cologne.

"How's your day going?" she asked, casually stepping back to hide her reaction.

"Long," he said, and she noticed he did look tired. Which he rarely did.

"Trouble in the Huntington empire?"

"Nothing you need to worry about."

She sat in a chair in front of his desk, while he returned to his seat behind it. "Oh, come on. I dump all my problems on you. It's your turn."

"It's fine. How's Cade feeling about Richmond?"

After Cade's wreck at Bristol, he'd had a run of bad luck and bad finishes. The whole team was worried and depressed. They were hanging on to eleventh in the points by a thread, and while May seemed too early to worry about the Chase for the NASCAR Sprint Cup, nobody wanted to go into summer on an unlucky streak. "You see him more than I do these days. You tell me."

He pushed his hand through his hair. "He's trying to keep it together, but the guys definitely need a boost."

So does somebody else. She'd never seen his eyes so dull. "You, too." She leaned forward, laying her hand over his, where it rested on top of his desk calendar. "What's wrong?"

His gaze searched hers for a long moment. "I'm not sure where to start."

CHAPTER NINE

PARKER KEPT his hand still and fought the urge to grasp Rachel's and pull her over the desk and into his lap.

Over the last few weeks, he'd buried himself at his office as he tried to push his feelings deep inside. Most of the time, he was fine. If she didn't touch him, he was fine. If he worked himself past exhaustion, he was fine.

But when he slowed down long enough to think, or when she unexpectedly touched him, his body responded, and he was forced into realizing he wasn't anywhere close to setting aside the attraction he'd promised both her and himself he would.

His role of supportive friend and business associate was wearing on him because it now felt like a badly played part in a rejected play. He'd truly been confident he could move past Rachel.

He *had,* he thought, clenching his fist and leaning back, away from her and the allure of her he didn't understand or want to deal with. For months, he had.

Or had he simply been fooling himself?

He hadn't been on a date in weeks. He thought about Rachel endlessly. About her dating that smiling surgeon, about what Cade had told him—Rachel's being a woman who expected and needed a long-term relationship. About his own inadequacies and reluctance to commit beyond dinner and sex.

His mother had left him and his father after they'd given her their hearts and devotion. The breakup had embittered his father, and while Parker dealt with his sense of betrayal by letting plenty of people into his life, he never let them get too close. He never wanted to risk rejection again.

But he wasn't prepared to share any of that with Rachel. With anybody.

And he certainly had other worries on his mind. "It's my grandmother."

"She's not sick, is she?"

"No, nothing like that. She's just interfering a great deal in the business. I feel like when I make a decision, I'm going to turn around and see her leaning over my shoulder, her lips set in a thin, disapproving line. She's reluctant to let me do things my way."

"But *you're* CEO. Tell her to back off."

He laughed. "You do know how to break things down to their simplest, most direct form."

"I grew up surrounded by drivers, remember. If you aren't firm and direct, you'll get run over. Literally."

"I'm sure. Unfortunately, directness hasn't worked

so far. At least my form of directness." He couldn't imagine saying "back off" to his formidable grandmother. She'd have him committed. "And it doesn't help that she and my father have formed an alliance on a lot of issues."

"Your father retired, and since when has your grandmother worked eighty hours a week at this company?"

"Ah, well, here's the interesting thing I've discovered. She was apparently the power behind the throne when my grandfather *and* my father ran the company. How she managed to run an international corporation behind the scenes, while she still supported more than a dozen charities and endless social functions, I'll never know. But she's determined to carry on her leadership role."

"Sounds to me as if she's trying to bully you just like your father did."

He shook his head. "He didn't bully. He blustered. She's the one who intimidates."

Rachel pursed her lips. "You're not the kind of man who lets himself be intimidated."

He didn't know what kind of man he was anymore. Not too long ago, he never would have believed he'd still be thinking about a woman who didn't want him. He spun his chair to face the window behind him. "I never have been."

"What about your mother? I know your parents are divorced, but she must have some role in the company. Maybe she could give you some advice."

He stiffened. His mother. In his life. What a laugh. "I haven't talked to my mother in a number of years," he managed to say, his tone rigid.

A brief silence ensued. "Oh. Sorry." Rachel cleared her throat. "What about offering to send your father and grandmother on a cruise? Maybe even one of those month-long ones. Glamorous vacation, relaxation. A reward for all their valuable insight into the company."

"I tried to send them to Paris a few months ago. They said they couldn't possibly leave me when I was obviously in need of their guidance."

"Well, that's a bust. How about setting them up on dates?" she added dryly. "Carmen could give you matchmaking tips."

"Grandmother has a full social life. My father doesn't date."

"Ever?"

"Ever."

"Oh."

Of course she didn't understand. She'd met his father, who was a handsome, physically fit man. Parker had no idea about his sex life—and frankly didn't want to know, but as far as companionship and romance went, there was none.

"My mother left when I was two. He never got over it."

His mother had, in fact, spent her life since traveling the world with her sizable Huntington settlement, never bothering to worry much about those she left behind. As a result of her abandonment, Parker had withdrawn, been shy and awkward as a child and teenager. Later, his charismatic uncle had taught him to be confident and charming with women, since his father had been too busy working and making sure his heart turned to stone to take an interest in his only son.

"He works," Parker added. "That's all he really does."

He heard Rachel move closer. She sat on the windowsill in front of him, her eyes shadowed with regret. "Divorce sucks."

Looking at her, he found he had a smile inside him after all. "Yes, it does."

"I guess he isn't handling retirement well, which is why he's driving you crazy."

"Pretty much."

"Keeping with my directness theme...if those two are so damn determined to run the company, why did they turn it over to you in the first place?"

"My grandmother pressured my father to retire. Apparently, she thought I'd be easier to deal with."

"Boy, was she ever wrong." She grinned. "I mean that as a compliment, of course."

"Of course."

"I don't know how to help you. Your troubles with your father and grandmother, I mean."

"You already have. It helps to talk about it."

"That's what friends are for."

Wanting more seemed greedy at the moment.

Having a trusted friend was a comfort he didn't realize he needed so much. "I guess they are."

She rose, pacing away so that he had an opportunity to notice her fitted black pantsuit, conforming to her trim, subtle curves. She also wore the shoes he'd had delivered to her in Bristol. She could, of course, wear a paper sack and look fantastic, but he still delighted in studying the way her blazer nipped in to emphasize her narrow waist, the way the pants highlighted the length of her legs.

And, just like that, the melancholy reflection lifted.

"I think we should go to each of them and try to talk about the situation."

He dragged his gaze to her face. "Talk to who about what?"

"The people you think took the money from GRI. That's what we were supposed to be meeting about, remember?"

"Right." On some level he recognized she was distracting him from his own problems, but, apparently, all she had to do to accomplish that was be in the same zip code as him.

He shook his head to clear it. "You want to talk to the embezzlement suspects?"

"Yes." She propped her backside on the corner of his desk. "I feel guilty. Like we're being dishonest by not talking to them."

"*We're* being dishonest?"

"Okay. Maybe not."

"We need to wait. We can't get access to their bank accounts without a court order, which we can't obtain unless we go to the police."

"No police," she said, her voice rising. "Police means press and—"

"I know," he said calmly. "That's why we wait. We'll have a chance to observe everybody, see if they've bought anything expensive, or if their life-styles have changed in some way."

She sighed. "That sounds like a long process."

"I told you this wouldn't be easy."

"But Rick and his staff are loyal. His secretary is dating Cade's car chief. They're so cute and happy. And Rick's wife recently had a baby."

"So money's tight, then?"

Rachel scowled down at him. "You're a cynic."

"But nobody's stolen fifteen thousand dollars from me."

"Maybe not, but you *like* Mark and Jim in licensing."

"Yes, I do," he said, hearing the accusation in her voice and knowing he needed to answer it. "That doesn't mean they're not guilty. Just because I've never wanted for money doesn't mean I don't understand it's vital to have and hard to earn. We don't have to hate anybody to prove anything."

"People make mistakes."

"Sure they do. They still have to pay for them."

"Fine." She crossed her arms over her chest. "We wait."

"For now, with the conditions of discretion you've asked for, I think that's the best way to handle things."

"I agree."

He understood the sting of betrayal lurking in her eyes. The money didn't matter a damn to her, but the disloyalty meant everything, and he'd cheerfully fire the jerk who'd upset her and taken that money without a second thought.

"I hear you're having lunch next door," he said in an effort to move away from the painful topic.

"Of course you know. You have Carmen as a spy."

"Spy?" Lifting his eyebrows, he leaned back in his chair. "Come on, now. She called me last week to ask if Cardoni's had an open reservation. She said she wanted to treat Isabel to lunch before her bridal gown fitting. I was supposed to turn her away?"

"No." He could have sworn Rachel pouted for a moment. "But you could have warned me. She ambushed me this morning." She paused, her measuring gaze flicking to his. "She has a thing for you."

"Isabel or Carmen?"

"Cute. You wanna ask Cade that question?"

"Certainly not."

"I always said you were smart. Carmen, of course." Rachel flicked at a piece of lint on her jacket that he never saw. "She's trying to get us together."

His heart gave his ribs a swift uppercut that he wished he could pretend he didn't feel. "No kidding."

"It's crazy, of course." Her gaze jumped to his, then moved away. "But it's probably better that you know."

Definitely. He wondered whether he should send Carmen flowers or get her advice on how to deal with unwanted attraction. He'd wrestled enough with this subject. Maybe it was time for a fresh perspective.

"So…" Rachel continued after an extended, humming silence, "are you coming to the go-kart races tonight?"

"I am. Though I'm better at poker. I think Cade got tired of losing at the tables and decided to substitute go-carts." Just as he'd substituted poker for pool, when he'd lost too often.

Her eyes sparkled. "Should be a good race." She glanced at her watch, then rose. "I should get going. If I'm late, Carmen will probably stop answering the phones in protest."

"Wait a second." He stood, then strode around the desk. "Are *you* racing tonight?"

"Could be." She lifted her eyebrows. "I have the track record there, remember." She headed toward the door with a definite swagger in her step.

Following her, he swung open the door. "Maybe you could show me a few tricks."

She turned toward him, her dancing eyes bordering on flirtatious. "I might. You'll have to prove you're worthy."

"Oh, I am," he said, offering her a confident smile. "I definitely am."

Her gaze searched his, and for a moment, the lurking attraction that had been there from the first rose between them. It was reflected clearly in her bright blue eyes, and he had no doubt she'd find the same, looking at him in return.

She'd denied it even existed many times. He'd accepted that and tried to move on. But, as the subtle, flower-with-a-hint-of-spice scent of her perfume drifted toward him, enveloping his senses, he called them both fools.

There was more between them than just friend-ship and business. *So much more.*

What that meant for him, for his sense of protec-tion and freedom, he wasn't entirely sure.

"Until tonight," he said quietly.

At his words, she seemed to come out of a trance. "Right." She cleared her throat and stepped back. "See ya."

She wasn't as immune to him as she liked to pretend. Maybe she was also having a hard time moving on. Maybe she felt as if she was playing a part these days. Was she tired of the charade?

"Chef is pushing his chicken pesto spaghetti today. You might considering trying it."

"Sure," she said, though she looked distracted.

Maybe her mind was on something besides food.

As she walked away, he closed the door behind her and considered the slow but certain shifting in their relationship. He'd never met a challenge he hadn't conquered or overcome.

Would Rachel Leigh Garrison be the first? Or simply the most rewarding?

"HOW ARE THINGS between you and that cute doctor, Rachel?"

Noting the probing, speculative smile on her future mother-in-law's face, Isabel glanced at her friend. Who wasn't smiling.

"They're fine," Rachel said.

Isabel retreated behind her menu. This whole lunch/girlie day—not to mention her upcoming wedding—had her personally on edge, so she was probably imagining the tension between Barbara, Carmen and Rachel.

"I'd like to offer you champagne," the waiter said, appearing beside the table with a cloth-wrapped bottle. "Compliments of Mr. Huntington."

Another waiter appeared at his side, setting elegant crystal flutes on the table in front of each woman.

Once the glasses were filled, Carmen was the first to hold hers aloft. "To Isabel and Cade. Happiness always."

They all clinked glasses, and Isabel frowned briefly into hers before taking a sip. She generally preferred beer to champagne, but having either in the middle of the day was weird. She, Rachel and Carmen had a million details to deal with back at the office. There were sponsorship and media obligations to handle, there were schedules to finesse, a championship to run…and a wedding in three weeks.

Beneath it all, she was scared.

And that ticked her off immensely.

"Mr. Parker," Carmen said, her eyes warm with pride, "he always thinks of the details."

Rachel frowned and set her glass aside. "I guess he does."

The waiter took their orders, and while the others chatted about Parker, his elegant restaurant and the racing season, Isabel sat back in her chair and sipped champagne. As long as she was blowing a whole day on silliness she might as well get silly.

There was something between Parker and Rachel. You'd have to be half-blind and stupid not to realize that, but Isabel could never seem to get a handle on where they stood. They seemed like friends lately. Before that, they'd been reluctant colleagues. Before that, wary adversaries. And even though the heat between them was palpable, they seemed to be trying to fight it. Yeah. Like *that* would work.

Still, love was complicated. Who knew that better than she did?

She loved Cade with everything inside her, and maybe with some depth of her emotions she didn't even know she possessed. And while their journey to find each other hadn't exactly been easy or without struggle, their engagement seemed even more overwhelming.

She'd survived a long time with her feelings held tightly in check. Now that they were out there— with family, friends and fans sending congratulations on their upcoming wedding—she felt the pressure to succeed in a way she never had before. She wanted to please Cade first, but she also didn't want his family and friends, his team, his *millions* of fans, to find her lacking either.

Rising to the top of her profession, she could be selfish, focusing on herself and her goals. Now, she was part of a team. She was, in fact, about to be part of the most intimate, vital partnership a person could ever join.

Marriage.

Their lunches were served, and Isabel was grateful to focus on her baked ziti. Parker had brought it to her many times over the last few months, somehow understanding that her Italian blood was soothed by food.

If Rachel didn't grab hold of that man with both hands, then she'd lost her mind.

"I'd like to meet him," Barbara Garrison said, drawing Isabel back to the conversation around her.

"Who?" Rachel asked.

"Your doctor friend. Maybe we could double."

"I'm meeting him in Richmond on Friday, but Charlotte's coming up, along with the wedding, so—" Rachel's head whipped toward her mother. "What do you mean *'double'?*"

Barbara's lips tipped up in a very feminine smile. "Date."

Isabel reached for her water in an effort to keep from laughing and choking. The stunned and appalled look on Rachel's face was seriously comical, but Isabel could sympathize with the weird idea of her parents dating other people.

She'd personally always thought Barbara and Mitch Garrison were made for each other and considered their divorce a weird blip in their relationship. But maybe their impasse couldn't be breached. If Barbara was dating, then she was obviously moving on.

"I met this really nice man at the florist's," Barbara continued. "Actually, he owns the shop. He asked me to dinner, so I went Saturday night. We had a lovely time." She paused, looking around. "Why are y'all staring at me like I've grown two heads?"

Everybody at the table got busy, drinking water, champagne, pushing pasta around on their plate.

"I think it's lovely, Miss Barbara," Carmen said, her dark-eyed glare flicking to Rachel, then Isabel. "Don't you, girls?"

"Yeah, sure." Isabel had no advice to give, though. She had no idea how she'd found her fiancé. Her prickly personality had always pushed most men away. But Rachel seemed to be doing okay in the dating department. Hell, these days she was dating a hot doctor and had Parker waiting in the wings.

She glanced at her future sister-in-law, and pretty soon so did everybody else.

"What?" she asked, looking up suddenly as if her chicken pesto had kept her mesmerized for the last several moments. "It's fine. Great, Mom." She made an obvious effort at forcing a smile. "Of course you should date. Dad certainly has been," she added in a lower tone.

Barbara sipped her champagne. "We saw him at the restaurant actually. He was with some girl half his age. I mean *really.* How tacky."

"You saw Dad when you were on your date?" Rachel asked, carefully laying down her fork.

Barbara shrugged. "I keep reminding myself Davidson is a small town, but it was still a little odd."

"I guess so," Isabel said, refilling her champagne glass. If they were going to talk about old family pain, men—both past and present—plus shoes, clothes and manicures, she was going to need more of a buzz.

Rachel laid her hand over her mother's. "Are you okay?"

"Of course." Barbara lifted her chin, and the determination in her eyes was fierce to witness. "He's moved on, and so have I." She squeezed Rachel's hand, then released it. "We have a wedding to plan. Let's talk about what color nail polish Isabel should get today. She should probably try out several shades, so she can have a few days to decide which one will suit her best on the big day."

As everybody's gazes shift to her, Isabel hunched over her plate, resigned to the inevitable.

ISABEL SCORCHED Rachel with a fierce scowl the moment she entered the dressing room.

"Are you having trouble with the zipper?" Rachel asked with forced brightness, noting Isabel's wedding dress was still hanging on the hook and the bride was sitting in the lone club chair in the room, wearing her jeans and plain white shirt, while her hair was curled in soft ringlets and her face artfully made up.

From the neck up, she was ready to go. It was the rest of her Rachel had been sent to deal with.

Isabel drummed her fingers on the arm of the chair. "My nails are painted five different colors, I want certification that that woman with the pincushion has had her eyes checked, since, the last time I was here, she poked me more than she did the dress, and you didn't say anything about hair and makeup."

"Didn't I?" She hadn't known herself. That was another one Carmen had sprung on her. At some point, she really needed to rein in her office manager, but since she was the only one not intimidated by Isabel, she wasn't about to do so before the wedding. "Well, don't worry. There's plenty of time to change things. This was just a practice run."

"Carmen said they—" Isabel jabbed a finger toward the shop, beyond the dressing-room doors where everybody, including the hairstylist and cosmetician were waiting for the bride's big entrance "—were *professionals*. Why do they need to practice?"

"Not practice for them. For you. You need to wear the makeup and hair, with the dress, so you'll be happy with the results on your wedding day."

Isabel crossed her arms over her chest. "Cade could care less what kind of makeup and hair I'm wearing."

"I'm sure that's true, but you're going to be in a million pictures, and most of the racing community, the press and your friends and family will be there. Wouldn't you feel more confident knowing you look your absolute best? You look amazing, by the way."

"I feel ridiculous, especially considering you people wouldn't let me look in a damn mirror."

"You need to get the full effect." Knowing Isabel's temper wasn't only about the primping, Rachel slid her hand down her future sister-in-law's arm. "You're not used to all the attention focused on you. You're used to being in the background."

Isabel looked up, anger mingled with a hint of fear in her eyes. "How do you handle it? All the press, the fans, the sheer *number* of people crowding around?"

"Experience. I've been on a stage, at least in racing, all my life. I'm used to it. You're not. You'll find your way." She knelt beside Isabel. "In the meantime, no one will find you lacking, least of all anybody in the family. And certainly not Cade. But don't you want to make the extra effort for this one day?"

"Hell."

Smiling, Rachel rose. "I'll take that as a yes. Let's get the dress on. I bet you'll see yourself in a different light."

"Cade is pretty edgy right now," Isabel said as she stood and started unbuttoning her jeans. "These bad finishes are seriously messing with him."

"I know, but both of you put way too much pressure on yourselves. There's a whole team around to support you."

"I should be doing something."

"Being there is enough."

"I think he needs something more."

"Mmm." She'd been reaching for the dress, but paused, looking at Isabel over her shoulder. "When *you're* in a pissy mood, what does he do to get you out of it?"

"What pissy mood? I'm the soul of even temperament." When Rachel snorted in disbelief, she added, "Okay, so he, ah…" Her eyes sparked, a sly smile appeared.

"He seduces you out of it." Rachel moved the wedding dress aside to reveal the undergarments designed to go with it, displayed on a delicate pink satin hanger. "Exactly my point."

"Oh, man." Isabel reached out and ran her fingers across the pale blue satin corset, trimmed in delicate white lace and complete with minuscule panties and a garter. "Where did this come from?"

"It's my gift to you."

Isabel's gaze jumped to hers. "No kidding." She looked back, longingly, at the lingerie. "I guess there are some perks to weddings."

"Indeed there are."

Isabel, holding the corset next to her body, glanced over. *"Indeed?"*

Rachel felt her face heat. The phrasing wasn't like her, and she blamed Parker. "It's designed to be worn under your dress," she said briskly, ignoring the amused undertone to Isabel's comment. "You need to wear it for this fitting, then the next time you wear it—"

"It'll be my wedding day."

For the first time, there was a tone of wonder in Isabel's voice. She wasn't much on ceremony; she only wanted her man. But Rachel knew there'd come a time when she looked back on the memories and pictures and would be glad she'd taken the time for a splashy wedding.

The spotlight *should* be on Isabel and Cade. Their love was an inspiration to so many.

Including her.

Rachel held on to the crazy dream that the ceremony might actually start to heal the troubles their family had been through over the last few years. Bryan's career-ending accident and divorce, her parents' breakup, her own lackluster love life and Cade's racing struggles had damaged them all in varying degrees.

But weddings brought people together, and Rachel could only hope everybody would pause for a moment to remember that.

"I don't like being poked and prodded," Isabel reminded her as they strapped her into her corset and dress.

"I know. It's almost over."

When they'd gotten everything on, Isabel glanced down at herself. "I'm me, with fussy hair and a fancy dress, right?"

You're exquisite.

But Rachel hid her reaction, swallowing the happy tears clogging her throat. "You certainly are," she said, steering Isabel out of the dressing room before she could balk at showing off for everyone else. "But let's see you in the proper light."

Isabel teetered out of the dressing room on her four-inch heels, then walked down the hall and up two steps to the round platform perched in the center of the bridal showroom.

Track lighting and angled mirrors reflected her white, strapless dress, highlighted her olive-toned skin and dark, curly hair. The simple design, a column of lace and satin, fell straight to the floor and made the most of her trim figure. The hand-sewn beads and iridescent sequins added a touch of sparkle and flash.

She looked stunning, and no one in the room seemed capable of speech. Barbara laid her hand over her mouth as her eyes filled with tears. Carmen nodded in satisfaction. The seamstress, makeup artist and stylist all sighed.

The scowling, jean-clad girlfriend had, miraculously, morphed into a brilliant bride.

"So, what do you—" Isabel stopped, her gaze catching her own reflection in the trifold mirrors. She narrowed her eyes, as if not quite recognizing herself, sliding her hands slowly over her torso, probably making sure it really was her wearing the stunning, wildly romantic gown that would carry her down the aisle toward her future and the man she loved.

Drawing a shuddering breath, tears rolled down her face.

Rachel nodded and smiled, knowing everything was going to be all right now.

CHAPTER TEN

RACHEL DROVE her SUV down the dirt road leading to the farm that had been in her family for three generations.

When her grandfather was a young man, struggling to make it in the racing business, the cows and chickens they raised fed the family or were sold at the local farmer's market. Nowadays, Grandpa still lived on the property in a huge Victorian house that everybody jokingly called the "cottage," since the garage used to be the entire living area.

She bypassed the house, though, knowing he'd be at the track with the boys. In his late seventies, he no longer ruled the world behind the steering wheel of a stock car, but he could still run with the best in a go-kart. She parked by the garage, up a small hill from the track, where, by the sound of the whining engines, the races were already under way.

As she approached the track, she noticed three go-karts whizzing around at top speed. Squinting, she realized the one in front was driven by Parker, in second place was her grandfather and the third driver was a mechanic from the shop. Cade and his buddies, Jay and Dean, stood off to the side, jeering good-naturedly at the competitors.

"Hey, guys," she called as she walked toward them.

"Where's Izzy?" Cade asked, glancing behind her. "I thought she was coming out with you."

"Um, well, she got a little emotional at the fitting."

Looking alarmed, he grabbed her arm. "Is she okay?"

"She's fine. In fact, I think you'll find her a lot more enthusiastic about the wedding plans. She seems to have made peace with all the fuss and preparations."

"Good." Relaxing, Cade let go of her arm and glanced back at the track.

What a competitive bunch those boys were, she thought, watching Grandpa tap—well, more like *slam*—the back of Parker's kart in an effort to move him out of the way. Since that streak ran strong in her as well, she almost regretted having to complete the mission Isabel had set her on. But then, with Cade gone, she'd be almost certain to wipe the track with the rest of the guys.

"She decided she needed to act a little more wifely," she said casually to her brother over the whining engines.

"Ah, man." Cade tunneled his hand through his hair, making the dark strands stand on end. "I told her not to worry about that stuff. I want her to be herself. I don't care about—"

"She's making you spaghetti." She paused at length. "In a black satin teddy."

Cade turned his head to look at her, his eyes wide, his face flushed. "She is?"

"Yep."

He thrust his helmet and gloves into her hands. "I'm outta here."

She waved as he ran off. "Have fun!"

"We gotta get girlfriends," Jay said, shaking his head, glancing at Dean.

"We can get 'em," Dean said. "It's keeping 'em that's the problem."

"What about you, Rachel?" Jay asked, nudging her arm and waggling his eyebrows. "You available?"

Long used to her younger brother's friends' sophomoric come-ons, Rachel simply shook her head. "Dream on."

"You wanna be our official starter?" Dean asked. "We can get you some hot pants and boots."

Rachel rolled her eyes. "Like *that's* happening. And I'll remember your lack of respect when I'm deciding whether or not to bump you out of the way before I lap you."

"Oh, no way," Jay said, nudging his buddy.

What a couple of goofballs. "Make yourselves useful, and go throw the checkers," she said, nodding at the electronic lap timer, which showed four laps to go.

They trotted off and threw the checkered flag a few laps later as Parker easily outdistanced the competition. Parker and Grandpa jumped out of the go-karts and Jay and Dean went in to race the shop mechanic. After kissing her cheek, her grandfather headed to the start/finish line to wave the next race on its way.

"Where did Cade go?" Parker asked, pulling off his helmet as the karts squealed off the start.

"His future bride is cooking dinner. In sexy lingerie."

He cocked his head. "I used to think marriage was overrated. Perhaps I should reevaluate."

Rachel rolled her eyes again. "You guys are so easy."

Parker flashed a quick smile. "And proud of it. I guess lunch and the gown fitting went well."

"It did."

"How long did you hold Isabel down to get her to comply?"

"I plied her with champagne and guilted her into it. She wound up in tears." When he looked worried, she added, "It was actually a good moment. You had to be there."

"Rachel rides to the rescue again."

She glanced over at him. "What the devil are you talking about?"

"You." She was pretty sure he smirked. "Call Rachel, she'll fix it. Call Rachel, she'll handle everything."

"That's *so* not true."

"Yes, it is." Though he must have caught sight of her annoyed expression, since he added, "It's a compliment, you know. Part of the matriarch's job."

"I'm not going into all that matriarch stuff again." No matter what he said, the title made her feel old and frumpy.

They said nothing for several minutes, watching the go-karts whir around the track. The scent of dirt, tire smoke and gasoline permeated the air, but Parker still smelled like exotic musky incense, the same as he did during a business meeting in his plush office. How did he do that? And how did he aggravate, intrigue and arouse her all at the same time?

"Do you really think I'm always rescuing people?" she couldn't resist asking.

Parker continued to watch the race, but she knew he was completely aware of her standing next to him. "I do." He turned his head to look at her. "It's one of your more amazing, selfless qualities."

Her eyes widened. "I— That's very sw—"

He laid his finger briefly over her lips. "Don't say sweet. It's simply true. I wonder if your family appreciates you the way they should."

She swallowed. "I'm sure they do." But it was nice to have someone else notice how hard she worked for them.

"Are you okay with what we talked about this afternoon?" Parker asked. "The plan to solve the financial problem?"

She rolled her shoulders, trying to shift the weight of her entire family's livelihood off her back without success. Was she crazy not to go to her brother Bryan about the crisis, or was she saving them all a lot of heartache? "No, I'm not comfortable with any of it, but waiting and watching is our best option at the moment. I agree with you, though. Since we'll never get our money back, I don't want to wait long and give anybody a chance to take anything else."

"You need to monitor disbursements closely. Don't worry. I'll be there for you."

"Thanks." She'd laid a lot on his shoulders as well. She could only hope and pray they were doing the right thing. "It helps."

"In fact," he said, his green eyes brightening, "if you find you have the urge to throw yourself into my arms anytime during this secret mission, please feel free."

She closed her eyes. The Bristol infield-care center was back to haunt her. "It was nothing. My brother had just been in a wreck. You were handy."

"And yet—unless I'm remembering the moment incorrectly, of course—there was a doctor nearby with two seemingly good arms. Did you choose mine for a specific reason?"

"To think I'd considered you too classy to bring this up."

"I'm simply a stickler for detail."

"It was an impulse thing," she insisted.

"I see. But just so you're aware, I could clear my social calendar if you like."

"Could you?"

His gaze roved her face. Desire flickered in his eyes. "My offer still stands."

"What offer?"

He raised his eyebrows and grinned wickedly.

For a moment—a weak and brief moment—her heart fluttered. Then all the reasons why her and Parker in an intimate relationship was a bad idea rushed back, and she shoved his arm lightly.

Vowing to set aside the problems at the office, along with the…whatever between her and Parker, she watched the drivers. Rachel found her fingers tingling with the urge to get on the track herself and show the guys that her success was well earned.

"When do I get a turn?" she asked Parker.

"You get a past champion's provisional. Let's wait for the loser's bracket to shake out."

"That is excellent sucking up, Mr. Huntington," she said, relieved they were back to their usual friendly banter. "Are you maybe hoping I'll have mercy on you during the race?"

"I am, Miss Garrison. I most certainly am."

"You're smarter than Jay and Dean."

"Is that supposed to be a compliment?"

"Definitely not."

A while later, she and Parker did get their chance to race against one another—and against the other big winner, her grandfather.

Nothing like racing motorcycle and stock-car champions to get the blood running.

Helmet in hand, Rachel climbed into the silver No. 500, which had been painted with blue stripes and red flames to look like Grandpa's championship-winning stock car from so many years before. She knew the track was slick and the cars light as air, so it took guts, concentration and skill to finish well.

Luckily, she thought as she pulled on her driving gloves, she had all three.

"You think you're gonna beat me in this old thing?" Grandpa asked, laying his hand on top of her head.

Craning her neck back, she flashed a grin at him. "You bet I am." She'd scored her record-winning run in the No. 500, and growing up with race car drivers had instilled a superstitious streak she was hopeless to get rid of.

"Don't count on it, little girl."

Shaking her head as her grandfather walked to his own kart, Rachel wiggled into her helmet. In her male-dominated family, she'd always be the "little girl."

"But who you gonna run to when there's trouble?" she muttered, gripping the steering wheel.

Jay waved the green flag, and the field roared off the start. Rachel, even though she started in the middle, ducked to the inside groove immediately, catching Parker by surprise. Focusing, knowing the dips and bumps on the track, she lost the lead only once to Parker, though her grandfather did pull up alongside her twice.

In the end, she nudged out Parker by half a kart length, and when she jumped out of her ride, her blood was pumping, her smile was broad. "*Girl,* huh?" she asked the men gathered around her.

"You're the man, uh…woman," Jay said, giving her a high five.

Dean grinned.

Parker grasped her hand and bowed. "A true champion."

Her grandfather hugged her to his side. "*My* little girl."

"If I'd lost, would you still claim me?" she asked him.

He kissed her temple. "Yep. A Garrison on the track always makes the competition more interesting."

"And tougher."

"Beer's on me," her grandfather said.

Rachel regretfully shook her head. "I've got to be at the office early. You guys go on and have fun."

"Sorry to bow out," Parker said, "but I've got to head home, too."

Dean and Jay razzed them for a couple of minutes, but, in the end, the idea of spending a couple of hours watching old races and drinking beer with the legendary Jack Garrison was a pretty tempting lure.

As the others climbed in their cars and headed toward the cottage, she and Parker cleaned up around the track, driving the karts back into the garage and storing the equipment.

"We're boring," she said, watching the garage door lower.

"We're conscientious," he countered.

"We're exhausted."

"We left it all out on the track."

Still, they leaned against each other, bracing shoulder to shoulder. "I gotta get in better shape," she said.

"I think it's more mental than physical."

"Sure it is."

Grinning, he grabbed her hand as they walked toward their cars. "It was fun as hell."

She returned his smile, noting how exhilaration lightened his eyes. "Yeah."

"You think we should stick to managing and accounting?"

"Probably."

He stopped and leaned toward her, brushing his lips across her cheek. "You were great, though."

"You, too."

And suddenly the moment changed from affable to something else entirely.

She was trying so hard to fit him into the *friend* box. To treat him as a valued colleague and nothing more.

But a moment or two of closeness, and she was breathing hard and longing for more.

"I'm not your brother, Rachel."

She swallowed hard, trying desperately to remember that she didn't need any more complications in her life. "No. You're my friend."

"Am I?"

The intensity of his gaze penetrated hers to the point that she briefly closed her eyes. But with the scent and heat of him inches away, she couldn't shut him out, so she opened her eyes and found him close. Too close.

They shouldn't be in this position. They were supposed to be colleagues. She should step back.

But she stepped forward.

He closed his mouth over hers as his arms slid around her waist. Angling her head, deepening the kiss, she slid her hands over his T-shirt–covered chest. His heart pounded beneath her fingertips.

Oh. Oh, my.

Fire coursed through her body as sure as the adrenaline she'd gathered on the track. And while part of her recognized she shouldn't be here, touching him like this, the rest of her simply didn't care. The scent and feel of him filled her with excitement and something else that trembled deep in her belly.

Lungs heaving, she jerked back. His eyes were dilated, his breathing coming in short bursts, just like hers.

"I—I should go." She backed away and practically ran to her car.

Safely inside, she laid her forehead on the steering wheel. "Oh, man, oh, man."

No kiss she'd shared with Damien—and there hadn't been that many in the first place—came anything close to resembling those intense moments with Parker.

What was she doing?

Should she be resisting Parker's allure? Instead, his offer of a weekend of sex and fun became more irresistible by the moment. And yet, she couldn't help wondering what came after. If she let her desire overwhelm her, then the aftermath caused problems for Cade, she'd never forgive herself.

Was she sacrificing her own needs over her family's wisely, or was she foolish to throw away the chance of something precious she could have for her own?

WALKING BRISKLY, Parker maneuvered through the crowded infield toward Cade's hauler. After racing tonight, his driver would marry the love of his life tomorrow.

Rachel was waiting for him in the hauler, so he only waved to other sponsors or owners he saw, when most race nights he would have stopped to talk. They needed to meet for an update on the embezzlement problem.

He had little to give her, and seeing her had its own rewards and tortures.

After the go-kart races and the kiss that followed, she'd been looking at him differently. Even at the Richmond race two weeks ago, when she'd had that smiling doctor in tow, her gaze had connected with his in an intimate way that hadn't been there before.

Before the kiss.

Usually her intimate look was followed by a quick frown of confusion and possibly regret, but he'd been having that same reaction for weeks, so he at least welcomed the companionship.

She was his driver's sister, he kept reminding himself. She was his business and marketing partner. She wasn't a casual weekend fling. If they gave in to the desire humming between them, then there would be repercussions.

Not to mention she was seeing someone else. They had to work together and he had to maintain control of his company. If his father or grandmother learned of any weakness in his strategy or relationships, they might petition the board of directors for a change of leadership.

He couldn't risk his lifelong dream, his *legacy,* of controlling HHI.

All these issues factored into a maelstrom of confusion and need, wonder and fear that seemingly had no end.

"Hey, Parker," Jamie, the team car chief said, stopping him outside the hauler. "the car's actually good, you know."

Clearly, his troubles had shown too obviously on the outside. He was a legend at poker in some circles. He might have the sense to show it.

"The car's good?" he asked, banking his personal issues.

"It's rocket fast," Jamie said.

The NASCAR Sprint All-Star Race taking place

later that night didn't count toward the championship points, but the payday more than made up for it. Money, plus pride and bragging rights, had the teams going all out for the Saturday-night crowd in Charlotte, which nearly every team called home. It was like winning the homecoming football game.

"Can't wait to see it hit the track," Parker said.

"Hey, a bunch of us are watching baseball tomorrow before the wedding. You know, kind of a bachelor party for Cade since we can't really have the strippers-and-tequila shots thing tonight."

And we can all thank God for that. "I'll be there. In fact, why don't we have the party in Cade's suite at the hotel." Which he'd already conveniently arranged in anticipation of some thrown-together gathering by the guys. "It has a full bar, and I can have the culinary staff make some snacks."

"Awesome. I gotta get back to the garage, but, hey, you wanna put some money in the betting pool? I got some serious cash on the Yankees."

"Sure. Count me in for a hundred. Are we getting a gift?"

Jamie grinned as he started backing away. "I got a blow-up doll."

"How—" Frankly, he was at a loss for words and barely managed to school his expression into amusement. He was also grateful he'd already sent a sterling-silver platter and coffee service to Cade's house. "How manly," he finally said to Jamie.

Jamie headed off toward the garage, and Parker,

shaking his head, turned toward the hauler. He greeted a few team members standing around outside. Cade's father was there, too.

"Big day tomorrow, sir," Parker said, shaking his hand.

"Yeah." For once Mitch Garrison didn't flash his signature wide grin. He looked distracted.

"Be nice to celebrate a wedding and a win."

"We gotta good track record for the victories." He glanced down, sliding his hands into his pants pockets. "Not so much with the weddings."

Two divorces in three years. A record not even his illustrious family could beat. "Then this will be a new beginning."

Mitch glanced up, his blue eyes finally showing some life. "You're good at always saying the right thing." He clapped Parker on the shoulder. "You'll make a good husband someday."

As he turned away, Parker fought a laugh and shook his head. Mitch was clearly a consummate optimist. Even in the face of overwhelming odds in the opposite direction.

In the hauler, he squeezed through the few crew members gathered beside the microwave, where a bag of popcorn was turning around on the tray. The scent of coffee was also strong in the air.

"Coffee and popcorn, boys?"

"We wouldn't have to stoop this low if you'd send over some of that fancy grub from the hotel," one of the guys pointed out.

Parker made a mental note to do just that for next weekend's big six-hundred-mile race, which was also in Charlotte. "I'll see what I can do."

He walked down the narrow hallway, with closed storage spaces on either side, and turned sideways once to pass Sam. He scowled at the crew by the microwave. "Don't eat too much," the crew chief called to them. "You'll be sluggish."

"What are you so worried about? I hear the car's a rocket," Parker said to Sam.

"Oh, nothin' to worry about, huh?" Sam's scowl deepened. "Only split-second timing on pit stops, calls for tires, adjustments, getting caught in a wreck, *causing* a wreck, blown motor, blown tire."

Parker held up his hand. "Okay. I get it. Sorry I asked the obvious."

"And we've had rockets before. Two wound up in the wall and one blew up with twenty laps to go."

"That's the way to handle it, Sam. Stay positive."

Sam paused, probably to decide if he was full of sarcasm or bull.

Naturally, it was both.

Parker opened the door to the back room, then walked inside—and found Rachel sitting on the couch beside Damien.

Oh, joy.

He battled back his increasingly short patience when faced with the doc and slid his hands into his pockets. "I thought we had a meeting," he said, trying to look a little confused and embarrassed to be interrupting them, though he felt neither. "Did I get the time wrong?"

Rachel rose. "No, you're right on time. Damien was about to head out."

Reluctantly, it seemed, Damien stood as well, but he never looked toward Parker. "I like walking around the infield with *you*."

"This won't take long," she said.

"I could wait here."

"It's GRI and sponsor business. We, ah, have confidential...things to handle." She cast Parker an urgent glance.

"I'm sorry, Damien," Parker interjected smoothly. "I have to discuss some of my company's financial data." He held open the door. "You understand."

Shrugging, Damien brushed his lips over Rachel's while Parker clenched his jaw. As the doctor walked out, Parker prided himself on not shoving him through the doorway.

"Not much of a kiss," he said to Rachel once he'd closed the door.

"He can do better."

"Can he?" Parker arched a brow. "Better than me?"

She lifted her chin. "That kiss was a mistake."

"So you've said. Several times over the last few weeks." He walked closer. He wanted to touch her, but didn't. His control was hanging by a thread these days. "Are you convincing me or yourself?"

"I'm dating Damien, not you."

"And that should settle things, shouldn't it?"

"Seems pretty obvious to me."

"Not to me." The scent of hothouse, tropical flowers drifted from her skin, and he found he couldn't resist after all. He slid his thumb across her cheekbone. "Do you tremble for him?"

She stepped back. She firmed the lips that had been shaking. "I thought you were here to discuss stolen money."

More avoidance, but he also noticed she hadn't challenged his assertion that he could kiss better than Damien.

Interesting.

"Yes, of course I am." He extended his hand, and they settled on the sofa. She kept a careful distance, which he found even more interesting. Obviously, his control wasn't the only one in question.

"I'm leaning toward Jim from licensing," he said. "Three of the four disbursements can be traced back to a project of his."

"But Jim isn't stupid. Wouldn't it be foolish to take from an account so easily connected with you?"

"It's stupid to take the money at all, and, yes, I've considered that whoever's embezzling is trying to shift the blame to someone else. But the plain fact is that they didn't hide their actions well in the first place. We're not dealing with a criminal mastermind here."

"They've been smart enough to get away with fifteen grand so far."

"Good point."

"I need some water. You want some?"

"Yeah. Thanks."

She walked to the minifridge, returning with two icy-cold bottles. "The whole situation is frustrating and depressing."

"I know." Without anybody else around, the tension she'd obviously been hiding rose to the surface. If somebody was stealing from his family, he knew the betrayal and anger would be ripping him apart. "On that note, I'd like, again, to express my desire to confront this in a more direct way."

She looked wary. "How direct?"

"Call each person into your office, tell them that money connected to their department is missing, see how they react."

"I can't accuse."

He held up his hand. "I didn't say accuse. I said *tell,* inform them, very matter-of-factly. You'll know who's lying."

"Like I told you, it's not my place to call anybody into my office."

"You're part of the family. It *is* your place."

She shook her head.

He very nearly sighed. "So tell Bryan. I guarantee he'll agree with my solution."

"Men." She huffed in disgust. "No finesse."

Parker raised one eyebrow. "Pardon me?"

"Hey, I'm surprised at you, too. Normally, finesse oozes out of your pores."

"Why, thank you, darling."

She narrowed her eyes—at the endearment or possibly his gender in general. "This is a situation that needs to be handled with discretion and grace, not bravado."

"Which is the reason you're not telling Bryan."

"Obviously. And you agreed to keep this between us."

"I did. But at some point, I think you're going to have to choose between discretion and expediency."

"I'm not at that point."

"Understood. Have there been any more unusual disbursements?"

"No. And I have Carmen watching the accounts. She knows something's up, but she won't say anything. I think she's simply happy somebody's taking her concerns seriously."

"She's a jewel."

"She's an interfering, matchmaker wannabe. *And* a jewel."

"An efficient jewel. You shouldn't take on so much. Give her—"

The door swung open, and Damien stuck his head around the edge. "All finished?"

"No, actually," Rachel said. "We need a few more minutes."

"I want to check out the media center." He walked across the room and sat beside her on the sofa, stroking her arm. "You guys can talk later, can't you? I'd love to see a press conference firsthand."

"Not just anybody can walk into the media center," Parker pointed out, gripping his water bottle a bit too tightly.

Rachel's gaze shifted between them. "I'm not part of the press conference, and the reporters are working, filing stories. We shouldn't be bothering them."

"Oh, come on. You're Rachel Garrison. Racing royalty." He flashed those perfect teeth. "Those reporters would drool on their shoes to talk to you."

Parker's jaw tightened, even as Rachel's face lost its pleasant expression. Damien didn't seem to notice either of them.

"But I don't have anything to say," Rachel said, her voice coolly calm. She rose, then crossed to the door, opening it. "Give me and Parker five more minutes."

Damien finally seemed to realize he'd stepped over the line. "Right. Sorry I interrupted."

Rachel closed the door behind him, then leaned back against it. Her face was flushed. "He's a little self-absorbed sometimes."

"Aren't we all?" Parker found himself saying, and could have kicked himself for opening his mouth. Did he really want this relationship between Rachel and Damien to *succeed?*

But then he and Rachel were friends. He was supposed to support her. It would do no good to point out Damien's flaws. She had to see them for herself.

She forced a smile. "Nobody's perfect, right?"

He nodded. "Right."

"What were you saying? About Carmen?"

"You shouldn't take on so much. Let Carmen help more."

"She can already run the office without me."

"Are you worried you'll lose your indispensable status?"

"No, of course not. It's a comfort to leave and know she'll take up the slack. Especially with all the traveling this summer and Isabel being gone on her honeymoon."

"She'll be gone three days."

"Oh, right." She paced the length of the sofa, then back. "We've been doing so much prep, it seems like it'll be much longer."

"I'm sending them to my hotel in Bermuda for a week as soon as the race season is over."

"Really? That's sweet."

Parker frowned. Sweet again, huh?

"You're awfully dressed up," she said, stopping to face him.

"I'm entertaining hotel clients in the suite."

She wrinkled her nose. "My dad's having a party in his condo. I'm supposed to go. But if that Desiree twit is there, I'm not staying."

"Isn't she the one he went to Hawaii with?"

"He has a picture of them dressed in hula skirts and bikini tops on his fireplace mantel. My father, NASCAR champion and legend, in a red polka-dot bikini. It's humiliating. For both of us."

"They're not together anymore."

"Really?" She planted her hands on her hips, staring down at him. "How'd I miss this? And how do you know more about my father's love life than I do?"

He shrugged. "Guys talk."

"That's the best news I've gotten all week. Now I don't have to dread going to his party." Her lips tipped up in a smile. "The view of the track from up there *is* pretty spectacular."

"Ah, well, you might want to be on the lookout for Bambi."

"Who's—" She stopped, shaking her head, her eyes widening. "Oh, no. You've *got* to be kidding."

"I'm afraid not. They met at the dentist's office."

"Please tell me Bambi is the dentist, and her parents, when they named her something so utterly, foolishly twitlike, were simply fond of cute, woodland creatures."

"Bambi is *not* the dentist, and I have no idea about the state of her parents' minds. Bambi was at the dentist's office to perform a strip-o-gram for the dentist—a birthday joke planned by his brother."

"She's a stripper."

"Was. Your father convinced her to give up her budding career and become his personal secretary."

"Oh, God." She sank to the sofa and dropped her head in her hands. "This is what divorce gets you."

"It does indeed."

"Does it ever get easier?"

He thought of his father, fiercely guarding his isolation. He considered his own issues with long-term relationships and their consequences. "Not really."

"Mom saw him a few weeks ago—on a date. She was on a date, too, of course. And all she said about it was that it was tacky of him to date someone so young. Silly, huh? She didn't even seem particularly upset. He's dating some twit named Bambi. Why isn't she upset?"

Knowing a thing or two about the people you wanted dating someone else, Parker said, "Maybe she is, and she's pretending she's not. Could be revenge dating."

"What step is that in the Eighty-Five Painful Steps After Divorce?"

He noticed the tears shimmering and grasped her hand. "You thought they'd get back together."

"Of course they will. They love each other. They just—they just got off track."

Such optimism. Had he ever felt the same?

"You're not twelve. You know how hard relationships are. They're complicated and ever changing. They involve a great deal of commitment."

She looked over at him. "Do you know why your parents broke up?"

"I can guess." And though he really didn't want to share his speculation, the fierce look in her eyes, blurred by tears, forced him to speak. "She married him for his money and social position. She gave him the required heir, then left."

"That's cold."

"Yes, it is. Not anything like your parents' marriage, I'm sure. But that doesn't change the circumstances *you're* in." He squeezed her hand. "You can't fix this."

She sighed. "Like I try to fix everything else?"

He brushed a lone tear off her cheek. "Like that."

"Yeah. I know." She blinked back her emotions and rose. "You're right. Of course you're right. Hey, what do you think Cade's chances are tonight?"

How had they gone from embezzling to Bambi to divorce to tears to race predictions? Friendship was exhausting. Seduction, really, was much simpler.

Still, he leaned into the sofa, laying his arm along the back and played along. "Jamie says the car's a rocket."

"Good. That's good. Jamie's a brilliant engineer, you know."

"I know."

"He's dating Laura. Did you know?"

"Who's Laura?"

"Rick Peters's secretary."

"Your accounting manager?"

"Yeah. They're so cute together."

"I'm thrilled to hear it."

It was a strange, rambling conversation. And not that he didn't enjoy spending time with her, but he couldn't help wondering why she didn't want to get back to her date—even if he was a self-absorbed date. She wasn't really afraid Damien was going to drag her bodily to the media center, was she? Rachel had no problems making her wishes known any other time, so…

He watched her pace in front of him. "Are you talking to me to avoid Damien?"

"What?" She stopped and whipped her head toward him. "No, of course not."

Studying the slightly panicked, annoyed look on her face, he smiled. "You are."

CHAPTER ELEVEN

RACHEL GAPED AT Parker. "I'm not avoiding Damien. I'm having a meeting. With you."

"We had the meeting about the embezzlement," he said in that calm, reasonable tone that never failed to aggravate and intrigue her. "In addition to that, we've talked about Carmen's status in the office and our viewing plans for the race. We've touched on divorce and the past and present love lives of family and team members."

He angled his head. "Is there some other crucial subject we've overlooked?" He paused, smirked, then continued. "Or we could discuss the ever-changing weather."

She glared briefly at him, then whirled. "Well, fine then. I'll go."

Before she reached the door, he'd caught her by the hand. "I'm not complaining."

The timbre of his voice sent warmth spreading through her body. She never got excited by the sound of Damien's voice. Why *couldn't* she get excited about the sound of Damien's voice? He was so great—moments of self-absorption notwithstanding.

"I'm simply curious," Parker continued, drawing her attention back to *him,* which he seemed to do effortlessly. "Why aren't you rushing out the door to see him? Your date, I mean."

She glanced over her shoulder. Heavens, he was close. She could see the flecks of gold in his green eyes. "I'm trying to. You're the one trying to stop me."

"But you only tried to go when I reminded you he was waiting. Am I that riveting? That irresistible?" He rubbed his thumb across her bottom lip. "Or is he that forgettable?"

She stepped back. She could think clearer when he wasn't so close, when he wasn't touching her. "I have to go," she said, tugging for him to release her hand, which he didn't.

She was a chicken, and she knew it. But she didn't know what do to about Parker. She wanted to dismiss him. To concentrate on Damien. And to lose herself in the happiness of Cade and Isabel.

She'd longed for a guy who wasn't involved in racing, who could belong to her alone and not be enthralled by her family. But she and Damien spent their weekends, not at hot clubs or great restaurants in Atlanta where he lived, but at the track, where she did.

Had she failed to escape, or had Damien drawn her back in? And how could she get them out of the pattern they'd fallen into?

Getting away from Parker would be step one.

"Let go," she said, pulling her hand harder.

"I'm not sure I can."

But he did, and when she was free, she darted from the room.

"MEN ARE SUCH wackos."

Isabel pulled on her seat belt. "Rachel, that's not what you say to a bride the night before her wedding."

Rachel started her SUV, shifting her gaze away from the window, through which she could see the limo Parker, Cade, Damien and several of Cade's other friends were climbing into. "How do you know? You've never been a bride before."

"It just seems like one of those obvious rules."

"No telling what kind of debauchery they're headed off to."

"No worries. Parker's in charge." She grinned. "He even printed out an agenda."

Rachel simply shook her head. "Sounds exactly like him."

She pulled out of the parking lot at Garrison Racing. They'd traveled from the speedway in the helicopter, avoiding the gridlocked traffic. Now, at nearly 1:00 a.m., they were on their way to Rachel's condo, where they could relax and get a good night's sleep in preparation for tomorrow's wedding day.

In less than twenty-four hours, her baby brother would be married. It was still kind of unreal.

"The guys are going to Midtown Sundries," Isabel said. "Eventually they'll end up at the hotel. Parker's turning over the penthouse suite to Cade and the groomsmen, where tomorrow they're all watching baseball and drinking beer until the ceremony. Cade promised to show up sober, but I'm not betting on anybody else." She shrugged. "Personally, I think Parker's kind of nuts to let them anywhere near his tower of luxury, but that's his decision."

"You've certainly got all the bases covered."

"I'm wearing a *dress*. A *white* dress, with little sparkly flower designs all over it. I'm wearing shoes that pinch my toes so tight, I'll probably wind up crippled after two hours. I've got you, my cousins, my friend Susan *and* Carmen wearing lemon-yellow halter-top dresses and lilies in your hair. Cade's not backing out now, or letting that skirt-chasing posse of his screw up the big day."

Rachel's laugh came out as a snort. "Skirt-chasing posse?"

"If I were you, I'd be concerned about my boyfriend falling under their influence."

"Damien isn't my boyfriend. We're simply... going out."

"I wasn't talking about Damien."

Rachel whipped her head toward Isabel, and the car swerved. "Are you trying to make us wreck?"

"You're the one driving." Isabel tried to look innocent, but didn't quite pull it off. "Who did you think I meant?"

"I have no idea. Who did you mean?"

"Parker, who else? When you kissed Doc goodbye, I thought Parker was going to grab the guy by the throat. He's got it bad for you."

"Don't be—" Rachel stopped. She couldn't disagree, since Parker had made it clear his *offer* was still open. So, he was attracted to her. She was attracted to him—when he wasn't going all Huntington Heir Apparent on her and using ten-dollar words, as if his sentences were required assignments for his doctorate in English lit.

Though, actually, she'd kinda gotten used to the fancy language. It was endearing in a weird—

"If it's taking you that long to work up an argument," Isabel said, "the feelings must be mutual."

"Well, they're not. And he doesn't *have it bad* for me." That description implied all sorts of deep-seated passions and longings. And while Parker certainly desired her, he also wanted every other woman in the county. If she didn't relive that dang kiss every five minutes, then she could go back to pretending she and Parker were just business friends. Which, even it was the safe thing to do, was also the wisest.

Wasn't giving in to desire when you *knew* things were going to turn out badly afterward a colossal mistake?

Did Damien have longings for her? Their relationship hadn't really progressed to the passionately naked part. She'd enjoyed taking things slowly, and the signs of speeding up weren't good. The kiss she'd shared with Damien before they'd separated for the night was quick and not hot in the least.

"You wanna talk about it?" Isabel asked.

"What?"

"Whatever man trouble has you biting your lip. That makeup woman you forced on me said that habit will ruin your lipstick."

Rachel glanced at her. "You're actually *inviting* me to share my troubled love life with you?"

"Sure. I've been dumping all my worries on you for the last several months. It's about time I returned the favor."

"I do have ice cream. And champagne."

"Together?"

"Okay, maybe not."

"Ah, what the hell." Isabel grinned. "Tomorrow's my wedding day."

AFTER THE THIRD glass of champagne and the second bowl of chocolate-chunk-turtle ice cream, Isabel had stretched out her legs on the sofa, while Rachel stood by the open French doors, looking at the moonlight dancing on the blackened lake.

"You know," Isabel began, "I gotta tell you, your issues aren't that dramatic. I know you don't want to get involved with a guy in racing, I know your track record with those guys hasn't been good, and you certainly seem to have an abnormal paranoia of divorce—"

"Oh, please," Rachel interrupted, "don't worry

about upsetting me by your dispassionate analysis of my deep-seated emotional traumas."

Isabel giggled. "Sounds like something Parker would say."

Rachel flung up her hands. "See! You see what I mean, the man is a terrible influence on me."

"I think he's really sweet. But still mysterious and captivating. And he has that whole rich-and-powerful-executive thing going on. Plus, he's really… well, I may be about to be married, but even I have eyes and can see how gorgeous—"

"Isabel!"

"Where was I?"

"My issues aren't dramatic."

"Oh, right. What I meant was that Cade and I had seriously dramatic problems. He was a driver. I was a PR rep for a competing company of his sponsor. If we were even *seen* together, it would have caused an international incident."

Rachel raised her eyebrows. "Really? An international incident?"

Isabel reached for her champagne glass, discovered it was empty, then set it down again with a sigh. "The point is, we were forbidden to get involved, and look what we overcame. We're getting married. We're gonna share breakfast and bank accounts and…"

Letting Isabel's plans for a blissful future fade into the background, Rachel refilled their glasses, then resumed her post in the balcony doorway. Maybe the moon would tell her what to do.

"…but the important thing I've discovered about relationships is that they're hard."

Rachel glanced at her, all flushed and happy and comfortably tipsy. "You think?"

She expelled a sappy sigh. "But it's worth it."

"I thought we were supposed to be solving my problems."

"We are." She lifted her head and took another swig of champagne. "Especially since I don't have any problems."

"Lucky you." Shouldn't she be focusing on something more critical, like the embezzlement? Wasn't the fact that two hot guys were attracted to her not really a problem at all, but something to celebrate? Why did romance have to be so confusing? "I shouldn't have kissed Parker."

Looking confused herself, Isabel propped up on her elbows. "You kissed Parker? How'd I miss that?"

"Nobody else was around. It happened a couple of weeks ago. After the go-kart races." When Isabel continued to look blank, she added, "Spaghetti-and-black-teddy night."

Isabel smiled widely. "Oh, right." She lay back down. "I guess I don't need to ask if it was a good kiss."

"Why wouldn't you need to ask that?"

"Because, Rachel, you're staring at the moon. Reflecting on the sizzling memory of kissing Parker Huntington, I'd guess."

"No, I'm not. I like Damien. I'm dating Damien."

"That's good. He's cute, too. Cade was great tonight, wasn't he?"

Clearly, they weren't solving her romantic issues tonight. And that was okay. It was Isabel's bachelorette party, after all. "He was."

"Third is great. He wanted to win, of course. He *always* wants to win. But he'll go into tomorrow with a lot of confidence."

"Marriage isn't a race."

"Isn't it? A really long one—well, hopefully. The love and passion has to be so strong to get through all those years. But it also takes determination, patience, compromise. Those last two Cade and I aren't big on.

"But we'll make it." Her voice grew quiet. "He's the most precious thing in my life. I don't know what I ever did to deserve him, but I thank God every day he's there, just for me."

Rachel blinked back a sweet rush of tears. If Isabel remembered saying any of this in the morning, she was going to be mortified. But it was so nice, so endearing, to see tough Isabel Turner Bonamici helplessly in love.

"Are you about to sing a power ballad?" Rachel asked her.

"I certainly hope not."

"No more champagne for you."

Isabel waved her hand vaguely. "Just as well. I need to get some sleep."

Rachel took a step toward her, and found, without the door frame for support, that she was a bit unsteady herself. Still, she pulled Isabel up off the sofa, then wrapped her arm around her waist. Together, they swayed down the hall.

Isabel's wedding dress was already hanging up in the guest bedroom, ready to be transported to the bridal suite in the morning. The ceremony would be held on the grounds behind the hotel, with the reception taking place in the grand ballroom afterward. Between the two families, nearly everybody connected to NASCAR would be there.

Including Parker *and* Damien.

She wished she knew what to do about both of them. Had the tension of the wedding and the stress of the missing money messed her up to the point that she was confused about everything?

"You could always cook spaghetti for him in trashy lingerie," Isabel suggested.

"For which one?"

Isabel patted her cheek. "Try both."

"I SAY WE TAKE one drink for every strike," Dean said, holding his beer bottle aloft.

"We'll be plastered by the second inning," Jay pointed out.

"If you guys throw up on your rented tuxes, Isabel will kick your butts," Cade said, popping the top on a bottle of water and dropping onto the sofa beside his buddies.

Leaning back against the floor-to-ceiling window several feet away, Parker watched the planning of the bachelor party drinking game closely. If things got out of hand, it would be *his* butt Isabel would kick.

He'd managed things well enough last night at the bar, though, keeping the beer flowing for Cade and his friends and moving along the female fans eager to congratulate the groom on his upcoming wedding. Waiting out the last few hours before the ceremony shouldn't require much effort at all.

Sam, Jamie and Mitch were sitting at the dining-room table, probably talking strategy for the next race. Bryan was slouched in a chair near the sofa, actually watching the baseball game on TV. Damien was standing in a group of guys with the Go! Energy Drink Girls, who had been Parker's compromise to the stripper request, which he was having no part of—in his hotel or otherwise.

Damien had Rachel kissing him. What was he doing smiling at the Go! Girls? Parker's mood only soured further when he recalled that last night he hadn't been in the least interested in flirting with Cade's fans, the way Jay and Dean had.

What's wrong with me?

Why was he wasting his time dwelling on Rachel, when she was obviously too busy playing it safe with Dr. Smiley to bother taking a chance with him? Though it wasn't often he was turned down by a woman he wanted—come to think of it, he couldn't recall that *ever* happening—he wasn't some pitiful beggar. He wasn't going to stand around, waiting and hoping she'd notice him.

"You don't look like you're having fun at your own party," John Bonamici, Isabel's adoptive father, said as he approached.

"It's Cade's party." He smiled slightly. "I'm only supervising. I hear the retirement day has been set," Parker added.

"Yeah. I've been training my successor all season, and he's coming along well, so I figured I'd give my wife an earlier Christmas present." He shook his head. "She already has us booked on a two-week cruise to Greece."

"It sounds lovely."

"Can I really float around on some boat, eating my way through the midnight buffet for *fourteen* days?"

"I wouldn't last two. But there are excursions, right? You dock in ports, and you walk around."

He winced. "My wife has the shopping route already mapped out."

"What about snorkeling? They have to have water-adventure trips, swim with the dolphins, that kind of thing."

"Right." His expression brightened. "Maybe even hiking or rock climbing on the island. I wonder if she'll let me take my laptop."

"I wouldn't push it. But most cruises have computer rooms these days. Send her to the spa, and you go there."

John clapped him on the shoulder. "Thanks. I may even ditch this—" he held up his can of Go! "—and have a beer to celebrate."

"Good idea."

John headed toward the bar, then glanced back. "Check on me once in a while, would you? Make sure I'm not making birdhouses or rocking chairs in my greenhouse."

"You can count on me."

Before Parker could stop shuddering and contemplate the scary idea of retirement, his cell phone vibrated, so he reached into his pocket, noting it was Rachel. "Hi, how are things going down there?" he asked.

"Isabel is surprisingly docile. She even let the makeup artist put on a few false eyelashes. Of course, it's possible she's hungover."

He lifted his eyebrows. "Hungover? What did you two do last night?"

"Champagne and ice cream. *Ugh.* Not a good combination."

He grinned. "I'll remember that."

"So how are things going with the strippers?"

"Really, Rachel. Do you think I'd be so obvious and tacky?" He paused for meaning. "Especially when you're the one being obvious."

"I have no idea what you're talking about."

"Sure you do. You're calling me to find out, and not too slickly, if we have scantily clad women in here."

"Isabel was concerned that—"

"I assured Isabel last night that we weren't doing the, ah…traditional bachelor party, and I seriously doubt she believes I broke my word and Cade is receiving lap dances—" he glanced at his watch "—four hours before his wedding. However, since you're only one floor down, you could come up and perform—"

"I'm hanging up now."

"You could always spend your time getting your own false eyelashes." When she didn't respond, he asked, "Rachel?"

Nothing.

She'd hung up.

He flipped the phone closed and returned it to his pocket. Clearly, women were touchy on wedding days, even when it wasn't their own.

At least the conversation with her reminded him of their friendship. In the interest of his peace of mind, and in honor of the wedding, their attraction could be set aside for the day.

Hopefully.

Deciding he'd be better company for the guys, he headed toward Bryan. For once, Cade's brooding brother was in a good mood. He undoubtedly felt that the third-place run from last night was a positive change in the tides. NASCAR drivers—and owners—were an insanely superstitious group. Whatever Cade and Bryan had worn, done or eaten yesterday, they would probably repeat next Sunday.

They talked about plans for the upcoming race, and Bryan assured him the special silver-paint scheme and decals for the car were being applied

Monday. The engineers were happy with the tests they'd done.

During their conversation, Bryan rubbed his knee several times, reminding Parker of the injury that had cost him his career, and, some said, whatever amiability he'd once possessed.

"Is your knee bothering you?" Parker asked.

Bryan stiffened. "It's fine."

"Rachel says you haven't found a physical therapist you like."

Bryan's tone turned icy. "It's none of her business and definitely none of yours."

Familiar with Bryan's dicey temper, Parker simply nodded. "If you ever do want to talk about it, I know someone who might be able to help."

"I don't need any help."

Definitely don't want to admit it, anyway. "I'll let you get back to your game." When he walked away, Parker headed toward the bar, where he retrieved a fresh bottle of water.

"Hey, Parker," Cade called, "get me one, too, would ya?"

He brought Cade a bottle and briefly tapped his against his friend's as he handed it to him. "Are you ready to do this?"

"Yeah." He grinned. "And I'm definitely ready to have my girlfriend to myself for a few days."

"You mean your wife."

His grin widened. "Right. Cool, huh?"

"Indeed it is." As long as it was Cade and not him.

Parker glanced at his groomsman. "Dean, don't forget to put the ring in your pocket before we go down."

Dean continued staring at the TV. "Oh, yeah. Sure."

"You do *have* the ring, don't you?"

"Sure. I, ah, I think I left it on the nightstand."

"You *think?*" Cade asked, his face paling.

Dean finally gave them his full attention. "Well, I'm pretty sure…"

"Why don't I check," Parker suggested, patting Cade's shoulder.

He headed down the hall toward the suite's back bedroom. In all the excitement last night, he'd forgotten to check with Dean to make sure he'd brought the ring and secured it in a safe place. He probably should have put it in the hotel safe, come to think of it.

He swung open the door—only to find the room, specifically the bed, occupied.

Damien and one of the Go! Girls were making out in a pretty determined fashion. They were still dressed, but he doubted they would be for long.

Hearing him come into the room, they hastily sat up, the girl's face bright red, her lip gloss smudged. Damien displayed a sheepish half smile, barely showing those perfect teeth.

Parker clenched his jaw in disgust. "Pardon me," he said tightly, then turned on his heel and left the room.

CHAPTER TWELVE

WHAT THE HELL was that idiot doing? Parker wondered furiously, pacing in the hall.

How far had Damien and Rachel's relationship progressed? How big of a betrayal was this? Had they slept together? Parker didn't like to think about Damien touching her at all, but rolling around on somebody else's bed, in the middle of the afternoon during a party, wasn't Rachel's style. How could she be dating a man who did that? Someone so coarse. And disloyal.

But he and Rachel had kissed. True, it had been more accident than seduction—at least on her part—and his hands hadn't been all over her, but it wasn't because he hadn't wanted them to be.

Still, it hadn't been cheap. Hot and amazing was a more accurate description.

And yet he hadn't asked Rachel to dinner, or offered her a relationship of any kind. He'd offered her a weekend. Honest as it might be, it was equally coarse.

Disgusted with himself and wishing like hell he'd

never walked into that bedroom, he leaned back against the wall. *What a mess.*

A couple of minutes later, the Go! Girl slunk out of the room, edging past Parker down the hall. He glared at her retreating back. He'd asked the Go! PR rep to bring the girls by with a case of the energy drink as an alternative to alcohol and to keep with the spirit of the bachelor party. The ladies were not there to make out with guests, and he'd be sure to let the rep know about her unprofessional behavior.

"Hey, man, you're not gonna tell Rachel about that little scene you witnessed, are you?" Damien asked from behind him.

Parker shifted his narrow-eyed glare to the doctor. "Are you and Rachel exclusive?"

"We haven't made any promises or anything. But I guess we're in a relationship."

And Parker knew, only too well, that Rachel wasn't seeing anyone else. "Have the two of you been intimate?"

Damien's friendly, just-between-us-guys expression vanished. "That's none of your damn business."

"Pissing me off by not answering my questions will get you nowhere."

Damien glanced at the floor. "No. No yet."

That was one small relief. In more ways than one.

But he still had no idea what to do. He'd made it clear *he* wanted to be with her. He hadn't made a secret of the fact that he didn't trust or like Damien. His credibility in this situation wasn't good.

Most of all, he didn't want to hurt her.

Shoving his hands in the pockets of his slacks, he stared at Damien. "I'm not sure what, if anything, I'll say to her."

"It wasn't a big deal. It didn't mean anything. It's a bachelor party, you know?"

"But not *your* party, nor your room."

"Do what you want," Damien said, storming off.

With a sigh, Parker walked into the bedroom and retrieved the ring, which was tucked safely in its box and sitting on the nightstand. Still not ready to face anyone and be able to successfully hide his anxiety, he paced beside the bed. He drained his water bottle, debating the difference between what he *wanted* to do and what he *should* do.

With one sentence, he could ruin Rachel and Damien's relationship. The power of that thought was as tempting as it was scary with responsibility.

A friend would tell her. If Isabel or Carmen had seen what he had, they wouldn't hesitate. But then Damien hadn't done much more than he and Rachel. Had she told Damien about their kiss? He seriously doubted it.

Could he really judge Damien for something he'd done himself?

But he hadn't kissed Rachel for a cheap thrill. The moment had come about impulsively, but he'd meant every breath and touch. Damien couldn't say the same. He'd admitted his *scene* with the Go! Girl hadn't meant anything. He was simply being a bachelor at a bachelor party.

Should intention have any bearing on his decision? If Cade caught Isabel with another man, would he care about intention?

No. Not even after he kicked the guy's butt from North Carolina to L.A.

But the reaction of an about-to-be-married man compared to a friend seeing his friend's date making out with another woman were two entirely different things. Had Damien even *cheated* in the technical sense?

He stopped pacing, staring at the bed and wishing fervently, again, that he didn't have the knowledge he did. Not only did he not want the responsibility, he also had to admit Damien's action shed new light on his own.

He'd flirted with Rachel, he'd attempted to persuade her into bed. He'd promised nothing and offered nothing substantial. It was no wonder she'd chosen to be with Damien over him.

His jealousy over the last few weeks, plus this crisis of conscience, were forcing him to admit a wildly daunting fact. Rachel wasn't just some woman he wanted to seduce. He cared about her. He cared a great deal.

Hell.

His knees actually wobbled a moment before he forced himself erect. Now wasn't the time to think about any of this. In fact, if he could manage, he wasn't going to think about any of it ever again. Today, thankfully, he had responsibilities to Cade for a distraction.

In the other room, he refused to so much as glance in Damien's direction and told Dean he'd take charge of the ring until they went down for the ceremony. He double-checked the bar supplies. He called down to the ballroom to make sure the reception setup was progressing on schedule.

As the afternoon progressed, more guys dropped by with congratulations and gifts, including Cade's fellow GRI drivers Shawn Stayton and Kevin Reiner. Kevin's wedding present even brought a genuine smile to Parker's face.

Splash laundry detergent had sponsored Kevin for nearly twenty years, supporting him through three championships, countless races, appearances and marketing campaigns. So the driver brought Cade a truckload of Splash, which he showed everybody by asking them to look out the suite window.

Way, way down on the street was a twenty-four-foot delivery truck, painted with the neon orange and green Splash logo, blocking the front driveway of the hotel. Imagining how many boxes of detergent were actually inside the truck sent the assembled crowd into fits of snorting laughter.

"You're the best, Reiner, really," Cade said, looking slightly panicked. "But what I'm I supposed to do with all that? *Today?*"

Holding a frosty beer mug, Kevin Reiner smiled widely. "I paid that guy triple time to drive the truck down here on a Sunday, Cade." He shrugged. "He's gotta unload somewhere."

Cade's gaze, of course, darted to Parker.

"I'll take care of it," he said, crossing to the phone near the door.

After he gave instructions to have the truck driver bring the delivery around the back of the hotel, where the boxes could be unloaded and stored, he walked through the party, reminding the groomsmen that they were due downstairs for pictures in an hour, so it was time to get ready.

He dressed quickly himself, reflecting, as he tied his sleek, black tie, that he and Cade had come a long way in the last year. He was a groomsman in his driver's wedding. But Cade wasn't merely a driver, a marketing campaign or business partner. He was a trusted friend.

When the wedding planner knocked on the door, he admitted her himself. She was impressed that all the groomsmen were dressed and only two of them—Dean and Jay—were tipsy. Reiner offered to take over as host in the suite, since Parker had to go with the wedding party, but Parker was still the last tuxedo-clad man to leave the room.

"Hey."

Parker turned at the sound of Damien's low, intense voice. "I need to get downstairs," he said coldly.

"This won't take long."

Parker noted the panic and anger on the other man's face had faded, replaced by a smug smile.

"You might want to remember, while you're judging me and deciding whether or not you want to hurt Rachel by telling her what you saw, that it's my word against yours."

Fully aware of that fact, Parker said nothing and continued to stare at the other man until he blinked and turned away.

Nobody needed to remind him what was at stake, or the risks tied up in speaking the truth. The fact that Damien would lie to protect his relationship with Rachel merely added another layer of complication to an already impossible situation.

"I'D LIKE TO PRESENT Mr. and Mrs. Cade Garrison."

Smiling broadly, Rachel and the other bridesmaids followed Cade and his new bride under the latticed archway and back down the rose petal–strewn aisle. The audience, seated in white chairs on the bright green lawn behind the hotel, clapped and stood as the bridal party passed.

Thankfully, the weather had cooperated, not only with a clear, cloudless sky, but also with a touch of cool breeze. May in North Carolina could be warm during the day and brisk at night. Or it could be sticky and smokin' hot.

The bridesmaids and groomsmen trailed behind Cade and Isabel as they made they way around the pool area, with its lush foliage, rock waterfalls and whimsical slide. Knowing the photographer was waiting and the wedding guests wouldn't be far behind, they rushed toward the ballroom where the reception would be held.

Still, as Cade opened the door for his bride, they paused and kissed. The touch of their lips was brief, but the intensity in their eyes, the way Cade slid his thumb across Isabel's cheek, communicated word-lessly, effortlessly, the depth of their love.

The beautiful moment reminded Rachel that despite the pace of racing, the struggles and even the anguish, there was love, passion and happiness inherent in people living their dreams.

Inside the hotel, as they moved into the foyer of the ballroom, everyone was buzzing about the re-ception, the need for food after a long day of getting ready, the anticipation of what the room would look like.

Rachel had seen the ballroom earlier when the wedding planner had double-checked to make sure the finished product would suit Cade and Isabel, but she'd allowed no one else inside, wanting guests to experience the wonder and ambience in the moment.

As they approached, the doors were pulled open by tuxedoed waiters, revealing the glittering room beyond.

Chandeliers rained down soft prisms of light, ac-centuating the white tablecloths and flickering golden votive candles. Red and pink roses domi-nated the centerpieces. Potted trees flickered with golden lights, and large ivy plants rested on pedes-tals and made the huge room seem alive and cozy. Tables of delicate and delicious-looking appetizers, desserts, plus two cakes, were positioned around the room, along with chocolate and champagne fountains.

Everything was luxurious and somehow simple at the same time.

The one homage to racing was the ice sculpture, which was in the shape of a waving checkered flag. Rachel figured it applied not only to Cade and Isabel's careers, but also to the astonishing feat of her brother making it to the altar without a shotgun next to his head.

"Wow," Isabel said quietly.

Rachel exchanged a warm glance with Parker, who was standing a few feet away. It was so rare for Isabel to be awed by anything, and she knew he was partially responsible for the effects of the room. He'd consulted with the wedding planner on every aspect of the decor, and his culinary staff had prepared and displayed all the food. She had no doubt the party would be everything the bride and groom, not to mention all the guests, had dreamed of.

Yet another reason to appreciate him.

Before they'd fully assessed the dreamworld before them, the entire wedding party was whisked to the back of the room for pictures and the cutting of the cakes. One dark chocolate, one white chocolate with white and pale yellow frosting. Cade and Isabel had wanted a few private moments with their friends and family before the crush of the reception.

As Rachel was wiping icing off Isabel's face, her friend—now her sister-in-law—grabbed her wrist.

"Thanks for not letting me go crazy. Or kill anybody."

"My pleasure, sis." She grinned. "I've always wanted to say that."

Isabel squeezed her hand. "Me, too."

The ultimate in sappiness—at least for Isabel.

Her duties done, Rachel stepped back so the photographer could get shots of the happy couple toasting and sipping their first glass of champagne.

"I think you've earned this," Parker said from behind her, pressing a glass of bubbly into her own hand.

She turned and, for a moment, her smile faltered as she took in the full length of the stunning Parker Huntington in an elegant black tuxedo. She must be getting somewhat used to the breathtaking sight, though, because when she'd first seen him for the preceremony pictures, her jaw had dropped until Isabel's friend Susan had not so subtly nudged her.

At least she managed to keep her mouth closed this time.

"Thanks," she said, trying to infuse some normality into her voice.

"It went well, don't you think?"

"It was beautiful. I even saw tears in Isabel's eyes."

He raised his glass. "Quite an accomplishment."

She nodded, lifting her glass. But when she started to take a sip, he wrapped his hand around her wrist, tapping his glass against hers. "To new beginnings."

She searched his gaze for some hidden meaning, but found none. In fact, now that she was standing so close to him, she noticed his eyes didn't say much at all. They were oddly blank.

Before she could ask what was bothering him, her father approached—with Bambi hanging on his arm. "Our Cade. Married." He shook his head. "Hard to believe. I always thought you'd be the first one, Rachel."

Rachel choked on her champagne.

Bambi widened her big, blue, vacant eyes and giggled. "The bubbles make me giggle."

Rachel had only had the opportunity to meet the young, buxom blonde briefly the night before at her dad's party, and she'd spent no more than thirty seconds in her presence today, but already she could officially say the woman was a twit. "Imagine that," she said, forcing a smile.

"You should go out more," her father continued, as if somehow the wedding had triggered a long-held need to give her relationship advice. "You work too hard."

"I tell her that myself all the time," Parker remarked.

She lightly jabbed his ribs with her elbow. "You work as many hours as I do. And I do go out, Dad. I've been dating Damien for a couple of months, remember?"

Her father looked blank.

"The doctor," Parker supplied in a tight voice. "He smiles a lot."

Her father shrugged. "Whatever. You should go out with a driver, Rachel. We need some more driver's blood in this family."

"Since I'm such a valuable mare, why don't you find me a nice, brown-eyed stallion?"

Bambi giggled.

Rachel ignored her. "And the last thing we need in this family is more driver's blood. We need accountant's blood."

Grinning, Parker cleared his throat.

"What?" Rachel asked.

"I have a master's degree in finance from Harvard."

Bambi giggled. "Oh, you two would make an *adorable* couple."

"Uh-huh." Rachel stared at Parker. "And you're available for marriage and babies?"

She had the great pleasure of seeing his smile fall away faster than the media hit the buffet line. "Ah, well, maybe we should all bask in the glow of Cade and Isabel's joy for at least twenty-four hours before we start trying to marry Rachel off."

"Hear, hear," Rachel added.

Bambi clung to Rachel's father's arm. "Maybe you won't be the next one getting married. Maybe my Pookie and I will get there first."

Pookie? Rachel's stomach rolled.

Her father was the son of a NASCAR champion driver. He was a champion himself, twice over. He was a championship-winning car owner. He was a *legend.* He was not, nor would he ever be while she had a breath in her body, a *Pookie.*

Parker slid his hand to the small of her back, as if realizing she needed the support. "Rachel, I hate to disturb your basking, but I need to ask you something about tomorrow's appointments. Do you have a minute?"

Rachel could have kissed him. "Business first, Dad," she said, kissing his cheek instead.

Wise man that Parker was, he led her to the chocolate fountain. With a plate in her hand and several skewers of chocolate-covered strawberries and pound cake to munch on, she quickly set aside the annoying Bambi and her aspirations to be the next Mrs. Mitch Garrison.

Not gonna happen, she decided, biting into a sweet strawberry dripping in chocolate.

"A couple more of these," she said, wiping chocolate from her lips, "and I'll forgive you for your nasty comments."

"Nasty comments? Me? Surely you jest."

"I do not jest, you eighteenth-century goofball. *He smiles a lot.* What's that supposed to mean?"

Parker took a sip of champagne, his eyes again taking on that strangely unreadable expression. "He should. He has excellent teeth."

"And you don't like people who smile a lot."

"Did I say that?"

"No, but it's what you're not saying that I'm curious about."

Parker sipped his drink again, staring off into the throng of wedding guests crowding the tables, filling their plates, laughing and enjoying the beautiful party.

"I'm not a fan of his," he said finally. "He's not good enough for you."

She swallowed. "Is that my friend talking, or the man who wants to spend a carnal weekend with me?"

His skin turned pale—a serious overreaction to her light comment.

"I didn't say I was worthy either."

Not worthy? Parker Huntington the Third? Did he have a fever?

The whole conversation was strange and moving into a deep and intense area that was very much at odds with the joyful atmosphere around them. Rachel couldn't deny her attraction to Parker, which seemed to have strengthened instead of lessened over the last few months. And as much as she claimed to want distance from racing and a personal life that was her own, she hadn't backed that up with her actions.

She still spent nearly every weekend at the track with a man who grew more involved in racing all the time. Recently, Damien had even consulted with another team's doctor on a driver's shoulder injury.

She was confused and frustrated.

"I'm sorry," Parker said, breaking into her thoughts. "Now's not the time to talk about this. We should enjoy the party." He smiled, though it was visibly forced. "Though I'd like to point out one last thing…we'd make an adorable couple."

"By all means, take the word of Bambi, the twit."

"Be careful. That's your future stepmother you're talking about."

"Bite your tongue."

"Maybe I could get her and Damien together. That would solve both our problems."

Since the teasing, flirty tone was back in his voice, her light mood returned, too. Maybe she was being a chicken to avoid the confrontation and serious discussion that had to be dealt with eventually, but for now she wanted to relax and have a good time with her friends and family. And she counted Parker among those friends. "Leave my date out of this."

"Where is the good doctor? He's usually glued to your side."

"He is not, and he's here somewhere." She gave the room a passing glance, but didn't see him and felt a pang of guilt that she hadn't looked for him before now. "He'll find me."

"Ah, so you're in control of this…relationship between the two of you." Parker nodded sagely. "Smart."

"Relationships aren't about control."

"Of course they are."

Fully aware of his issues with his parents, as well as his seeming inability to commit, she shook her head. "That's a cynical approach."

"They're not *all* about control. They're also about sex."

She ignored the fluttering of her pulse. "Of course they are," she said dryly, holding up a chocolate-laden skewer of pound cake. "Shut up and eat some cake."

Instead of taking the skewer in his hand, he leaned toward her and slid the piece of cake off the end. Holding her gaze, he bit into the treat, then held the rest in front of her lips. She opened her mouth without thinking, and his fingers brushed her skin as she accepted the bite.

Even as the sweetness warmed her mouth, she had second thoughts. What were they doing? Feeding each other in public?

The bride and groom did that, not the guests. Plus, there were hundreds of people milling around—her date among them.

Clearing her throat, she stepped away from him. "I'd better go find Damien."

"Rachel, I…"

She pretended not to hear him call after her. She desperately wished she didn't want to turn right back around. Regardless of the way her feelings for Parker continued to intensify, she had a date with someone else tonight. She was also supposed to be watching out for Isabel, making sure she had something to eat and that her feet hadn't gone completely numb in those fantastic satin white stilettos she hated so much.

Winding her way through the crowd toward the

bride and groom, she made a pass by the buffet tables and filled a small plate for them. She looked for Damien, but saw no sign of him anywhere. She couldn't call or text him. Her cell phone was upstairs in her room. She should have designated a meeting time and place.

She needed to see him. She needed to remind herself of the connection they shared. He was fun and easygoing. He didn't challenge her. He didn't distract her to the point that she said and did things she normally wouldn't. Plus, their time together was all about him and her. Work didn't interfere.

Unless Parker interrupted them.

Reaching Cade and Isabel without seeing Damien, she politely broke into the conversation between them and John Hepner, the president of NASCAR, who had issued more than a few penalties and stern lectures to her brother in the past. It was nice to see them both relaxed and joking around.

She handed Isabel the plate of food, and she and Cade gratefully accepted.

"Rachel, you and Isabel organized an excellent party," John said. "It's not often we can all get together for an event not racing related."

"Thank you, sir," she said, exchanging a brief glance with Isabel. "We had a lot of help from the wedding planner and a very particular mother of the groom."

He laughed. "Barbara knows how to keep everybody in line. It's a shame about her and Mitch," he added in a more sober tone. "I always thought they'd be together forever. The racing life can be hard on families."

Since this subject was not only relevant to Cade and Isabel, but to her struggles with dating and relationships as well, Rachel couldn't resist probing the older, wiser man for insight.

"How do you do it, sir?" John had been married for nearly forty years, had raised three kids, and he was as intricately involved in racing as anybody. He traveled to every race, plus he was the leader of a large staff with tons of responsibility. Nothing happened in NASCAR unless he said it did, and somehow, he was able to have it all, a successful career and marriage that had stood the test of time.

"Every Monday night is family night. Or was, when the kids were still at home. These days it's couples night." He winked. "My wife has me in ballroom-dancing classes for the next three months. Don't let that get around," he added in a lower tone.

"I wouldn't dream of it," Rachel said.

"That sounds like a pretty simple philosophy," Cade said.

John nodded. "Sounds, yes. In reality, it's not. Races get rained out, emergency meetings come up, throw in a crisis or two with a driver and his sponsor getting physical…"

Cade sighed. "You couldn't resist tossing that in there, could you?"

"No," John said, rocking back on his heels as if

he was pleased his dig had hit its mark, "but I can be easy about it now, especially since I have faith in Isabel to keep you in line, so I won't have to."

"I'll do my best," Isabel said, sending her husband a superior look.

Cade shook his head. "You know, I've spent the last five months getting razzed by my buddies. I thought that would stop after I actually strapped on the old ball and chain."

Isabel swatted him.

Rachel laughed.

John clapped him on the shoulder. "You've got a lot to learn about marriage, son."

"Please tell us," Isabel said, her eyes sparkling with humor. "We want to make sure Cade gets it right."

"It's all about priorities. Not that your parents didn't do that," John added hastily with a glance at Rachel. "But remember that when I go home, I mostly leave racing behind."

Rachel nodded. "We don't have that luxury."

John's thoughts only confirmed what she'd believed for a long time now—she needed a life outside of the family business.

"Sure you do," John surprised her by saying. "If you want to. Cade and Isabel are active in the Davidson Historical Society."

"Ah, my involvement was by court order, after my and Parker's…altercation," Cade said.

Isabel laid her palm over his chest. "It started out that way, but now those projects are really important to you. I see what John's saying. It's something we do together that's not racing business, another part of our lives that bonds us."

John smiled. "Exactly so."

Isabel wasn't often prophetic—at least not without a sarcastic edge—so Rachel was again plunged back into her maelstrom of confusion. Isabel and Cade worked together, in the racing business, and still loved each other and made their relationship viable. True, everything was new and shiny at the moment, but Rachel knew her brother, for all his wild bachelor days, had found "The One." He wouldn't stray or become lazy or forget that. *Ever.*

Just because her parents hadn't made it, just because the confusion and disillusionment of that still lingered, just because she'd chosen badly several times and racing had claimed many other relationships around her, didn't mean there weren't plenty of people who made it all work.

Damien slid his arm around her waist. "Hey, I've been looking for you everywhere."

Lost in thought, disturbed by so many of the emotions and decisions that dominated her life, Rachel struggled to smile. "You, too."

He stroked his hand up her back. "Are you okay?"

No. Definitely not. "Yeah. I'm fine." She made the introductions between Damien and John Hepner, then fell back into silence while the rest of the group chatted.

Damien glanced at her curiously several times. She knew she was acting strange. She *felt* strange.

It wasn't long before the circle around the bride and groom became a line. Everybody wanted to greet them and wish them well.

Grabbing Damien's hand, she walked around the crowded circle and approached Cade and Isabel from behind. "You have a lot of people who want to talk to you," she said, sliding an arm around each of them. "I'm gonna circulate."

"Bring more food," Cade said.

She kissed his cheek and felt a surprising rush of tears. Her baby brother was all grown up. "Mom and I will make sure you get fed. Don't worry." She gave them a quick squeeze and whispered, "You're both so amazing. You inspire me."

"Ten o'clock at the service entrance," Isabel said, reminding her of the send-off time, limited to family and close friends.

Rachel nodded, and with Damien in tow, they moved away and hit the buffet tables for themselves. They quickly fell into the rhythm of the last few months— easy conversation, light flirting, her educating him about the racing world and introducing him to people he hadn't already met.

"Let's do something besides going to the track this weekend," she said after polishing off her slice of chocolate cake.

He angled his head. "Like what?"

"We'll go out to dinner and a movie, like normal people."

"Isn't the race here in Charlotte next Sunday?"

"Oh, shoot." She bit her lip. She couldn't miss that. She and Isabel were hosting a party for Cade's sponsors in the suite. "Well, the race after that is Dover. I can skip that one."

"If you want. But we have to make sure we go to New Hampshire in a few weeks. There's this great restaurant one of the crew guys told me about. It's right on Highway 106 near the track and has the most amazing lobster you've ever put in your mouth. Even the White House is a customer."

Rachel stared at him. When had he become such a superfan? "Aren't you getting tired of moving in and out of the airport every weekend?"

"I could drive over Thursday and fly up with you."

"What about your patients? Don't you usually have surgeries scheduled on Friday mornings?"

He shrugged. "I'll bump them to Monday for that week."

She tried to hide her astonishment. He was going to put off surgery on sick people, so he could avoid the airport and go hang out at the race track in Loudon, New Hampshire, all weekend?

She'd casually told Parker that Damien could be a little selfish sometimes, but as a surgeon he was used to being the center of attention. When your hands stood between somebody living or dying on a daily basis, that small flaw was understandable.

Still, all surgeons put their patients' well-being first. Damien did, too. At least in the time she'd known him. Had she so misjudged—

Before she could complete the thought, Damien snapped his fingers. "On second thought, I don't think that'll work. That may be the Friday I have a patient flying in from Texas. But we're definitely on for a weekend in Atlanta instead of going to the Dover race."

Relief flowed over her. He wasn't abandoning his patients. *Of course* he wasn't. Parker had planted that negative seed in her brain. *He smiles a lot.*

As if that was a bad thing.

"Sounds great," she said.

He stroked her back, his eyes gleaming with desire. "You could stay with me."

"At your apartment?"

"I have two bedrooms. No pressure."

But there was inherent pressure in the invitation. She'd been dating Damien for months with simple kisses to sustain them. Where was the heat? The intense can't-not-touch-you need? If they were going to continue dating, if they were going to take their relationship to the next step, sex was bound to be a factor.

Why hasn't sex come up before now? her conscience whispered.

If she'd been dating Parker, would they have slept together by now? Their one kiss had been hotter than anything she'd shared in the entire time she'd known Damien. Was that fact, in itself, the answer?

"I'd prefer to stay in a hotel," she said finally. "I'm sorry. I'm not ready to take that step."

"Yeah, okay. You said you wanted to take things slow."

She noted the understandable frustration on his face. "But we're crawling."

He smiled slightly. "Yeah."

To make a relationship work, there had to be commitment *and* heat, and she didn't know if she or Damien had that between them. She laid her hand on his arm. "Maybe—"

"Come on, sis," Bryan said, suddenly appearing next to them. "They're about to do the first-dance thing. Mom wants us together."

Her brother's eyes were dark and moody, which was normal for him these days. She wondered if he was thinking about his own wedding and figured the bad ending had ruined the happy memories.

Moving toward the dance floor, she never got a chance to tell Damien that maybe their relationship would grow stronger away from the track. *Away from Parker.* After hearing about all Isabel and Cade had gone through to be together, shouldn't the intensity, the sparks for her and Damien have exploded by now?

Or had her caution and fear set them up for failure from the start?

The bandleader approached the microphone as Rachel, Damien and Bryan reached the edge of the dance floor. "Let's have our happy couple's first dance." Amidst the applause, the room's lights darkened, he extended his hand in a dramatic sweep from left to right. "Ladies and gentlemen, Cade and Isabel Garrison."

A lone spotlight hit the center of the floor, then, hands joined, her brother and his wife glided into the center. They didn't bother with the proper hands joined on one side and propped on each other's waists. She looped her arms around his neck, pulling him against her, and he folded his arms around her body, tucking her head next to his shoulder.

Beautiful and simple.

Happy tears clogged Rachel's throat.

"And how about the parents joining them now?" the bandleader invited.

There was an awkward moment when John and Emma Bonamici joined hands, then glanced at the Garrisons. Her father had brought Bambi, but her mother hadn't brought a date. Was her father supposed to dance with Bambi and leave his ex-wife alone on the sidelines?

Clearly, the wedding planner had failed to inform the bandleader of the awkward relationship between the groom's parents. The tension in the room was palpable.

Naturally, Parker stepped in to save the day. He bowed formally in front of her mother, then took her hand.

A smile tugged at Rachel's lips. The man did know how to command attention.

Then, unexpectedly, her father moved toward her mother. He said something to Parker briefly before he led his ex-wife out on the floor beside Cade and Isabel.

Before Rachel could pick up her jaw off the floor, Bryan said what everybody else was thinking.

"Well, I'll be damned."

CHAPTER THIRTEEN

PARKER SLID his hands in the pockets of his tuxedo pants and watched the Garrisons move smoothly around the dance floor. Two generations of Garrisons. Together. Smiling in harmony.

But did this mean he had to dance with Bambi?

The decision was taken out of his hands as the bandleader invited all the guests to the floor, and Bryan took the giggling Bambi by the hand. Rachel and Damien followed them, leaving Parker standing alone.

There were any number of single women in the room who would dance with him if he asked, but he wasn't in the mood. He clenched his hands into fists as Rachel and Damien passed in front of him, her delicate yellow dress setting off her glowing skin and glossy dark hair. What was he doing, gazing at her like a love-starved kid?

Yet he didn't move. He watched Rachel laugh in Damien's arms and let the anger and jealousy wash over him, knowing any minute, he'd grow disgusted with himself, drag himself out of the ridiculous and futile self-pity and go find someone else.

Minutes later, he still hadn't moved, and he'd lost them in the crowd of dancers.

With envy bubbling beneath his skin, he turned away and headed toward the bar. He certainly didn't feel like celebrating, so he asked for a glass of Merlot. Maybe the familiar vintage of deep red wine, full of berries and pepper that he'd personally selected for the reception, would remind him of refinement and self-control. Two qualities he prided himself on.

He didn't know or want to acknowledge the green-eyed monster lurking in his chest at the moment.

Sipping the wine, he noticed Jay and Dean approaching the bar. They'd apparently abandoned the idea of beer and moved on to sipping his premium whiskey. They each had their arm wrapped around an attractive woman, and he envied their careless smiles. For so many nights this spring, the three of them had cut a wide path through the female population.

What had happened to him? When had he lost control of his emotions and his life?

He managed to make polite conversation with people as he moved around the room, making sure the guests were having a good time and his staff was keeping everything running smoothly. He astutely avoided looking at, or going near, the dance floor.

"Good evening, Carmen," he said to the GRI office manager, who looked lovely in her bridesmaid's dress and had a delicate lily pinned behind her ear. He brushed his lips across her cheek. "You're a true gem."

Her face flushed. "It's such a wonderful party, Mr. Parker. *Muy caliente.*"

"You certainly fit in perfectly with the hotness."

The redness in her cheeks deepened. "You," she said, waggling her finger, "are a shameless flirt." She glanced around. "Where's Miss Rachel?"

He shrugged. "I haven't seen her in a while."

Carmen's lips flattened into a thin line. "With Dr. Findley, I assume."

Parker sipped his wine and nodded. He knew Carmen wanted to see him and Rachel together, but he didn't see how she could help at the moment.

Carmen patted his arm. "Not to worry. You're the right man for her. She'll see it soon enough."

But I'm not right. She deserves more than the doctor or I can offer.

But he didn't comment further to Carmen, and when Barbara Garrison approached and complimented his attention to detail for the party, he was grateful to move away from the subject of Rachel.

As he continued to circulate the party, several other guests complimented the hotel, its staff and facilities. If nothing else, he'd solidified his reputation for superior service and quality among the NASCAR community.

Great, I'll be rich, successful and alone. Just like dear old dad.

ON THE WAY up to her room, Rachel leaned against the elevator wall and closed her eyes. She was afraid to look at her watch, and she was pretty sure her feet were so swollen inside her satin heels that she'd need a crowbar to get them off.

Her brother and new sister-in-law were off to their secret island honeymoon. Their guests had partied long after they'd left, and everyone seemed to have had a fabulous time. Her parents had danced together. She and Damien had enjoyed a date that didn't include a race track. Carmen and Jay had even entertained the crowd with a rousing salsa that ended with Carmen bent backward over Jay's arm, clutching a rose between her teeth.

With the long summer stretch of races coming up, the chaos and silliness were a welcome break.

For now, though, she had an appointment, for at least twelve hours, with cool sheets and a firm mattress.

Lost in thinking about the moment she would finally be horizontal, she jolted when the elevator dinged its arrival to her floor. Squinting in the bright hallway light, she limped down to her room. After sliding her card into the lock, then opening the door, she sighed, deeply and thoroughly.

"Getting in pretty late, aren't we, Miss Garrison?"

Parker. She laid one hand over her galloping heart and braced the other on the wall, noticing him sitting in a chair, in the dark, on the other side of the room.

"You scared me to death. What are you doing in here?"

"Waiting for you."

"How did you get in?"

He rose slowly, unfolding his long, lean body like a looming shadow, blocking the pale light from the window behind him. "It's my hotel."

The silky, proprietary tone in his voice forced her anger to the surface. "So that gives you the right to barge into your guests' rooms?" She glared at him, though she doubted he could see her in the dim light. "I don't think so. I'm tired, and I don't want to talk to you, so you can just—"

"Where's the doc?"

"In his own room. Which is where you should be." She pried off her shoes and kicked them under the desk, flexing her aching feet. "We can talk in the morning."

He wrapped his hand around her arm. "You let him touch you, but you dismiss me?" He leaned toward her, his voice low and husky against her ear. "I don't think so."

Her heart was hammering now, not only from the surprise of finding him in her room, but with a strange kind of excitement, as if something unexpected was about to pounce. And that something was six feet two inches of an angry, gorgeous man, who wanted her, who was jealous of her dating another man.

The heat between them flamed to life. And

though part of her longed to explore and understand his effect on her, she didn't have the strength at the moment to deal with Parker and all the complications he presented.

She jerked her arm from his grasp. "I'm tired. Please go."

She headed into the bathroom and slammed the door behind her. She wanted a shower and to forget all about men, their egos and their issues.

Under the hot spray, she closed her eyes and imagined her tension raining down, circling the drain. She wished she could wash away her troubles so easily. And though she was proud she'd helped give Cade and Isabel a day to remember forever, and she'd smiled as she'd watched her father and Bryan relax as they hadn't in a long time, she worried that she wasn't doing right by her family.

Should she tell her brother about the missing money? Maybe Parker was right, and they should be confronting everyone involved. Maybe they should be contacting the police, or at least their attorney. Who had taken his or her sticky fingers to their bank accounts? Who had betrayed their trust among the people she considered extended family?

And what was with Parker? Lurking in her room like a parent making sure his child got home safely? Or hanging around to confront her like a spurned lover?

He certainly wasn't either.

When she had all her wits back together, she

and Parker were going to have to have a serious discussion.

Out of the shower, she slid into the cushy hotel robe and towel dried her hair, glancing at her sallow-eyed expression in the mirror. *Bed.* She glanced down at her swollen feet. She was getting to the bed if she had to crawl.

As she opened the door, steam billowed out. And Parker was leaning against the wall a few feet away.

She nearly sighed, but he'd turned on the desk lamp, so she could finally see his face clearly, which was even more drawn and tired than her own. He also held a plate on which lay a piece of chocolate cake. "I can't go. What I have to say is important."

"Is this a friend thing, or another dissection of my love life thing?"

His lips tipped up on one side. "Take the cake."

She took the cake.

Sitting cross-legged on the pillow-strewn, king-size bed, she ate and even tried to share, but Parker simply shook his head. By the time she'd drained the glass of milk he'd also brought, she was in a significantly better mood. "If the cake was a bribe to keep me awake, it worked," she said as she set the plate and glass aside and tucked her hands in her lap.

Parker, who'd taken off his tuxedo jacket and loosened his tie, was sitting across from her in the desk chair, one leg crossed over the other. He wasn't smiling.

Rising, he slid his hands in his pockets. "We need to talk."

Though she'd thought the same thing mere minutes ago, she swallowed hard. "Okay."

"I'm not sure where to begin."

"You? You're *never* hesitant. You're always in control."

He laughed. "That's me all right. Mr. Self-Control." He shook his head and added softly, "Not anymore apparently."

She angled her head, beginning to worry a little. His hair was rumpled, as if he'd speared his hands through it many times over. His face was pale. Yet his eyes were bright with intense determination. "Are you all right?"

"No. I'm not all right."

"Parker, you—"

"I'm crazy about you."

Her pulse raced, pounding in her veins. "I see," she said, though she really didn't.

"I don't *want* to be crazy about you," he said fiercely. "I've tried everything to make it stop. It doesn't."

She wasn't exactly flattered by this revelation, but she felt a similar combination of frustration and desire toward him. She flung her hand toward the bed. "Maybe you're just lonely tonight."

"That's insulting."

"Is it? Seems pretty accurate to me. You've probably had most of the women in Charlotte in your bed. Think it's time to move on to another city? Maybe you could go for the whole region."

"You're seeing that doctor." A muscle along his jaw pulsed. "And you shouldn't be. He's not good enough for you."

"So you've said. Several times. But you don't want me, not really, so why should you care who I see?"

His eyes widened in shock. "Not *want* you? Of course I want you."

There'd been a lot of heat and innuendo between them, some teasing and one mind-blowing kiss, but not much honesty or directness since that night five months ago when he'd made his notorious offer. Since he'd cracked that door, it was time she flung it open.

"You want to sleep with me," she said briskly.

"I—" The shock in his eyes was quickly replaced by caution. "Where is this going?"

"To Direct-Land. Answer my question."

"Was there one?"

"Do you want to sleep with me?"

"Yes."

"How about have dinner with me?"

"We have dinner together all the time."

"Movies? Plays? DVDs in my condo?"

"Sure."

"How about long talks about our feelings?"

He hunched his shoulders. "We're talking now, aren't we?"

He just didn't get it. Given what he'd told her about his mother abandoning him and his father cutting himself off from romantic feelings, she could understand his reluctance to commit, but they were now supposedly friends. They couldn't simply sleep together on Friday, then have everything go back to normal on Monday. All that messy sexual tension nicely dealt with and conveniently removed.

"That's a relationship, Parker, and there's more to relationships than temporary liaisons."

"I know that," he snapped.

"Which is why you don't have them."

"I—" He fell silent, looking away from her.

"No point in denying the obvious." She sighed and grabbed his hand, pulling him down to sit beside her on the bed. "Sex isn't just a physical connection. It's an emotional one. At least it is for me. I don't take that step casually or lightly, no matter if most of the rest of the world does."

"I know that, too," he said, his tone gentle this time. "Why do you think I'm so miserable?"

"I agree the attraction between us is frustrating, but you can't give me what I want. Damien can. We have a real relationship."

"No, you don't. You want me, not him. You can't deny that."

"I do want him." Maybe the physical heat between them wasn't as strong, but she hoped it would be, given time.

Parker cupped her face in his palm. "When Cade wrecked, you turned to *me*. When you needed someone to help you with the missing money, you trusted *me*. When you felt desire, you kissed *me*. You don't have a relationship with Damien, you have a crutch. He's simple and uncomplicated. He keeps you from going after what you really want." He paused, his gaze flicking to her lips. *"Me."*

"Damien may be simple," she said tightly, "but he's loyal."

A hint of a smile appeared on his lips. "Is he?"

"Yes." She grasped his fingers and flung his hand back as she stood and moved away. "I'm not a whim to him."

"Like you are to me, you mean?"

She crossed her arms over her chest. "Exactly like I am to you."

"The reason Cade hit me two seasons ago was because we argued over you."

No one could accuse Parker of not understanding the art of the dramatic announcement. That was twice he'd blindsided her. Maybe that was his goal—to knock her so off balance she'd fall back on the bed.

Crude as her thoughts were, at least they were honest. Something her feelings about Parker could seriously use.

"He told me it was because you criticized his driving," she said.

"It was—to a certain degree. The last straw was me telling him I was going to ask you out."

"But you didn't want to ask me out. You only wanted to sleep with me. I could see that driving

Cade to slug you one. For once, an overly protective brother is right. I'll have to congratulate him."

He rose, moving toward her. "My point is that you're not a whim."

"No, the point is, nothing's changed. You don't want to date me. You want to use me to get this... *whatever* out of your system, so you can move on to the next swimsuit model."

"Originally, when I made my offer that was true. Not anymore."

"But you don't want a relationship with me."

Shadows filled his eyes. "I don't know what I want."

"Other than me in bed."

"Yes."

She shook her head, sad for them both. "Sorry, Parker, that's just not good enough for me."

CHAPTER FOURTEEN

PARKER KNOCKED on Cade's motor home door, then entered after he heard Isabel's call.

"Hey," she said as he walked inside, her eyes warm with welcome. "Want some manicotti? My dad finally let me see his recipes." She comically rolled her eyes. "I had to get married to have them entrusted to me. How crazy is that?"

"Crazy, and I'd love some."

"Where've you been lately?"

"Busy." *Busy brooding.* But he hoped she wouldn't press too hard for details. His mind was troubled enough without having to actually talk about the mess he'd made in his life.

At the beginning of the season, when he'd been drowning himself in women, proving to himself and Rachel that she didn't mean anything to him, he'd been happy. When she started dating someone else, he'd been mildly annoyed. Now that he'd actually acknowledged—to her and himself—that she was important to him, he was miserable.

In his opinion, that entitled a man to a good, long brood.

"Aren't we all? Can you believe Daytona is next week? Where'd June go?"

"I have no idea."

"I've got soda and water." She rounded the bar that separated the kitchen from the living area and opened the fridge door. "And I have Go!, of course."

He cleared his throat as he slid onto a bar stool. "I'm trying to cut back. I'll have water. Thanks." At least, during the brooding, he'd managed to remember the bonds of friendship and make an important decision. "Is Rachel still dating Damien Findley?"

If Isabel was surprised by his sudden switch in topics, it didn't show on her face. "Last I heard." After dishing up a plate of manicotti and marinara, she set the meal in front of him. "What's up?"

He took a bite of manicotti, which was delicious. "I have reason to believe he's not honorable."

"Oh, Parker, you're a mess." She raised her eyebrows. "Not honorable? What's that supposed to—"

Staring at him, she obviously decided he was serious, because she leaned forward, her dark eyes narrowed ominously. "Not honorable how?"

"He sees other women. Which is fine, I guess, as long as Rachel is aware."

"She's not. At least I can't imagine she is." Isabel bit her lip. Leaning against the counter, she twisted off the top of a water bottle for herself. "They don't come to the track that much these days, but she's always shooting off to Atlanta to see him. She's doing that this weekend, in fact. I think they're getting pretty serious."

He nodded briefly, belying the confirmation of his fears. "I figured."

"Damn," Isabel said suddenly. "I should've seen it."

"What?"

"Dr. Player. I'm surprised. He seemed so genuine. But I've been so wrapped up in my own life lately, I guess I let a lot of important things slide."

"You're not going to question how I know this?"

Isabel's gaze slid back to his. "No. Why should I?"

"I thought I'd need some kind of evidence to back up my credibility."

"You've got credibility with me." She grinned. "Especially credibility on Rachel issues. Good grief, man. Everybody knows you love her."

He felt the blood drain from his head. "I don't— I'm not—"

"Oh, please." Isabel waved her hand. "I'm an expert on these things."

His hand shook, so he dropped his fork onto his plate. "What things?"

"Falling in love when you don't want to."

"Isabel, I'm not…well, what you said." He pushed back from the bar and wished he could run from the room. "I *like* Rachel. I'm attracted to her, *really* attracted to her, but that's as far as it goes."

Isabel stared at him. "Uh-huh. Why aren't you telling Rachel yourself about Damien?"

"She wouldn't believe me."

"You sure it isn't because you can't bring yourself to hurt her?"

"Of course not."

"It's sweet," she said, ignoring his protest. "Self-sacrificing."

It's stupid.

If only he'd made sure Rachel found out about Damien *before* he'd made his crazy confession the night of the wedding, she might have turned to him for comfort. But, no, instead of thinking through the situation rationally and strategically, he'd let emotions like jealousy overwhelm him, and he'd blown it.

And Rachel claimed she didn't understand why he wasn't interested in a relationship.

"That's me," he said mockingly, "coated in sugar."

"And, hey, with Damien out of the way, the road will be clear for you."

"No, it won't." He shook his head. Love, eventually, made you bitter and alone, like his father. He wasn't having any part of it. "I'm not getting involved with Rachel."

"What do you mean *getting involved?* You're involved up to your eyeballs already."

"We haven't spoken in over six weeks. We barely exchange e-mails anymore." And those only about the embezzlement investigation.

"Because you've been avoiding her."

He could hardly deny that.

"It's okay, you know," Isabel continued, her eyes dark with understanding. "To be scared."

He rose, shutting down the emotion that had gushed to the surface. "I'm not scared." He headed toward the door. "I need to go. I have a meeting scheduled."

She snagged his hand and pulled him around to face her. "You, Parker Huntington, are not running from a fight." She squeezed his hand. "Or your feelings."

"Yes, I am."

He was going back to New York, where he belonged. There was no way his lust—and that's all it was—for Rachel would survive more than six hundred miles apart.

"Not while I have a say in this," Isabel said sternly.

"You don't."

"I do." She pointed at the sofa. "Sit."

Familiar with Isabel's Italian temper, Parker sat. Though he was amused at himself for taking her orders, when he took no one else's. Not even his formidable grandmother's. Maybe, just maybe, he was a little curious about what Isabel was plotting.

Because she was definitely in plotting mode.

He watched her pace the living area, gesturing with her water bottle, which, thankfully, wasn't very full.

"No way are you giving up," she said after a few

minutes. "We're warriors, doers, directors. We make things *happen*."

Amused by her frenetic pacing—and accurate assessment of their personalities—Parker echoed dutifully, "We make things happen."

"We've got to come up with a plan, a brilliant, no-way-to-fail *operation* that will get Rachel's attention."

"I don't want to—"

She silenced him with a glare.

"Okay, *maybe* I still want to. But why are you helping me?"

"Like I'm gonna go down on Dr. Smiley Face's side?" She snorted with laughter. "That'll happen." She tapped her lips with her finger, continuing to pace. "So, let's see. She likes flowers, fancy dinners, champagne, new clothes, shoes. Have you seen that collection of mile-high stilettos?" She shuddered. "She loves all that girlie, romancy stuff. If you tried to come at *me* with that stuff, I'd think you were trying to pull a con, but Rachel gets into it."

From working with Isabel over the last year, Parker knew when she was on a roll, it was best to let her roll. Some of their best promotional ideas had come from Isabel's restless pacing. Since he'd screwed up his...*whatever* with Rachel so thoroughly, he was more and more curious about what his marketing partner could come up with.

"So how about we set up a fancy date, surprise her

at her condo. We do the candles, roses, champagne, the works. I've got a key, so—"

"Ah, the last time I surprised her," he interrupted, thinking of the ambush in her hotel room, "things didn't go so well."

"No? Hmm. Well, then something planned. You're worth a gajillion dollars. You have to be a strategic thinker to be that successful."

"I inherited most of that money."

She frowned briefly. "Right."

Thinking of the wasted weeks of worrying about Rachel, *pining*—there was no other word for his state of mind lately—for Rachel, he wondered how his friend and driver had managed to land the volatile and wildly independent Isabel. "How long did Cade chase you?"

She ground to a halt. "Cade didn't *chase* me," she said, eyes narrowed. "I stood my ground and flat out told him we weren't getting involved."

"Uh-huh." He glanced at the wedding ring on her finger. Clearly, that hadn't worked. "Then what happened?"

She grinned. "I seduced him." Her hands on her hips, she looked him over from head to toe. "You know, Parker, you're a pretty cute guy. Not my type, of course, but not bad."

"Please, don't gush."

"Some women might even say you're hot. Clearly, Rachel has way more willpower with you than I had with Cade."

"Thanks. My ego really needed that kick in the teeth."

Isabel waved her hand. "Oh, come on. We'll figure this out. It's just going to be a bit more of a challenge than I anticipated. Cade and I had— have—a lot of heat, so the—"

"Rachel and I have plenty of heat," Parker said indignantly.

"Good, then you need to get her in the sack ASAP. Trust me, that would solve most of your problems."

"I'm sure it would, but I have four words for you—*six months, one kiss.*"

"What the devil are you waiting for?"

He sighed—deeply. "You've been a great help, Isabel," he said, rising. "Lunch was wonderful, but I need to go."

Isabel attempted to block him. "But you didn't eat."

And he certainly wouldn't be able to now. "If you get inspired—"

A knock on the door stopped the rest of Parker's words.

"Come in!" Isabel called.

"Hey," Rachel said, walking in, "I was just wondering—" She halted as she noticed Parker. "Sorry. I'll come back."

She started backing up, but Isabel grabbed her hand and pulled her into the room. "Stay. Have some manicotti."

Her gaze slid to Parker again, frosted over, then moved away. "No."

"I should go," Parker said, his tone as cold as her eyes.

Isabel plastered her body in front of the door. "Nobody's going. You—" she pointed at Rachel "—eat. You—" she pointed at Parker "—don't move."

Rachel stiffened, then she marched toward the bar, sitting on the bar stool next to the one Parker had occupied. "I'd love some manicotti."

Parker said nothing, though he considered, then discarded, making a break for freedom.

"Not much heat, but there sure is a lot of ice," Isabel muttered as she passed him and headed into the kitchen.

Parker returned to his stool and tried to pretend he didn't smell Rachel's perfume over the pasta sauce. He didn't look at her either. He hadn't seen or spoken to her in nearly two months. But a few frosty words and one long stare and desire was roaring over him like a tidal wave.

He had to go. And soon. Or else he'd wind up begging.

For Isabel, and to prove to himself that he wasn't a weak-kneed idiot, he made an effort at polite conversation. "I didn't know you were here," he said to Rachel. "Isabel said you were going to Atlanta."

"I am," she said tightly. "Tomorrow. I wanted to see qualifying this afternoon."

Isabel served Rachel her manicotti. "Eat up. You'll feel better."

"I feel fine," Rachel said, shooting her a quick glare.

Parker clenched his jaw. "You're angry at me. You shouldn't be shouting at Isabel."

Rachel shifted her glare to him, and he felt the chill in his veins. "I'm not shouting. Believe me, if I ever shout, you'll know it. And I'm not angry at you. I just have nothing to say to you."

"Ah, guys," Isabel began. "Why don't we—"

"And what are *you* doing here anyway?" Rachel asked him, cutting off Isabel as if she hadn't heard her speak. "You've made yourself pretty scarce over the last month."

"I've been busy."

"Obviously, I've talked to your secretary more times in the last few weeks than I have in a year."

"You ask Carmen to screen my calls."

"News flash—I don't want to talk to you."

"I think I hear my cell phone ringing," Isabel said, scooting around the bar, then disappearing down the hall.

Glaring at Rachel, Parker barely noticed. "I don't particularly want to talk to you either. I'm not *good enough* for you, after all."

"Are you not? I just *don't know.*"

Now that they'd thrown each other's words back in their face, they fell silent. Rachel ate. Parker stared out the window.

His anger drained away suddenly. He'd been resentful for six long weeks. Now he was left with simple confusion.

"I grew my hair for you," he said into the charged stillness. "Dumped my designer suits and ties."

He sensed, rather than saw, her set her fork aside. "You grew your hair for me?"

His face flushed. "You suggested I loosen up, not be so formal. Cade said the same thing, but you were the one…well, changing my appearance was my way of showing you I cared what you thought of me."

"I asked you about that months ago," she said. "Why did you lie?"

"Acknowledging it gave you too much power over me."

"Dammit, Parker," she said quietly but fiercely, glancing at him. "Relationships aren't about power and control."

"The ones I have are."

"They don't have to be." She turned, angling her body toward him. "You know what I think? I think you're afraid of me. Of what I make you feel."

Isabel had also accused him of fear. He considered his attitude astute self-preservation. Plus, he had other interests in his life besides romance. He had a company to run, and if he wanted to stay at the top, he had to make some changes in his life.

He met her gaze and was proud he didn't flinch from the frustration he saw reflected in her beautiful blue eyes. "I can't be more than I am."

"We'll have to disagree there, because I think you can be."

"I'm not the marriage and happily-ever-after type,

Rachel," he said, rising and backing away from her. "If that's what you're thinking, you're wrong."

She blinked, then lifted her chin. "No, you aren't."

"I'm going back to New York permanently."

She half rose from her bar stool, her eyes firing with fury. "You're abandoning Cade? How can you—"

He held up his hand to stop her outburst. "I'm not abandoning Cade. I'll assign the sponsorship responsibilities to one of my senior managers. I think it will be easier on us."

"Yeah," she said. "I guess it will."

"I'll still be available to help you handle the embezzlement investigation."

"I'd appreciate that."

"I'm sorry. I handled things badly between us." For once, his fancy speeches failed him. "Well… bye."

He turned and walked out the door.

"WHERE'S PARKER?"

Rachel glanced at Isabel, walking toward her, a frown on her face. "Gone."

Isabel knelt in front of her. "Are you okay?"

Rachel looked around, noting that she was sitting on the coffee table and had no memory of getting there. "I think so."

"You're crying."

She laid her hands on her cheeks. They were wet. "Am I?"

"Let me get a tissue and some water." She moved

away, then returned moments later with a box of tissues and a bottle of water. She twisted off the top. "Drink."

Rachel did, the icy water somehow sliding past the lump in her throat.

"What happened?"

Isabel's sharp tone penetrated the haze Rachel had fallen into. "He left."

"Why?"

"We argued—sort of. It was all very quiet and dignified. Actually, I'm wishing now I'd yelled." She sighed. "He wants me, but not enough."

Isabel said nothing for several seconds. Finally she asked, "Huh?"

Knowing she had to help Isabel understand Parker and all that had happened in the last several months, Rachel explained about his proposition back in December, their confrontation the night of the wedding, his parents' ugly divorce, the mother who ignored him, the father without feelings.

"Well, bye?" Isabel asked incredulously when Rachel finished her story. "I gave him more credit."

"So did I."

"Explains a lot, though. We all know how a lousy childhood can mess up adulthood."

"You overcame it."

"I had help. Does he?"

She lifted her gaze to Isabel's. "I don't know. What's wrong with me? I *always* know what to do."

Isabel sighed and sat next to her on the coffee

table. She wrapped one arm around her shoulders. "You could do one of two things. One, you could cry a while, tell me what a bunch of trouble and aggravation Parker is, while I remind you what a loyal friend and amazing man he is—or at least could be. Then you'll tell me how he's seriously on the run from the feelings between you two, and I'll tell you to give it time, take a chance, what've you got to lose?"

"Only my heart." Rachel felt the ridiculous urge to laugh. Or cry harder. "What's the second thing?"

"I could just tell you what to do."

"Which is?"

"Break up with Damien Findley and go after Parker. Make him see what he could have."

Rachel jutted out her chin. "Wasn't I clear? Parker doesn't want me."

"But he does. He just doesn't know what to do about it. You didn't fall into his usual plan—charm, seduce, enjoy, move on. You're a—" she pursed her lips, as if thinking of just the right word "—*anomaly* to him."

"Oh, and, gee, abnormality has been my lifelong goal." Frustrated, she glanced at Isabel. "Damien's perfect for me, you know. He's smart, kind, successful. And he's a doctor, not a driver."

"I guess it doesn't matter that I don't think the two of you fit. Or that I don't care for him, and I *am* wild about drivers. The big question is—how do *you* feel about him?"

Rachel mopped her eyes with a tissue. "I don't know."

"How does he feel about you?"

"I don't know."

"I suggest you find out."

"Yeah." Her heart pounded as she recalled the panicked but hopeful look in Parker's eyes when he'd told her he couldn't be more than he was.

Damien had never looked at her with that much emotion. *Nobody* had ever looked at her with such a volatile combination of longing and regret.

Maybe she and Damien weren't going anywhere and just floating along. She was comfortable floating. No waves. No wild gushing of emotions. No risk.

No reward.

It was obviously time to face the fact that it was never going to happen between her and Damien. She'd been hoping so hard for it to feel right, to settle for safe instead of roaring into the turn with her foot pressing the gas pedal to the floor. She wanted a quiet turn around the park when her blood craved a superspeedway.

And Parker? Well, he was a whole other mess entirely.

There were so many things already against them, not the least of which was him running back to New York.

"I have no idea how to handle my feelings for Parker, whatever they are, but at least I know what to do about Damien now." She gripped Isabel's hand. "And you can't let Parker move back to New York."

"Since when—" Isabel drew her lips into a thin line. "You can't drive away my husband's sponsor."

"See!" Rachel jumped to her feet. "This is why I don't want to get involved with somebody in racing. It's all too personal. *And* it's all business. As long as we're on the subject, what are we going to do if I actually convince Parker to stay, we start seeing each other, and it doesn't work out? I don't want to get divorced!"

Isabel shook her head, apparently trying to clear it. "Wouldn't you have to get *married* first?"

"You know what I mean. Look what happened to my parents. Aren't you worried racing will ruin your relationship with Cade?"

"No."

"*No?* Just no?"

"Just no. Not that there haven't been moments I was concerned. But I got over it and got married to the man I love."

Rachel ignored her sister-in-law's exasperated expression and begged, "Please, Isabel, I need help here."

"Okay, okay. Don't get teary again. I can do advice." She patted Rachel's arm, then paced. "Sure it's hard," she said after a few moments. "All relationships are hard sometimes. The travel in racing makes it more difficult than if Cade owned a dry cleaners, and some couples *don't* make it. But when was the last time you gave up on something because it was going to be a challenge? When have you been too scared to even try?"

"I'm pretty scared right now."

Isabel grasped Rachel's hand. "You and Parker both. But somebody has to take the next step, don't they?"

Rachel blinked back another rush of tears, at the decisions in front of her and at the unconditional support from her friend. "Parker said he'd bring in someone to manage the racing business. Cade isn't going to lose his sponsor."

Isabel pressed a wad of tissues into her hand. "You could have led with that."

"Sorry. I'm off balance."

"You're entitled. But, just so you know, I don't want another manager. I want Parker."

Rachel sighed. "I'm sure Cade does, too."

"The question is—what do you want?"

CHAPTER FIFTEEN

"DINNER WAS GREAT," Rachel said as she walked out of the Atlanta restaurant and into the humid summer night with Damien. "Thanks."

"Some friends of mine are having a party tonight. You want to go over there?"

She drew a deep breath. "Actually, I was thinking we could have a drink at my hotel. There's something I need to talk to you about."

"Okay. It's just two blocks up. You want to walk and talk?"

"Sure."

Holding hands, they started off down the sidewalk. "Why do I think I'm not going to enjoy this conversation?"

She glanced at him, then back at the street. She hadn't exactly been a heartbreaker in her life, and though she didn't think Damien's heart was too deeply vested, they *had* been dating for several months.

Had she led him on? Had her confusion and indecision over her life—and Parker—kept his life on hold as well?

"I'm leaving first thing in the morning," she said finally.

"I see."

"You're a great guy, Damien, but the sparks aren't there between us."

"They would be, if you'd give them a chance."

He'd invited her to his bed more than a few times in the past few months, which she hadn't accepted, so she didn't blame him for the stiffness in his voice. "I don't think so. I like being with you. We have a good time together, but it isn't enough. For me or you."

He pulled her to a stop. "Parker told you about the Go! Girl, didn't he? He told you about the girl I was with at Cade's bachelor party," Damien went on as Rachel's whole body went rigid with shock. "He wants you himself, you know," he said, his tone harsh and angry, as she'd never heard it before. "You can't trust him."

"You were with somebody else?" she asked, eyes wide, looking at him as if she'd never seen him before. And maybe she hadn't.

His hand flinched, then relaxed. "He didn't tell you."

Chest tight, she shook her head. "No."

"Damn. Well, I blew that, I guess. I've been waiting for him to tattle." He bowed his head. "He got me in the end anyway, didn't he?"

Finally released from surprise as anger set in, she jerked her hand from his grasp. "I would say you did pretty well all on your own."

"It wasn't a big thing. We just kinda made out. It was a bachelor party, you know. We had our clothes on."

She gritted her teeth. What an idiot she'd been. "Oh, gee, I feel so much better now. This went on *during* the party?"

His face darkened to a deep red. "Well, ah, back in one of the bedrooms. Parker walked in on us."

"And the girl? She works for one of my brother's sponsors?"

"She was one of the Go! Energy Drink Girls."

Her stomach rolled. "The ones who wear the boots, shorts and fishnets and have their pictures taken with fans at the track."

"Yeah." He reached for her hand, but she stepped back. "We never said we were exclusive."

"Please stop." Every word out of his mouth made him sound worse. Did he even realize it? He wasn't bailing himself out; he was digging himself deeper into a hole. With a front-end loader.

But, oddly, she didn't imagine this girl and Damien locked in an embrace, hands roaming over each other, and feel anything but embarrassment.

She felt ridiculous and stupid for trying to fool herself into making something work that never had a chance. No telling how much more "kinda making out" he'd done behind her back. And she hadn't exactly been innocent herself. She'd kissed Parker. She'd longed for something beyond the friendship they claimed they shared.

She'd been so worried about the complications of a guy involved in racing, of being used for her family

connections, she hadn't considered the other relationship pitfalls, the ones everybody faces.

"I'm sorry. I didn't mean to hurt you," Damien said.

She laughed, but the sound wasn't cheerful. How
much time had she wasted trying to make him into
the right man for her? Trying to accept fine and
easy? Safe and uncomplicated. All in an effort to
avoid risking her heart on something real, possibly
dangerous, but ultimately amazing?

"You didn't hurt me," she said, meeting his gaze
straight on. "But it does bother me how easily you
could have embarrassed me and my family." She
angled her head. "Haven't you learned anything in
the last few months? Didn't I tell you that there've
been spotlights on me and my brothers since we were
born? When sponsors are your livelihood, and you
socialize with them, a party is never simply a party.

"Did it occur to you for one single second the humiliation you could have caused Cade at his own
bachelor party? Did you wonder, at all, if that girl
had gone to some tabloid with her story how you
would have disgraced me to my entire family and the
racing community? And while that may not seem
like a *big deal* to you, it's a very big deal to me."

He extended his hands, then pushed them through
his hair. "Rachel, I— Damn." His gaze was bleak
when it met hers. "I didn't think about any of that. Obviously, I didn't think about anything I should have."

She touched his cheek. He wasn't a complete
jerk. He just wasn't for her. "It's okay." She grinned.
"I kissed Parker, and you know what? I liked it a lot

better than kissing you." She wiggled her fingers in a wave. "Bye, Damien."

Then she turned and strolled toward her hotel.

In her room, she stripped off her clothes and put on the hotel robe. It wasn't as cushy as the ones Parker provided. She'd stayed at his competition out of some kind of petty revenge that was even more childish than throwing her kiss with him in Damien's face.

And while she wished she had the cushier robe, she couldn't help but smile over the memory of the stunned expression on Damien's face when she'd tossed her insult.

Groping a Go! Girl in the back bedroom during a party with sponsors, her *father*, brothers, any number of NASCAR's elite only a few feet away?

"Yuck."

She snatched the chocolate off her pillow and ate it to dispel the image of the what-might-have-beens, wasted time and missed opportunities.

Using the remote, she flipped around the channels until she found a pay-per-view movie she liked, propped the pillows behind her head and settled down to watch, hoping only for more chocolate.

She avoided thinking about Parker, and why he hadn't told her about Damien groping that girl. Besides all the other stuff between them, they were *supposed* to be friends.

All men were pains in the butt.

Monday morning, she was throwing herself right back into work. She was going to get the investigation moving forward again. And she was going to

find a hobby. Knitting or crocheting—one of those
crafty, creative things. Isabel always sang the praises
of kickboxing. Maybe she could expand her tread-
mill workout. Plus, she was buying a kick-butt pair
of hot shoes.

Wearing them, she'd admire herself in the mirror
at her condo while she ate ice cream and seriously
pondered her future, reminding herself she was as
hot as the shoes.

She soon called room service and ordered chocolate cake. By the time it was delivered, she was into
the romantic comedy on the TV and floating pretty
blissfully on a sugar high.

When her cell phone rang, she picked it up and
noted her mom's number. "Hey, how are you?" she
asked brightly.

"Why is your father still with *that woman?*"

Her mother's fury all but made the phone vibrate,
and now the sugar made her feel nauseous. She and
her mom had been through tears, faked amusement
and revenge dating, she supposed it was time for a
little anger. "Mom, he's—"

"Is that what he *wants?* Some empty-headed, big-
boobed nincompoop?"

Apparently so. "Didn't you tell me how nice it
was for him to ask you to dance at the wedding?
Everyone thought it was lovely."

"I. Don't. Need. Pity."

Oh, boy. Rachel muted the TV. "He doesn't pity
you, Mom. He's just going through a phase. You two

are made for each other. He'll come back. You'll find a way—"

"He's *engaged.*"

"Who?"

"Your *father.*" She practically spit the words.

Rachel wanted to laugh, but didn't dare. "How do you know that?"

"It's on Racing Surfer."

"It can't be. Mom, all press releases go through me and Isabel."

"It's listed as a rumor, but Racing Surfer always knows."

Well, that was certainly true. The insider Web site had started several years ago and always had amazing accuracy. There were even rumors that drivers had discovered they'd been released from their teams on Racing Surfer before the owner had even called them officially.

"Dad isn't marrying that twit Bambi," Rachel said with pretty reasonable certainty. *He wouldn't, would he?* "I'll find the source of the rumor, and I'll bet it goes back to her. There were pictures of them at the wedding all over the Internet—as well as ones of you and Dad. This is probably her idiotic way of staking her territory. I'll take care of it."

"No, Rachel, I don't think you will."

The resolve in her mother's voice made her stomach clench. "He loves you," she said desperately. "You guys are going to get back together."

"We're not." She cleared her throat. "And maybe it took this for me to realize that. He turned away from me. He chose what *he* wanted over me. He's moved on. I will, too."

"Mom—"

"Thank you, sweetie. Over the last few months you've helped me see that I have so much more in my life. I don't need him. You'll be here for dinner Monday night?"

"Of course, but—"

"'Night, honey."

Super. She flipped her phone closed and crossed her arms over her chest, no longer interested in the amusing, happy ending on the TV.

Her mother was moving on.

Her father was dating, possibly engaged to some girl named Bambi.

She'd broken up with the guy she'd been dating for the last several months after he made out with a fishnet-clad woman and she had rebuffed a guy who said he was crazy about her, then had watched that same guy run the other way when she asked him for more than a roll between the sheets.

Romance, quite frankly, sucked.

PARKER WALKED through the backdoor of the GRI shop on Monday and felt an immediate sense of coming home.

As much as he'd spent his life in elegant dining rooms and boardrooms, nothing satisfied him like knowing the people in this building were fulfilling their dreams through his support—both financial and promotional. Leaving them behind was going to be extremely difficult, but he couldn't give the team all they needed at the moment.

Eventually, he hoped he'd find his way back. But, for now, he had to step away. He had to get away, go in a new direction, both personally and professionally.

He had to get *her* out of his head.

Several people called to him or waved. He'd worked hard at the relationships here, and he'd become one of them—at least somewhat—over the last several months. A couple of guys ragged him about his "fancy designer suit," which was out of the norm for him. He usually changed into jeans before leaving his office.

But then today was different—in a lot of ways.

As he strode past the fabrication section and headed toward the interior hall that led to the offices, he thought of the first time he'd walked through this gleaming shop, expecting a typical, grease monkey–type garage, and had instead been treated to a pristinely clean, ruthlessly organized manufacturing facility worth tens of millions of dollars in personnel and equipment.

There were computers, simulators, dyno machines, welding stations, specially enclosed painting rooms and engineering checkpoints. Racing NASCAR style was no longer a backyard garage sport, which was both exciting and regrettable, depending on where you fell in the historical arch.

"Hey, Parker," Sam called before he could open the door leading to the office portion of the building.

Turning, he spotted Cade's crew and car chiefs huddled over a stack of printouts. "Sam." He shook his hand. "And Jamie," he added, clapping his shoulder. "Nice work at New Hampshire yesterday. Second keeps us solidly in a run for the Chase. You guys pulled out of that spring slump nicely."

Sam's bushy eyebrows arrowed together. "We need a win."

"Always pushing," Parker said. "That's why you're the best."

"I keep telling him the Cardinals need a win worse than we do," Jamie said with a shake of his head.

"Baseball." Sam looked annoyed enough to spit. "Who cares about dang baseball?"

"How does the Daytona car look?" Parker asked, knowing arguments between these two could escalate rapidly. They were classic old school/new school. Sam had been around since the first wrench was forged, and Jamie was an engineering genius with a computer for a brain. But together, working in sync, they were a formidable team.

Sam scowled. "Wind tunnel says it's good."

"And you don't?"

"We'll see at the track" was all he'd say.

"The car's great," Jamie put in. "We got a winner."

"Don't jinx it," Sam said with a sharp look at Jamie. Then he immediately shifted his gaze to Parker. "You still got it, don't you?"

Sighing, Parker reached into the pocket of his

pants and pulled out a penny. He opened his palm and showed it to Sam. "Shouldn't Cade be the one carrying around the lucky penny?" he asked for probably the twentieth time.

"No," Sam said. "You keep it."

The afternoon of the NASCAR Sprint All-Star Race, a young boy, who was a fan of Cade's and the team's special guest at the track, had found the penny on the ground and given it to Parker for luck. Parker had intended to give it to Cade, so he could tape it to his dash, but in the confusion and excitement of the race getting under way, he'd forgotten.

That night Cade had finished third, breaking their streak of wrecks and bad finishes. Sam insisted Parker keep the penny with him at all times ever since. Even forcing him to agree to wear the same jeans to Sunday's six-hundred-mile race.

Obviously satisfied he'd covered all the bases to win the race—wind-tunnel testing, engineering genius, a perfectly balanced chassis, a lightning-quick engine and keeping the bad luck gremlins at bay via the magic penny—Sam led Jamie off.

Parker dutifully returned the coin to his pocket.

He walked down the hall toward the elevator, which would take him to the third floor where Cade's offices were located. Even though Carmen had called and told him Isabel and Rachel had gone out for lunch, his stomach clenched as he strode out of the elevator. He didn't want to see Rachel.

He *couldn't* see her anymore.

"Don't you look handsome, Mr. Parker," Carmen said, rising as he walked toward her desk in the reception area. "Do you have an important meeting today?"

Grasping her hands, he leaned down and brushed his lips across her cheek. "Only with you, beautiful lady."

She flushed and smiled briefly, then her eyes narrowed. "Are you gonna tell me why I had to call you when Miss Rachel left?"

"Later. Is Cade in his office?"

"He's there," she said as he moved past her. "But I don't like any of this. You and Miss Rachel need to kiss and make up."

Don't count on it.

"You have a minute?" Parker said, pausing in the doorway of Cade's office.

"Sure." He grabbed a Sharpie off his desk and headed toward a folding table on the other side of the room, where dozens of model cars—intricate replicas of his NASCAR Sprint Cup Series race car—were lined up in neat rows. "I promised Rachel I'd sign these while she was gone. I can talk and write at the same time. I keep telling her we could get double the work done if she'd just learn to forge my name, but she keeps reminding me fans want authenticity."

"And it's the least you can do for them."

"Right." He grinned. "I used to get through these sessions by thinking each one was going into the gentle and lovely hands of some hot brunette."

Bending over the first row, he shook his head. "Times change."

As lead-ins, it was as good as any.

"They do indeed." He tucked his hands into his pants pockets. "I'm going to send one of my senior managers here to be my liaison to Garrison Racing from now on."

Cade's hand froze in the middle of his autograph. Straightening, he stared at Parker. "You're leaving?"

"It's out of the norm for the president of the sponsor company to spend three days a week at the race shop."

"Since when have you worried about what's the norm?"

His friend knew him too well. "I need to spend more time in New York. It's important that the people in corporate headquarters actually see the boss on a regular basis."

"You fly up there at least once a week."

"It's not the same."

"You can't leave. We need you here."

"My money stays. And you always have my support. It's simply time for me to move on. I have other projects I'd like to focus on."

"Uh-huh," he said, sounding skeptical. "Seemed like you were happy here—for a while."

"I was. This is merely a business decision, Cade. It's nothing personal."

"Uh-huh," he said again, and there was no mistaking the doubt in his tone this time. "But you sure seem to have had a sudden change of heart." At the word *heart,* his gaze flicked to Parker's and held there for a long, silent minute. "Was there something I did to run you off?"

"No, of course not."

"The guys? They're not ragging on you as much these days." He paused, looking thoughtful. "There's not that much to rag about, though, I guess. You've gone to a lot of trouble to change— growing your hair longer, the goatee, the jeans-and-T-shirts thing." He paused again. "At least before today."

This was going somewhere, but exactly where, he couldn't be sure. "Have I? I wasn't aware you'd noticed my wardrobe and personal hygiene."

"I can see just fine. You shaved. You're wearing a suit."

"So I am. I'm sorry. I can't be here anymore."

"Near my sister."

For obvious reasons, Parker hadn't shared his desires toward Rachel with Cade. But now he didn't see any point in lying. "Yes."

"You fought about something."

Evidently, his avoidance of Rachel over the last several weeks hadn't been quite as discreet as he'd thought. "Yes." And it was apparent she'd told her brother about his intentions to go back to New York. "You knew I was planning to leave."

"Yep. And, sorry, buddy, but I can't let you do that. I've got orders to keep you here."

He hated himself for the surge in his heart rate. "From her?"

"From my wife."

Of course. Isabel had some grand plan regarding him and Rachel. *You, Parker Huntington, are not running from a fight,* she'd said.

He scowled at Cade. "I can't make business decisions around Isabel's feelings."

"I agree. Thing is, you're not making a business decision, are you?"

"It's complicated."

"Women always are." Cade resumed signing the cars. "If you can't do it for her, do it for me and the team. We need you here. We're finally back on track. We got past our slump. Sixth in the points. I don't want to do anything to upset the chemistry we have going."

"You sound like Sam."

"I wouldn't knock his methods if I were you. He's won two championships. You still have the penny, don't you?"

"Yes, I have it." He, heavily, felt the weight of friendship and responsibility. And his shoulders were already burdened with plenty. "Fine. I'll stay until you get in the Chase." He turned to leave. "I can't promise more than that."

"Not that I'd give advice to a guy who wanted to get physical with my sister, or anything, but I like you a helluva lot more than I do that doctor."

"Glad to hear it," Parker said, turning away.

I think you're afraid of me. Of what I make you feel.

Rachel's challenge flipped through his memory

again, as it had many times over the last few days. He shut off her voice, as he had so many times over the last few days.

He strode back down the hall, stopping beside Carmen's desk. "Do you have any scissors?"

She smiled. "Sure." She retrieved them from her center desk drawer, then handed them to him. "Is Cade signing those cars? Miss Rachel will have his hide if he doesn't get them done today."

"He is." He held out the scissors toward her. "I need you to cut my hair."

"What?" Her dark eyes widened. "Why?"

"I want it short again. Will you do it?"

She rose, her face pinched with concern. "But it suits you so well, and you spent so much time growing it. You and Miss Rachel will make up. You don't need to do something so drastic."

Denying the haircut had nothing to do with Rachel seemed pointless, so he didn't. "Yes, I do." He had to move on. The sooner he cut ties with the past, literally, the sooner he could get back to his normal life.

She shook her head almost violently. "No. You're the perfect mates. You're so sweet and—"

He winced.

She planted her hands on her hips. "What's wrong with being sweet?"

It's something I'm not. His intention had been to seduce Rachel, not eat chocolate chip-cookies with her. He couldn't bear to have Carmen think of him as some noble and pure-hearted hero. "Sweet is something a friend is," he said for lack of any other, more personal argument.

"And you want to be Miss Rachel's dark and dangerous lover."

Parker actually felt himself blushing. *So much for personal.* "Ah…Carmen, this really isn't a subject I feel comfortable going into with you."

She waved her hand dramatically, then planted it on her hip. "I'm a hot Latina woman with three grown boys. I know a thing or two about dark and dangerous lovers. You can be all that and still be sweet and caring."

For some reason, he thought of his father, who would laugh in derision at those qualities. Parker didn't want to be him—cut off from emotion—but he wasn't sure he could be anything else.

"I appreciate the vote of confidence," he said finally.

Carmen smiled. "You'll work things out."

He certainly hoped so, though probably not in the way Carmen intended. "Sure I will." He handed her the scissors. He would have a professional stylist clean up the cut later, but he wanted to start moving on now, not later. "Now cut."

Her dark eyes were troubled, but, with a resigned sigh, she took them.

CHAPTER SIXTEEN

"Is THERE a particular reason we're having lunch at your condo instead of the office?"

Rachel unlocked her front door, then urged Isabel inside. "I told you—I need to talk to you in private."

Isabel sent her a skeptical glance. "I *am* going to get to eat, aren't I?"

"Of course."

"Your cooking skills rank right below mine, and that's not encouraging. I'm hungry."

"I can cook just fine." Though what she'd actually done was get takeout the night before to reheat in the microwave. "And you're the marinara queen now."

"After I slave over the stove for four or five hours. I don't have that kind of time for lunch."

Rachel walked into the kitchen. "Just sit."

After reheating the grilled chicken and vegetables, she set plates on the table, along with two glasses of sweet tea.

Isabel sniffed experimentally. "Smells good. You cooked this?"

You could never get away with anything with
Isabel. "Martha at the Main Street Café did, actually.
Happy now?"

"I'm half-Italian, remember? I'm picky about
food." She cut her chicken, then chewed thought-
fully. "Nice. Now what's up?"

Rachel took a bracing sip of her tea. "You knew—
about Damien and the Go! Girl, didn't you?"

"The who? What's a Go—" Isabel frowned. "You
mean those girls who wear the boots and fishnets at
the hospitality tent? What do they have to do with
D—" She nodded. "Ah, not honorable."

"I knew it!" She jumped to her feet, her lunch still
untouched. "Parker told you. Only *he* uses words
like *honorable*. Why didn't you tell me? Why didn't
he tell me?"

Isabel gestured with her fork. "For the record,
sister, I tried to tell you."

"You said you didn't think the two of us fit, that
you didn't care for him. *You,* Isabel, *you* were vague.
It's like waking up and finding out the sky is really
green instead of blue. Couldn't you have said, 'Hey,
did you know Damien made out with the Go! Girl
at Cade's bachelor party?'"

"I didn't want to upset you." Isabel grabbed her
hand. "And *that* certainly worked. Good grief. Calm
down. In fact, sit down." She tugged her into her
chair. "I didn't know about the girl and the making
out. Parker told me he thought Damien was seeing
other women. That's all."

So the question still lingered, why hadn't Parker *tattled,* as Damien had so childishly put it?

"I broke up with him," she said to Isabel.

"It's about time."

"And I ate chocolate cake."

"Even better."

They ate in silence for a few minutes, but Rachel might as well have been eating sawdust. She'd done the right thing in breaking it off with Damien, but looking back over the past few months, she knew she should have done it sooner. There were so many signs that he wasn't the guy for her.

His selfishness and tendency to ignore the rules always annoyed her, even as his kindness toward people impressed her.

But, really, hadn't it all come down to chemistry and avoiding her true problems? Damien was a nice enough man. Intelligent and interesting, but safe. He was a way to avoid getting her emotions too tangled. A reason for her to ignore her attraction to Parker.

Rachel pushed her remaining vegetables around on her plate. "Did you hate Damien from the beginning?"

"No, I liked him fine. Parker and Cade said he smiled too much—whatever that meant." She rolled her eyes. "But I knew you guys wouldn't last."

"You did?"

Isabel nodded, then stood to clear the table. "I knew you were only dating him to avoid focusing on how much you were attracted to Parker."

"How do you know that?" she asked, staring after Isabel. She knew her sister-in-law was perceptive, but that was a little spooky.

"Because I notice details. And because you've spent most of the last six months looking away whenever Parker threw you one of those hot looks of his."

"I have *not*."

"In between the hot looks, he did his absolute best to look devoted to whichever member of the opposite sex happened to be standing around at the time."

"He did *not*."

Isabel flipped the dishwasher closed, then crossed her arms over her chest. "I can name off the four million times I saw him smiling at you in a way-more-than-friendly way, then we can call Carmen, and she can add her recollections, then we'll ask your mother. Hell, we'll ask *Cade* how many times he's muttered under his breath about men, specifically Parker, stepping over the line by imagining you naked. You still wanna go with the *I haven't/he didn't* denials?"

"I guess not." She looked at her irritated sister-in-law. "You've been holding this in a while."

"Yeah, I have. I kept waiting for the two of you to take those looks to the next step. Instead, I find out— *six months, one kiss.*" She paused, angling her head. "And I'm getting a real sense of déjà vu here. You people really need to get a move on. I can't keep having this same rah-rah discussion every other day."

"Well, that's going to be a little hard to do with him running in the opposite direction."

Isabel shrugged, then grabbed a rag to wipe down the counter. "So get his attention. Take him up on his offer."

Rachel rose slowly and walked into the kitchen. "You're not serious."

"Sure I am. Give in to all that scorching chemistry. Enjoy each other. Quit worrying about why, and go for it."

"That's it? That's your advice. *Go for it.*"

"Hey, remember I told you last weekend to break up with Damien and go after Parker. Part one worked out pretty well."

She supposed it did. "But *all* he wants is chemistry."

He hadn't thrown himself at her feet, declaring his undying love.

I'm crazy about you. What the devil did that mean? And according to him, he didn't even want to feel *that* much for her. He didn't really care about her. He felt lust, which he planned to sate, then move on. *She* had to be the crazy one to sign up for that disaster.

"And you know why he says that?" Isabel prompted.

"He's afraid of what I make him feel," Rachel said, just as she had to him last weekend.

"More than that. He's afraid you'll reject him."

Thinking about causing Parker pain, Rachel's throat tightened. She wouldn't do that.

But you have. Over and over again.

She'd turned him down back in December and

spent all the time since dating someone else and denying Parker was anything more than a friend.

It was hard to believe wealthy and powerful, arrogant and suave Parker had such deep-seated uncertainties, but she knew Isabel was right. He was rejecting her before she could hurt him. He wouldn't let her have power over him.

That's why he was going back to New York.

More troubled than ever, Rachel leaned against the kitchen counter. "He's afraid of becoming his father."

"It's kind of poetic actually."

"How's that?"

"You're afraid of becoming your mother."

Rachel opened her mouth to deny Isabel's words, then snapped it closed just as quickly. Her fear of divorce had caused plenty of problems in her life.

"For the record," Isabel added, "I think you've both got serious issues."

"So how are we going to make a relationship work? If he even wanted to *have* a relationship, that is."

"I'm so glad you asked." Isabel laid her arm around Rachel's shoulders and led her back to the table. Rachel sat, but Isabel paced. She did her best thinking that way, so Rachel was grateful. "My seduction plan is step one. I mean, let's be real, the way to a man's heart *isn't* through his stomach. Though the whole romantic-dinner-and-candlelight thing would be a nice touch. Parker would appreciate the effort."

She paused, tapped her finger against her lips, then started moving again. "Step two may be a bit risky, certainly more complicated, but let's look at the evidence and decide. Why do you think Parker didn't tell you about that girl and Damien?"

"I—" Rachel frowned. "He didn't think I'd believe him?"

Isabel shook her head. "No, no. Obviously, because he didn't want to hurt you."

"How do you know that?"

"Why do you think he chose *that particular* night to tell you how he felt about you?"

"I don't—" She stopped, because she remembered clearly the moment she'd walked into her hotel room after the wedding reception and found him in her room, lurking in the dark, solemn and determined. "Because he'd just seen Damien with that girl earlier in the day."

Isabel smiled proudly. "Now you're thinking. If you accepted his offer, so to speak, and fell into his arms, he wouldn't have to tell you about Damien at all. You'd end things with him to be with Parker."

"And all those women," Rachel said slowly, realization dawning. "You really think he dated those swimsuit models to make me jealous?"

"Yes. Though I suppose he justified all the dating by telling himself he was moving on after you turned him down."

"He grew his hair to please me."

Isabel stopped suddenly. "How do you know that?"

"He told me."

"Oh, he's *so* in love with you."

"Let's not go crazy."

Isabel ignored her. "I get to be maid of honor at the wedding. Let's see how *you* like being stuck with pins by that sadistic seamstress."

"Ah, that's *matron* of honor, Mrs. Garrison."

Isabel curled her lip. "Yuck. Then I wanna be best woman."

Rachel thought they were seriously jumping the green flag to be *thinking* about weddings, much less talking about them. Parker had told her he wasn't the happily-ever-after kind, and she certainly had issues of her own with marriage.

Plus, understanding their problems was an entirely different thing from fixing them.

"So, we know he wants you, we know he cares about you. The last part on the strategic-planning list—how do you feel about him?" Isabel stopped and stared at her, waiting for the answer.

"I—I have no idea."

Isabel shook her head. "Come on. That's not good enough."

Rachel knew Isabel wasn't pushing to be annoying, but part of her wanted so badly to turn away from Parker and whatever joy and pain might lie with him, she was reluctant to put her feelings into words.

"Okay, so I'm crazy about him," she said after a long silence.

"What, exactly, does that mean?"

"Something more than like and less than love." *I think. I hope.*

Was that what Parker had meant by the words? Were they really going to take a shot at this… whatever they had?

After all the flirting he'd done over the past months, what would he do if she actually reciprocated? The one time she'd given in to desire had led to a wildly blazing kiss. That couldn't be a bad thing to repeat, could it?

Remembering the feel of his heart pounding beneath her hand, the heat they generated, the way his lips had moved over hers with easy confidence and the promise of plenty of satisfaction ahead…

She jumped to her feet. "So, seduction it is." She grabbed her bag and Isabel's and headed toward the door.

Isabel fell into step beside her. "Zippy. Now we plan the details."

"Sure. I need to talk to my mom sometime soon, too."

"Okay, well—" She looked confused. "Your mom?"

The divorce held the roots of her fears. It was time to dig them up and deal with them. "Yes."

As they walked toward her car, one of those fears jumped out at her. "What if I seduce him, and he still walks away?"

Isabel shrugged. "You can't be more miserable than you are now, can you?"

"That's cheerful."

"It's practical."

"You're such a romantic."

"Hey, sister dear, remember I'm the one who's married and blissfully in love."

It was hard to argue with that simple logic.

RACHEL WAS GIGGLING as she stepped off the elevator with Isabel.

Though the emotion felt good, she clamped her hand over her mouth. People would think they'd been drinking booze for lunch.

As they walked toward Carmen's desk to check for messages, Rachel kept her voice low. "So, let's plan to—"

"Parker, how nice to see you," Isabel said.

Rachel ground to a halt at his name.

But shifting her gaze in the direction where Isabel was staring, all the breath left her body. And it wasn't only the unexpected sight of him—standing, tall, lean and gorgeous next to Carmen's desk.

He wasn't wearing jeans, but an expertly tailored black suit, pale gray shirt and charcoal tie. His lustrous, chin-length, wavy black hair and rakish goatee were gone. In their place was a short, just-above-the-ears style with the wave ruthlessly tamed, and a clean-shaven jaw.

As always, he looked alluring. Expensive. Commanding.

Just as he had last December. As if the last seven months never happened.

Her stomach rolled. "You cut your hair," she said with stupid obviousness.

"It was time," he said, his voice cold and remote.

She nearly backed up a step. "And you shaved," she added dully.

He nodded and said nothing.

Had she really done this to him? Had her rejection, her refusal to take a chance, changed him so much? What had happened to her teasing friend? Her kind and trusted business partner?

Part of her realized that Carmen and Isabel were also in the reception area, standing stock-still and silent. They had to feel the tension between her and Parker.

Nobody seemed to know how to break it.

All she could think of was how his vivid green eyes stood out as they stared coldly through her and how sorry she was for not noticing his now-transparent pain sooner. For not only being a lousy friend, but also doubting she could ever warm that chill.

"I need to get back to the office," Parker said finally, as always, saving the day. He kissed Carmen's cheek, then Isabel's. "Married life agrees with you," he said with tender affection to her sister-in-law.

To her, he merely nodded, strolling past on his way to the elevator.

Rooted to the floor, stunned by the hard expression on his face, Rachel couldn't think of a single thing to say.

The moment the elevator door closed, Isabel lightly smacked her on the back of the head.

Rachel spun. "Hey!"

"It's an Italian thing," she said, her eyes clearly communicating her aggravation. "A gentle way of calling somebody an idiot, which you are for letting him walk out of here."

Rachel rubbed the back of her head. "That didn't feel too gentle."

But then the sharp anguish in her soul was so painful she was almost glad for some other hurt to focus on.

DAYTONA BEACH Saturday night.

July Fourth weekend.

The excitement and anticipation was as palpable as the humidity. Fireworks on the track as well as in the sky.

The Chase for the NASCAR Sprint Cup would begin in barely two months. The predictions, pressures and vying for positions had already begun and would only get hotter the closer they came to that final race in Richmond.

Parker intended for his team to be high enough in the championship-points standings that they wouldn't be scrambling for one of those last few positions.

For once, he was watching the race from the war wagon above and behind Cade's pit stall. He'd let Isabel handle the invited VIPs watching the race from the suite high above the enormous superspeedway. Thankfully, Isabel had also promised to recruit Rachel for the business networking, so he didn't have to worry about running into her around the garage.

The pit crew was standing behind the pit wall wearing their helmets and red-and-white uniforms, watching the cars being led around the track behind the pace car. The engines barely rumbled at the lower speed, like a group of tigers purring until they attacked. Though with forty-three of them moving, the noise was still substantial.

Cade had qualified fourth. His normally white car had been painted silver for the night race. Black flames had been added to the red, which made the car look slightly devilish and otherworldly.

Sitting next to Sam and Bryan with his headset on, Parker could hear the nerves jangling in his friend's voice. He'd posted the highest speeds in one of the practices, so the media were listing him as the one to beat. With the added pressure and expectation of Sam's drive to win, not to mention they were racing at *Daytona,* there was an added element of stress mixed into the already tense situation.

Normally Parker left the race communications to Sam and the spotter, but he couldn't help saying, "I still have the penny, Cade. This one's all yours."

Cade cracked up, and even Sam smiled.

In another two laps, the race was under way. The freight-train roar of the cars across the start/finish line brought every fan to his or her feet, and the flash-bulbs exploded like neon popcorn.

The noise was deafening. The ground rumbled like an earthquake.

Parker grinned like crazy.

He should have done this long before now. Even the combination of jealousy and longing he'd felt so often lately didn't have a chance against the all-out assault the full-field start of a NASCAR Sprint Cup Series race at a hundred and eighty miles an hour.

Instead of smiling politely, serving cocktails and appetizers in the suite, he should have been down here, where the real racing happened. Where the blood vibrated in his veins, and the roar of the cars stole his breath.

As nothing had distracted him before, the intricacies of drafting, the call for pit stops, three- and four-wide racing and the nonstop action eased his troubles. He dreaded the end of the race, when he'd have to go back to work, when he'd have to face decisions, when he'd have to think about the full board meeting his grandmother had called for Monday afternoon, the one where his leadership would be called into question, the one that might lead to him losing the only job he'd ever wanted, the one that might sever a three-generation legacy.

And, of course, when he'd have to think about Rachel.

A flat tire and spin by a car near the end of the pack brought out the caution twenty laps from the finish.

"Four tires," Sam said into the headset. "Clean and quick, boys. No mistakes."

"Car's great," Cade said. "But I can't do this without Shawn."

"He'll stay with you as long as he can," Bryan returned.

Shawn was Cade's younger teammate, but that didn't mean he was less hungry. Cooperation among the three GRI drivers was encouraged by Bryan, but he never asked anybody to hang back for anybody else. Even his own brother.

Wins were too precious, too rare, and every driver wanted his shot at Victory Lane.

The green flag flew again, the cars roaring off the start, the jockeying for position beginning before they'd even reached Turn One. Cars shifted and wiggled. Everybody was looking for the fast lane, everybody was searching for the air that would send their car to the front. Front, back and side drafting was the norm. Precision movements and calculated decisions won at Daytona.

A healthy dose of luck didn't hurt.

Parker stood along with every fan in the stands during the closing laps. He held his breath just like anybody wearing a red-and-white T-shirt or ball cap. Sweat rolled down his back along with every team

member who sweated and bled for that No. 56 car
and their driver.

The inside train of cars had the lead heading out
of the second turn, but on the front straightaway,
coming out of the final turn, Shawn tapped Cade's
back bumper, shoving him into the lead. The momentum held, and Cade blazed across the finish line first,
Shawn just behind him.

The pit box erupted with shouts and high fives.
Before the rest of the field had even crossed the finish
line, they'd thrown off their headsets and were
running full out toward Victory Lane.

Parker glanced back long enough to see Cade
complete another full lap, then spin his car in a smoke-
filled burnout under the flag stand. The crowd was in
a frenzy. The media converged on Pit Road as the
nonwinners rolled their cars into the pits. The garage
area, quiet during the race, surged to organized chaos.

War wagons were dismantled and rolled toward
the haulers. There were smiles for the ones who'd
finished well; scowls for the teams who'd fallen
below the standards they'd set for themselves.

For team No. 56, their destination was the one
everybody craved.

They'd spend hours with media members and
sponsors, taking pictures and doing interviews. But
the duty was joyful. Even relished. Parker was already
mentally planning a blowout party for Sunday night
to celebrate the precious win.

By the time he reached Victory Lane, Cade was

climbing out of his car. As he stood on the window frame and pumped his fists in the air, confetti rained down, fireworks exploded, flashes ricocheted off the car, and Parker laughed out loud.

It was their first win as NASCAR Sprint Cup Series partners.

Though Parker had been around when Cade had won with Huntington Hotels before, the company had been controlled by his father. Parker had merely been on the periphery—part of the company, but somehow not really part of the victory.

But this one was all his.

The giddy relief and elation was amazing. All their teamwork, cooperation and heartache spun into this culminating moment of triumph.

Isabel stepped forward and kissed her husband briefly, then the live media interview commenced.

"You guys started off great this season," the reporter began, "but had a frustrating spring. What does this win mean to your team?"

Cade's grin was wide even as his body had to be exhausted. "Everything," he said, breathless, his face slick with sweat. "My team was amazing. Sam and Jamie made all the right calls, and I can't thank my teammate Shawn enough. He gave me that last push to the end." He wiped his face with a towel. "My sponsors are awesome." He turned, caught Parker's eye and high-fived him. "We needed this one, and I'm grateful for the equipment from Garrison Racing and the support of Huntington Hotels."

As the interview continued, Parker glanced around at the jubilant team, covered in bright confetti and spraying each other with shaken-up cans of Go!. It was a moment to remember, to cherish when times got tough, which they inevitably did.

"You still got it?" Cade asked Parker a few minutes later, pulling him close for a quick hug.

"I'm never taking it out of my pocket again. I'm wearing these pants, shirts, shoes, hell, underwear every single time you race."

Cade laughed. "Afraid you'll jinx us if you don't?"

"Absolutely."

Pride in his eyes, Cade braced his hand on Parker's shoulder. "You've gone and done it, you know."

"What's that?"

"Become one of us."

Not even thinking about the meeting less than two days away, where his biological family would question his leadership and direction, could hold back Parker's joy. Not even the thought of Rachel and the uncertainty looming over them could prevent his heart from filling with happiness.

He'd been accepted by Cade and his team. With all their differences and troubled history, with all the struggles of the last two years, he'd at least accomplished that one, simple, amazing thing.

As if his simultaneous light and dark thoughts had conjured her, Rachel appeared out of the cheering crowd, her mother behind her. He'd never seen Barbara Garrison at a race. Given the dance she'd shared with her ex-husband at the wedding, he wondered if acceptance and healing was contagious.

The women approached Cade, each giving him a hug and kiss, then, before Parker could step back, Rachel raised on her tiptoes and brushed her lips across his cheek.

"Congratulations," she said softly.

"Thanks," he returned stiffly and prayed she would step back, so he wouldn't be tempted to lean into her on the bare chance he could catch a whiff of her perfume.

She didn't move.

Around them, the celebration continued. Bryan, Mitch and Bambi joined the circle around Cade.

Parker couldn't take his gaze off Rachel.

Why had he agreed to stay these extra weeks? He should be running as far and as fast as he could. She didn't want him on the terms he'd established, and he'd continue to futilely want her as long as he was anywhere near her. She was a tornado to his peace of mind.

When the NASCAR officials moved in to hustle Cade and Sam off to the press conference, Rachel grabbed Parker's arm. "I need to talk to you. Privately."

"Not now. I need to go with Cade."

"He'll be tied up with the media for a while, and I won't take up much of your time."

He crossed his arms over his chest. "So talk."

She extended her arm. "Can we at least go over there, so I won't have to shout?"

Sighing heavily, as if she'd asked for him to shoulder a particularly heavy burden, he moved away from the crowd.

"Isabel said your grandmother called a full meeting of the board," she said when they were alone. "Is everything okay?"

"It's fine."

"That's not the impression I got."

"I'm telling you it's *fine*," he said, his jaw clenched. "Isabel shouldn't have said anything."

"She's the only way I get information about you."

He deliberately made his tone mocking. "And you've been asking about me, have you?"

"Yes." She met his gaze and—he'd give her points for courage—didn't back away from the skepticism she had to see there. "I have something I need to tell you, and since you won't take my calls or answer my e-mails I'm down to pursuing you at races or showing up on your doorstep."

He'd ignored the e-mails and cell-phone calls, and, at his directive, his secretary had stopped telling him when she called the office. "Here I am."

"I broke up with Damien."

His heartbeat ceased, then started again with a lurch. But he refused to acknowledge his heart's idiotic tendency to hope. "Have you come to me for the consolation prize?"

She flinched, her head snapping back as if he'd hit her. "No."

He'd never, ever consider touching her in anger, but he figured he was doing pretty serious damage with his words. Some part of him was screaming at him to stop, to just walk away. They'd already said enough to each other. Maybe too much.

"So why tell me?" he asked.

"To thank you. You asked Isabel to talk to me, to warn me."

"You're welcome. Is that it?"

She shook her head. She looked at the ground, then back up at him. Her gaze was direct, even blazing. "I accept your offer."

A jolt of elation struck him. His fingers tingled. "What offer?" he asked, though he *knew*. He knew, and didn't want to acknowledge the combination of hope and fear.

She lifted her chin. "The one involving you and me, a hotel room and good wine."

She echoed almost his exact words from so many months ago. How did she remember? *Why* did she remember?

Still, he drew a deep breath, then forced the words from his lips. "It's too late."

CHAPTER SEVENTEEN

RACHEL BLINKED against the closed expression on Parker's face.

Isabel had warned her he wouldn't, well…come quietly, and she'd seen for herself the coldness Parker could summon when he was determined to push somebody away.

But, good grief, was all this worth it? Was she really going to chase a man who said he wanted nothing to do with her, even as his eyes smoldered with need?

When was the last time you gave up on something because it was going to be a challenge? When have you been too scared to even try?

Isabel had asked her those critical questions last week. The answer was *never*—and she wasn't about to break her perfect record. Not when taking on this challenge might prove to be the most important fight of her life.

"It's not too late," she said. "We never even tried."

She risked taking a step toward him, hoping he wouldn't back up. Again. "I accused you of being afraid of me, of feeling anything for me. Truthfully, I'm just as scared. You tempted me, even when I was sure getting involved with you would end in disaster. So I went the easy route with Damien.

"I thought our attraction to each other would fade. I *hoped* it would. It hasn't."

For a second, she saw a glimmer of something warm in his eyes. But he shut it down quickly. "It has for me."

"And that's why you cut your hair?"

"Yes."

The confidence from Isabel's pep talk was wearing out faster than tires at Darlington, but she made herself touch him. She laid her hand against his chest, pushed her face close to his. "I think you're lying. I think you cut it, hoping to cut me out of your life, because nothing else is working."

"You're reaching," he said sarcastically.

Feeling his heart pound beneath her palm, she raised her eyebrows. "Am I?"

He shook his head, whether at her words or his own thoughts, she wasn't sure, but he stepped out of her reach. "Regarding the financial situation at GRI, I think I know who's taking the money and why."

She struggled to adjust to the quick change in topics. She'd never realized how good the man was at rendering people speechless. Probably worked like a charm during all those big-time business negotiations. "You're barely speaking to me, but you're still going to help with my problems?"

"The company doesn't only belong to you. I'm concerned for Cade as well."

She wondered if he'd leave her twisting in the wind if she was the only one affected. "So who and why?"

"I'd like to do a bit more digging. I'll contact you when I'm certain."

"Me? Or Carmen?" Her frustration leaked out enough that her tone was sharp. "Or maybe you'll have your secretary call?"

His expression remote, he turned to leave. "I'll let you know."

"Parker, don't." But he'd been swallowed by the still-celebrating crowd before she could think of something to say that would stop him.

She stood, rooted in place, unable to find the energy to even be happy for Cade and the team.

"Well, that went super great," she muttered.

"He'll come around."

Rachel turned to find Isabel behind her. Immediately, the tears gathered, then started to fall.

Isabel pulled her into a tight hug. "'Bout time."

Through her tears, Rachel managed a weak laugh. "You never cry."

"I do when it's important."

Confetti littered the ground around them, flash-bulbs continued to explode, smiles lit everyone's faces. Rachel had never been more miserable in her life.

"I love him, Izzy," she said in a choked voice.

"I know."

But even through her despair, a heart of hope beat,

sure and strong. She wasn't certain if it was Isabel's support, or her own self-ingrained determination, but if Parker Huntington thought she was going to give up easily, that he could freeze her out with his dismissal and indifference, he was very much mistaken.

"YOU AND DAD had a nice conversation last night," Rachel said to her mother as they cleaned up after Sunday's lunch.

"I can be civil to the man," she said stiffly.

"There's no engagement ring on Bambi's finger."

"Really?" Her mother turned away to put a plate in the dishwasher. "I didn't notice."

Rachel didn't believe that for a second. She wrinkled her nose in distaste. "He shouldn't even be *dating* her. He wouldn't be, if you two would just talk this out."

"Talk what out?"

"Your relationship."

Her mother stared at her briefly. "Our problems can't be fixed with a conversation, honey."

Neither of her parents would ever explain what, exactly, had gone wrong in their marriage. Rachel had deduced it had something to do with the business, the racing.

But maybe her conclusions were wrong. What if there was a simple solution? What if there had been a misunderstanding?

"What *are* your problems?" she asked casually.

"They're complicated."

"Maybe I can help." *Maybe I can finally understand.*

"It's private."

"Private? I'm your daughter. Who else—"

Her mother banged the plate on the counter. "That's enough, Rachel Leigh! I'm not discussing this with you." She drew a deep breath and visibly made an effort to calm herself, which only left Rachel feeling more confused and upset than ever.

"Are you going to the party at Cade and Isabel's tonight?" her mother asked, breaking the awkward silence as they dried the crystal by hand.

Rachel tucked away her resentment and forced a smile. "No. I'm going to New York."

"Shopping? Oh, I'll come with you."

"Sorry, Mom. It's business." She winced over the lie, but there was no way she could have her mother be party to the bold plan she and Isabel had cooked up. "We'll go back in a few weeks and shop."

Isabel appeared in the opening between the kitchen and dining room. "You got a minute, Rach?"

"Go on, dear," her mother said. "I'll finish this up."

Rachel hung her drying rag over the sink, then followed Isabel through the dining room and out the front door.

"Everything's all set," Isabel said in a dramatic whisper.

Rachel's eyes widened. "His secretary agreed?"

"I told you, her son is a huge fan of Cade's. She got you a room down the hall from the suite where

Parker always stays." She smiled, her eyes twinkling. "Though, hopefully, you won't need it. She'll leave a key to his room, which is 2546, in an envelope at the front desk. You'll pick it up when you check in."

"And she's sure he'll stay at the hotel and not at his apartment?"

"She says so. The meeting's at three, and she figures there's no way it'll be over before five. But if it is, and he leaves the office, she'll call your cell phone."

"Meanwhile I order room service, light candles and hope for the best?"

"Don't forget the champagne."

It all seemed way too easy. Rachel bit her lip and considered flaws. "You're sure this will work?"

"Fairly. And it was better than your idea to bash him over the head and lock him in your condo until he admits he cares about you."

"You didn't see his face last night. I figured bashing was the only way to get him to spend more than ten minutes with me." Sighing, she leaned back against the porch railing. "He'll probably throw me out."

"He won't."

"He'll leave."

"He won't." Isabel paused, considering. "But if he tries, start taking off clothes."

"Mine or his?" Rachel asked dryly.

"Yours. And don't panic. No matter what he says,

stay calm and in control. He's scared and hurt. You have to channel that into lust."

"I can't believe I'm going to manipulate him with sex."

"You're not manipulating. You're seducing."

"Right." She felt her face heat. All she did these days was think about their single kiss and fantasize about what might have happened afterward if she hadn't been denying and pretending and fooling herself in a desperate attempt to save herself from the possibility of heartache. "Though it seems like we're leaping over a lot of steps in the dating process."

"Seduction doesn't have to be *all* about sex. Don't go all the way, if you don't feel comfortable. There are plenty of ways to be intimate. Reassure him. Comfort him. Get him to tell you about the meeting, his worries about his grandmother trying to take over and run the show. You've been friends for a while. You'll think of something."

"We *used* to be friends."

Isabel shrugged. "Sex works, too. It did for me and Cade." She paused. "Well, eventually."

"Eventually?"

"It took about eighteen months."

"Eighteen *months?*"

Isabel waved her hand. "Different situation entirely. Don't worry. What could go wrong?"

His head felt like the gleeful target of about twenty jackhammer operators.

The moment he got to his room, he was lying alone, in the dark, in the blessed and complete silence, and not moving for at least twelve hours. The thought of food made him physically ill. And if he ever saw another champagne bottle, he was going to run in the opposite direction.

But it had been a helluva victory party.

Certainly better than the childish battle for control he'd just fought with his grandmother. And the look on her face when the board had thrown their support behind him…well, he'd seen less petulant expressions on a three-year-old.

He slid his key into the electronic lock, then pushed open the door, dropping his briefcase in the entryway and heading straight to the opposite side of the room to close the curtains.

If he'd been on top of his game, he would have seen her sooner. He certainly would have come up with a better, more dignified reaction than grinding to a halt with his jaw unhinged.

"Hi, Parker," Rachel said cheerfully. "How was your meeting? Did you kick Grandma's butt?"

He blinked.

She was still there. And this time he noticed she was wearing a low-cut, sexy red dress, and her hair was soft and tousled, as if rumpled by a lover's greedy hands.

He closed his eyes, counted to ten, then opened them again.

Still there.

She was standing beside a white linen–draped table. Candlelight flickered from elegant white tapers. China and silver gleamed. Champagne chilled in an ice-filled bucket.

His stomach rolled even as his heart leaped. "How did you get in here?" he managed to say, moving warily toward her. "What are you doing here?"

"Isabel convinced your secretary to give me a key, and I'm here to have dinner with you. Our first date." She held up the champagne bottle. "Champagne?"

This isn't happening.

But if it was, what did it mean? What was she up to? After he'd said all those spiteful, angry things to her, after he'd told her he didn't want her and walked away, she'd jumped on a plane and followed him to New York?

No, that didn't make sense. None of this made any sense.

"We're not dating," he said, proud of the calm in his voice.

"We would be if you'd sit down." She popped the cork on the champagne and poured two glasses. "I ordered steak. It should be here in a little while."

He pushed his hand through his hair and headed toward the bar, pouring himself a shot of whiskey. "I'm not in the mood to argue with you, Rachel," he said wearily. "I'm hungover and exhausted."

"Then what are you doing at the bar?"

He downed the whiskey in one gulp, then poured more. "Numbing the pain."

He wasn't sure he had the strength to walk away from her again. But self-preservation demanded he try. She meant too much. No matter how hard he'd tried to exorcise his feelings for her—putting her in the category of every other woman he'd seduced and enjoyed, accepting simply friendship, clumsily trying to admit he was the only man for her and, finally, leaving her.

None of it had worked.

Wasn't it important to remember all that? To keep control over his feelings?

I have to.

Without his control, the only thing left was pain. And emptiness.

She laid her hand over his as he brought the glass to his lips again. "Please don't."

He let her take the glass from his hand and closed his eyes as the alluring scent of her perfume, spiced flowers and vanilla, drifted toward him.

"Did the board fire you?" she asked quietly.

"No."

"What happened?"

He opened his eyes to find hers, startlingly blue and worried, locked on his face. "I won. She lost."

"She hurt you, though. With her doubts, questioning your decisions."

"*You* hurt me." He turned his back on her as the ache in his heart swelled, then spilled over. If he let her fill that emptiness, and she left him, he wouldn't be able to bear it.

She laid her hand on his shoulder and stroked, comforting and arousing at the same time. "I know. I'm sorry."

He clenched his fist. "Is that why you're here? To apologize?"

"Yes." Her voice was soft, contrasting with the abruptness of his. "But not only that." She walked around him, sliding her hand down to his chest as she faced him. "I'm here to tell you I think you're the most beautiful, amazingly frustrating..." With a smile, she stroked her fingers along his jaw. "...extraordinary, generous man I've ever known." She wrapped her arms around his neck, pressing her body against his. "I'm here to show you I want you, like I've never wanted anyone else in my life."

She brushed her mouth over his, her tongue flicking against his bottom lip, and his whole body tightened with need. "I know it took me a long time to get here, but I am here. I'm here—for as long as you want me."

Hands shaking, he cupped her cheek in his palm, astounded by her beauty and bravery. "I want you. I've always wanted you."

He crushed her against him, kissing her with all the pent-up emotion, lust, hope, hunger and wishes he'd stifled for so long. The fear that he'd never touch her again fell away, drowned in a wave of relief that made him giddy with its cleansing.

She clung to him as he lifted her off her feet, carrying her toward the bedroom. He wondered for only a second if he was taking a step he could never take back, if they could go from despair to intimacy in a heartbeat. But everything inside him urged him to let go, to let the passion bind them together with its intensity.

He undressed her slowly, forcing himself to gentle his shaking, greedy hands. They made love without words, but with sighs and touches that spoke for them, fueling the chemistry that had been building between them for so very long. No more denials or pretending. No more cold, angry words.

Her eyes were bright with passion, lovely with heat. The slim body he'd desired for what had to be forever warmed his as her smile and laughter warmed his soul.

Later, as they lay beside each other, trying to regain normal breathing, he lifted her hand off the sheets and weakly kissed her palm. "I feel so much better."

Laughing, she turned on her side, propping up on her elbow. "How's your hangover?"

He grinned. "Cured. It's miraculous."

"We could put me on the market and make a fortune."

He laid a possessive hand on her hip, rolled to his side and pulled her closer. "No way. You're all mine."

She wrapped her bare leg around his. "Yes, I am."

Brushing a strand of hair off her face, he felt a quiver of panic. He wasn't tempted to say something light, clever and meaningless. His mind hadn't gone to dozens of deals and problems sitting on his desk. He wasn't temped in the least to leave.

In fact, he could lie here, content with her, for a very long time.

"You…scare me," he blurted out, knowing, somehow, that he needed to admit what she already knew.

Her fingers danced lightly over his jaw. "I don't think it will be so frightening to face things together."

"Okay."

"Though it *is* a bit surreal," she said, her gaze capturing his. "After all this time."

"For me, too."

"Maybe it will be for a while."

A while. His heart jumped a beat, then rolled along as if nothing had interrupted. "Maybe so. I've never done this before, so I'm not sure."

Her eyebrows drew together. "Done what?"

"Had a relationship."

"Is that what we're doing?"

His mouth hovered over hers as he absorbed the breathtaking beauty of her face. "Sure. Why the hell not?"

She smiled. "Kiss me, and let's be really sure."

"YOUR CHEF HERE could give the Cardoni's guy a serious run for his money." Stabbing the last bite of luscious steak and lifting it toward her mouth, Rachel angled her head. "But maybe with cooks they'd compete for special sauce."

"Bite your tongue."

She lifted her eyebrows.

Parker cleared his throat, and, she could have sworn, blushed. "I just nibbled on it earlier." He leaned back in his chair, sipping champagne. "I don't need a culinary war to go along with a corporate one. Especially since Chef Andre—the master of the steak you inhaled—is a key part of the battle."

"Your grandmother."

They'd eaten dinner in lush white hotel robes, and even after all the tension and turmoil of the last few weeks, they'd quickly fallen back into the rhythm of friendship and easy conversation. She guessed it was time to turn their attention to more serious subjects.

"She asked the board to remove me," Parker said, his gaze fixed on the champagne glass, even though he was obviously reliving the afternoon meeting. "I knew she was…displeased, but I never thought she'd betray me that way."

"Working with family's tough sometimes."

He looked up, offered her a half smile. "You'd know."

And his grandmother's lack of confidence had come on the heels of their fight and her rejection. No wonder he'd shut down his emotions so completely.

You don't want me? Fine. I'll force myself not to want you.

She hoped that with time his reaction would change. A tentative bond of trust had begun between them tonight. Maybe, with time, he'd accept and believe in the love she carried so carefully in heart.

Gripping his hand, she led him away from the table to the sofa, where they sat close, her feet tucked beneath her and her hand on his thigh. "So, what's her deal?"

"She thinks I'm paying the chefs too much, giving them too much power. She doesn't like my friendliness with the staff or my letting the regional managers call me by my first name."

"Sounds like a difference in managerial styles to me." She raised her eyebrows. "And an unwillingness to give up the power your father and her husband must have let her have. You want me to go over there and kick her butt?"

"She's very formidable. You'd never threaten that to her face, believe me."

"I sure as hell would." Envisioning the cold green stare Parker could command on some blue-haired biddy's face, she took a bracing sip of champagne. "But I'd take Isabel as backup."

"She thinks I'm weak."

Rachel laughed. "You're joking. She didn't say that."

The disappointment in his eyes said it all. "She did."

She gripped his jaw, turning his face toward her. "You, Parker Huntington, are a great many things, but weak isn't even part of your vocabulary. And your vocabulary is pretty extensive."

He didn't laugh, as she'd hoped. "I was kidding myself all these months, dating anybody I could find, smiling and pretending I was happy, when what I wanted was you. And you alone."

Frankly, she really didn't see the parallel between Grandma's attack on his character and their relationship. "So? I did the same thing." She narrowed her eyes as she thought about *all* those bikini models. "Though with much less quantity."

He gripped her hand, held it tight in his. "Fear is a weakness."

She shook her head. "Fear is normal. And you're not fearful in business. You're strategic, careful and smart. You and Isabel together—brilliant. Bold when necessary and never afraid to take a chance.

"But you're also patient, thinking long and hard before committing your resources to a risky project, finding just the right moment to launch, then working like crazy to making it successful long term."

He studied her for a long moment. "I'm not sure whether to be flattered or humbled by all those compliments."

Grinning, she slid into his lap, looping her arms around his neck. "Be flattered."

"When you sit in my lap, the idea of business goes out the window." He cupped her chin in one hand while tugging on the ties of her robe with the other. "I get other ideas."

She lightly slapped his hand. "Hold 'em. I've still got things to say."

"How long are you staying in the city?"

"As long as you're here."

He wrapped his arms loosely around her waist. "Then I can be patient."

She seriously doubted that, but then neither was she. When you finally realized what you wanted— *who* you wanted—you tended to be anxious about moving on down that road.

"The board chose *you*," she said, locking her gaze onto his. "They probably think your grandmother is an annoying control freak, too. And take it from somebody who's had plenty of battles with family members, let her stew awhile, let her realize she's taken a business decision and made it way too personal. Then send her flowers and take her to lunch."

"Flowers?"

"Sure. Even formidable grannies like flowers. Talk to her and tell her she's hurting you. Unless she's a complete dingbat, she'll back off. And if she doesn't…" She shrugged. "The board chose you."

"That's good advice," he said, tangling his fingers in her hair, his gaze dropping to her lips. "Practical and succinct."

"I'm here to please."

"If it doesn't work, you'll kick her butt for me?"

"Definitely."

He smiled, and she caught her breath. She liked seeing him happy. "Rachel Leigh, my protector," he said. "Defender of the legendary Garrison racing dynasty, standing guard for a Yankee."

She wrinkled her nose. "You're not a Yankee— exactly." She thought a moment. Really, he was. Well, if NASCAR could go multicultural, she supposed old-school drivers could, too. "We'll adopt you."

He pulled her face closer to his, and she could tell she'd lost the businessman and awakened the lover. "Just part of the family."

"Speaking of family, we have to talk about the embezzlement."

He kissed the side of her neck. "Later."

"You know who and why?"

His lips slid across her skin, and she closed her eyes, absorbing the pleasure, the closeness she thought she'd never find, even if the commitment she longed for was still a bit out of reach. "Yes."

"Then who—"

He captured her mouth with his, angling her head to take the kiss deeper. She sighed into him, her mind going fuzzy.

Maybe she *could* be patient.

At least, for now, she knew his touch was enough.

CHAPTER EIGHTEEN

TWO WEEKS LATER, in the same hotel suite where she and Parker had christened the beginning of their intimate relationship, Rachel studied the selection of lingerie she'd laid out on the bed.

Before the all-important race at Indianapolis, they had a rare weekend off, so she and Parker had come up to New York with Cade and Isabel for some couples-only time, and, of course, to make use of room service and the sensual luxuriousness of the rooms.

The guys had headed to a sports bar in Times Square, where Cade was being interviewed. They were due back within the hour so they could all go to dinner. In the meantime, she and Isabel were, for once, taking their time getting ready.

"Oh, good grief," Isabel said, walking out of the bathroom. "Pick already."

Rachel glanced briefly at her. "How? The pink is sweet. The red is, well, obvious. The black is seductive. The green matches his eyes."

"Heaven save me from new love."

Rachel ignored the sarcasm. "I guess you're an old married woman now?"

"Married, yes. Old, no."

Rachel studied the robe her sister-in-law was wearing. "What've you got on underneath there?"

"Red. It's one of Cade's favorites."

Rachel had no idea what Parker's favorite color was. On her or otherwise. They'd shared a great deal, months of intimacy crammed into a couple of weeks. Even if so much was missing.

"Have you told him?"

"No."

"Are you gonna?"

"No."

"He might be ready to hear it."

Rachel shook her head. Parker was definitely not ready to hear she was in love with him. "It's only been a few weeks."

"I know." Isabel waved her hand, as if moving the topic aside. "You're happy. He's happy."

Rachel told herself the same thing every day. Still, there were a few things she needed to settle. They were issues that stemmed from her own fears and hesitations—the last strands holding her back from complete trust and belief in their future.

The issues holding Parker back were something else entirely and weren't likely to be solved tonight.

"Cade's in fifth and food is in your immediate future," Rachel said.

Isabel high-fived her. "Life's good." She approached the bed, staring down at the selection of lace and satin. "I like the black."

Rachel swooped up the lacy panty-and-bra set. "Black it is."

By the time the guys showed up an hour later, she and Isabel were relaxing on the sofa, with a glass of wine and a beer, respectively.

Cade plopped down between them and snagged Isabel's beer bottle. "*Drinking?* We men are out there working our fingers to the bone to keep you in silk and lace, and you're here drinking?"

Rachel swatted him. "See if I balance your checkbook next month, brother dear."

Isabel snatched back her drink. "Get your own beer, race boy."

Parker leaned over to kiss Rachel, then he picked her up and settled her onto his lap. "No comment from you?" she asked.

His face took on the familiar, but now endearing, Huntington arrogance. "I can balance my own checkbook, I prefer wine, and I am *not* a fool."

Cade levered himself off the sofa. "Thanks a lot, buddy. Way to stick with the boys. Well, this fool needs to get ready." His eyes gleaming, he glanced back at Isabel. "Wanna come help me with my tie?"

Isabel looked at him, and her eyes warmed. She shrugged and set her beer aside.

"Now you've done it," Parker said as they walked hand in hand out the door of the suite. "We'll be late for our reservations."

"*Me?* He was just pretending to be mad so he could have an excuse to leave."

Parker appeared to consider this. "You think?"

Rachel stared at him. "You know he did."

"Mmm." He grinned. "I was supposed to pick a fight with him, but you ladies handled things nicely on your own."

"Sneaky. You're—"

"A very lucky man." He plucked her wineglass out of her hand and set it on the coffee table. Then, with her giggling in mild protest, he picked her up.

"Parker, I'm already dressed. I wanna hear how the ESPN interview went."

"Fine, and don't worry, darling, I'll help you with your zipper."

He carried her into the bedroom, where she found out his favorite color—for the moment anyway—was black.

By the time the four of them had assembled by the maître d' stand in the restaurant downstairs, they were all flushed and thirty minutes late for their reservations, but since they had a close relationship with the owner, none of the staff mentioned their tardiness.

Dinner was delicious and elegant, as with everything Parker had his hands on. Every day it seemed her feelings deepened and her admiration increased. He was as gracious with his staff and patrons as he was with the crew and fans at the track.

The envious looks sent her way were understandable, and the hot, possessive looks *he* sent her way were even better.

But there were also times he looked at her as if he wasn't quite sure why she was next to him. Other times, he clung to her with an almost desperate hope.

She'd avoided all conversations about feelings or the future. Anything beyond what they were doing that day or that night seemed premature and asking for conflict. Still, she had a question to ask and things to say. If she'd settled her hang-ups, then she could be patient about his.

At least there was one potential problem with her and Parker's relationship that hadn't materialized. Her brother gave no sign that he'd like to slug his sponsor and friend for sleeping with his sister.

Causing problems for the race team was not a guilt she wanted to carry around, especially with the embezzlement looming over them all. Though Parker had told her who was guilty, they were still gathering evidence and planning a confrontation carefully.

After leaving Cade and Isabel lingering over dessert, she and Parker got in the elevator to return to the suite. "You seem distracted," he said.

"I guess I am a little."

He slid his arms around her and maneuvered her out as the car reached their floor. "I bet I can distract you better."

She fought a twinge of disappointment that he didn't want to know what was bothering her and pulled back.

He held her tighter.

She laid her hand on his chest and pulled back again. "We need to talk about something."

"Is this part of the relationship-discussion stuff you said I'd have to participate in?"

"It is."

"Humph."

Parker Huntington, out of fancy words. She'd have to make a note on her calendar.

She led him to the sofa, where they sat, her angling her body toward him. "Did you cut your hair because of me?"

His eyes widened. "What does that have to do with anything?"

"It does, and you know it." She scowled. "Be honest this time."

He lifted his hand to the back of his head, which was still fairly short from Carmen's snip job. "So maybe I did." When she stared at him and said nothing, he sighed and continued, "I was symbolically moving on."

"Well, you symbolically sent me into a panic." She lifted her shoulders, feeling the weight of guilt all over again. She'd known that haircut meant *the end.* The remoteness on his face and in his voice had chilled her to the bone. "But maybe that was a good thing. It made me realize I had to do something drastic, too. Symbolically."

"Surprise dinner."

"Actually, Isabel and I were already planning that before I saw your hair." Since then she'd gone a bit further, a little more obvious with the symbols, and she still wasn't sure she could be that bold. "Are you going to grow it back?"

"It did add a nice, rebellious touch in the board-room. Do you want me to grow it back?"

"If you want," she said, trying to act casual. It was stupid to have a hang-up about hair. He was gorgeous either way, *any* way. "I like it short, too."

"You do, huh?"

"So maybe I liked it long." Self-conscious, she cast him a quick glance. "A lot. It's even possible I had this fantasy about tangling my hands in all that luscious, silky, jet-black—" She stopped, pressing her lips together so nothing else idiotic would escape. This was not going as smoothly as she'd planned.

"Luscious?" he asked, lifting a brow and smiling way too smugly.

"It's no big deal either way."

Of course he wouldn't let it drop. "It's a fantasy."

She cleared her throat. "So I have a *thing* about your hair. Not just anybody's hair, by the way." When he continued to grin, and she knew she was being made fun of, albeit silently, she decided she could definitely play the card she had up her sleeve. "How do you feel about shoes?"

He cocked his head, as if suspicious of a hidden motive. "I like shoes. I know *you* like shoes."

"You bet I do. But shoes are just shoes unless they're really hot, red patent-leather stilettos. Then they become a *thing*. Hair is hair, unless it's silky, black and frames your face. Make sense?"

"Not really, no."

She hadn't figured it would. Visual aids were always more effective. She kissed him briefly, then wriggled off his lap. "Hang on. Don't go anywhere."

"Where would I go?"

She ran into the bedroom and dug into her luggage for the shoes she'd worn a few weeks ago, the ones that were supposed to seduce him should her words not have reached him.

Her symbolic moving on. She wanted him to know.

Confidence, she thought, sliding her feet into the four-inch, red patent-leather stilettos that matched the dress she'd worn that night.

She recalled getting ready, when she'd decided to take a chance instead of the easy path, even though hope seemed beyond her reach. If he wanted her physically, she'd told herself, she was going to give him that. And, somehow, she'd find a way to reach past his fear and find his heart.

So far she'd succeeded, and she intended to keep reminding him.

When she returned to the other room, wearing the shoes and one of the hotel's cushy robes, his gaze swept her. "They're hot."

Smiling, she walked slowly toward him. His gaze followed every step.

"Isabel told me guys don't care about shoes," she

said, untying the robe, then opening it. She wore nothing underneath. "What do you think?"

When he lunged toward her, she ran, giggling into the bedroom.

LATER, AS SHE LAY beside Parker, her eyes drifting closed, she laid her head on his chest. He didn't move, his breathing was already deep and even.

"I love you," she whispered in the dark.

Maybe he wasn't ready to hear the words, but they sounded pretty nice to her.

AS PARKER EXITED the elevator on the third floor of the GRI offices, he flashed back to the week before the Daytona race, when he'd been miserable and devastated, when he'd been prepared to leave racing, and the Garrisons, behind.

That was two months ago.

By contrast, today his happiness was a living, breathing entity. The race team was doing phenomenal. His bond with Cade and the crew was stronger than ever.

This weekend the last race before the Chase for the NASCAR Sprint Cup would be held under the lights in Richmond, Virginia. Cade was already guaranteed a spot in the run for the championship. The team was firing on all cylinders. They'd won Indy and Michigan. Cade, along with longtime Garrison rival Chance Baker and teammate Shawn Stayton, were the favorites to win it all.

And then there was Rachel. Their friendship, which started as a professional liaison, had deepened, with several layers of intimacy added. With so many emotions tangled through.

Part of him kept waiting for her to leave. To realize he wasn't enough for her, that she needed more.

But she loved him.

She said so all the time.

Of course, she didn't *know* he knew about her feelings. She whispered them at night, after she thought he'd fallen asleep. He was afraid to tell her he could hear her, because he didn't know what to say in return, then she would stop saying them. And leave.

It was a vicious cycle of thrill and denial and confusion that he didn't know how to resolve, though he knew he'd have to, and soon.

Today, however, he was at GRI on a different mission.

Embezzlement.

It was an ugly word. An intimate betrayal. Over the last couple of months, he and Rachel had done nothing, even knowing who was responsible, trying to decide how best to handle the delicate situation and not send the company into a negative spin. But then another phony check had been presented two days ago, and they'd had no choice. The confrontation was at hand.

Parker wanted to break the guy in half for causing Rachel one minute of worry and grief.

"Mr. Parker!" Carmen exclaimed as he walked

toward her desk. After he kissed her cheek, she leaned back, eyeing him closely. "You look happy."

He smiled. "I am."

Rachel talked freely about her worries regarding the pressures of racing, and the toll the business took on relationships. He realized her parents' marriage ending had triggered a long-held fear of growing up and watching families fall apart, only to find her own, once tight-knit family a victim as well.

She obviously understood his own reluctance to discuss the future, since she never brought it up and never asked for a commitment. He kept waiting for some kind of substantial proof that he was the man Rachel would always want. That some grinning doctor wasn't going to come along and lure her away. That happily-ever-after really existed.

Both of them were holding back giving their hearts. Neither wanted to rock the boat, so they floated along, happily enough.

But, eventually, somebody had to cash the check.

"Miss Rachel's waiting for you in her office," Carmen said, her eyes twinkling. "The others should be here soon."

Parker grasped her hands, squeezing them lightly. "We're both in your debt, you know. You never gave up—on either of us."

"I know passion when I see it. I'm a hot Latina woman."

Grinning, Parker kissed her knuckles. "You certainly are."

Carmen's face flushed for a moment, then her eyes narrowed. "And because I'm hot, I'm angry."

"Rachel told you what's happening today?"

"Yes, she did, and I think he should be fired. *Jamie!* Cade's car chief, our brilliant engineer, betraying us all. It's horrible. It's—"

"It needs to be kept quiet."

"I don't want to be quiet. I want to roast his tamale. I want—"

Parker squeezed her hands again. "I know." He, too, had trusted Jamie. But if there was any racing-business mantra he'd learned this year it was *chemistry is key.* One blip in leadership, sponsorship or communication, and your season could be over. It was as devastating as an engineering or mechanical failure—the difference between first and fortieth. "Cade is running for the championship. This is the last thing he needs to worry about."

"You're too calm."

"Believe me, I'm not calm on the inside."

Carmen nodded. "I'm counting on you to make this right."

"I will."

He headed down the hall toward Rachel's office, pausing in the doorway. She hadn't noticed him yet, and he smiled, leaning against the frame, enjoying the opportunity to watch her. She was glaring at the computer screen as if it had called her a foul name moments before.

He could have stood there for ages, staring at her,

thinking about how far they'd come, how far yet they had to go, but Max wasn't as distracted as his mistress. Eyeing Parker with glee and superiority, he hoisted his fat orange body from his comfy quilt, padded out of his basket and leaped onto Rachel's desk.

Absently, without glancing over, she reached out her hand and scratched his head.

Max turned his head toward Parker, his self-assured yellow eyes gleaming. *See, I'm her favorite.*

See if I don't kick you off the bed tonight, Parker thought, sending the cat his own superior glare.

"I wish you two would call a truce," Rachel said, glancing from Max to him, obviously aware of him after all.

"I will if he does." Parker strode into the room, and, bracing his hands on Rachel's chair, leaned down and kissed her with slow thoroughness and long enough to have desire ringing in his ears. "You were gone when I got up this morning."

She reached up, trailing her hand through his hair, which had grown into waves that fell into his eyes, but that she seemed to adore.

He'd grow his hair to his hips if she continued to look at him the way she was now.

"I couldn't sleep," she said, stroking his cheek with her thumb as she sighed. "Today's going to be lousy."

"Mer-owww," Max echoed, ducking his head toward Rachel in sympathy.

"Yes, it will be." There was no way to soften this

or protect her, much as he'd like to. "Good thing I've come equipped with mood boosters."

Her eyes brightened. "Food or presents?"

He'd given her a custom-made checkered flag consisting of onyx and flawless white diamonds hanging from a sterling silver chain, which he'd never seen her take off. Dozens of times, he'd also brought her lasagna from Cardoni's in a plastic container. Both gifts had been received with equal enthusiasm.

"Food," he said, reaching in his pockets.

From one he retrieved a tin of caviar, from the other a four-box assortment of truffles. The cat got the fish eggs; the girl got the chocolate. They both pounced, and he stepped back, smiling as he watched them devour the treats.

"You're amazing," Rachel said, her eyes sparkling as she licked melted chocolate off her fingers.

And you love me.

Would he ever get used to the comfort of just the *thought* of those words? If she actually faced him, looked him right in the eyes and said them, would he run the other way, or would he want to say them in return? If she said them often enough, would he finally believe they were true?

As he forced the questions back, he straightened. They had other questions to answer at the moment.

"Are you ready for this meeting?" he asked.

"No." She shook her head. "No way. But it has to be done."

He drew her close. "I'll be here when it's over."

She wrapped her arms around his waist and laid her cheek against his chest. "I know. I need you here."

He kissed the top of her head. "I'm not going anywhere," he said, then turned as somebody moved into the room.

"Sorry," Bryan said, starting to back out.

"No, come in," Parker said, stepping back. "I'll go."

Rachel held on to his hand. "Oh, no, you won't." Her gaze found his and clung. "You promised to explain to Bryan about the financials."

"I thought you might need a moment to talk, privately, to your brother."

"Please stay."

Bryan flopped into the chair in front of Rachel's desk. "If you guys need violins for this tender moment, you're out of luck."

Rachel glared at her brother. "Nice. You were always the nice one, come to think of it."

"Nice is overrated."

Parker eyed him, his slouched posture, his narrowed eyes and the proverbial chip the size of Montana on his shoulder. From talking with Rachel about him, he knew that she and her mother had coddled him, talked reasonably and even shouted. Nothing seemed to get through to the stubborn guy, and his continued bitterness over the loss of his career and his wife was painful to witness.

Apparently, they didn't call him "Steel" for nothing.

Bryan's personal problems, however, were better

saved for another day. They were about to seriously piss him off with a completely different set of issues.

"Where's Dad?" Rachel asked him.

"Right behind me," Bryan said. "He got stopped in the hall by Sam. You want to tell me what's so important that you wouldn't talk about it on the phone, and you needed both of us here?"

"When Dad gets here," she said.

Bryan's gaze slid from her to Parker. "You two getting married?"

Parker, with extreme skill honed from endless high-level negotiations over the years, managed to keep his expression neutral. And ignored the cold sweat breaking out on his back.

Rachel glanced at him, her face flushing. "Ah, no."

Thankfully, her father came in before he could spend too much time worrying about whether the Garrisons still believed in shotguns.

Mitch Garrison, in contrast to his son, came into the room grin first. He kissed Rachel's cheek, shook Parker's hand, then plopped down into the chair next to Bryan. "What's up, guys?"

Rachel's gaze slid briefly to Parker's, then she blew out a breath and faced her family. "It has come to our attention—actually, Carmen was the first person to notice—that one of our employees has been stealing from the company."

The smile fell away from Mitch's face with startling abruptness. Bryan's lazy pose vanished.

"Stealing?" Mitch echoed.

"How much?" Bryan asked, his eyes lit with angry sparks and turning dark gray, like the steel to match his nickname.

"A bit over fifteen thousand dollars," Rachel said.

Bryan shot to his feet, looking furious enough to spit nails. He was normally a cool negotiator and businessman, but Rachel had told him her brother also had a formidable temper. The proof had leaped like a striking snake.

Mitch closed his eyes briefly. "You're sure?"

Rachel looked over at Parker. "Carmen and I suspected, and Parker helped me confirm. We're sure."

Bryan, who'd been pacing behind his chair, braced his hands on the back of it. "Who?"

"Cade's car chief, Jamie. He has a serious gambling problem, and he's using his girlfriend, who works in accounting, to dig himself out of debt."

Bryan let loose a stream of curse words so vile Parker was tempted to hold his hands over Rachel's ears.

"That's not possible," Mitch said, looking stunned. "He's been such an asset to the team. He'd do anything to help Cade win."

"He has an illness, Daddy. We need to get him help."

Bryan didn't look as though he cared about the reasons. His gaze drilled into Parker's. "Let's go over everything. Step by step."

CHAPTER NINETEEN

"IT WENT OKAY, I guess," Rachel said to Parker, watching her father and brother talk quietly in the corner of her office. "They weren't nearly as mad at me for keeping the embezzling a secret as I thought they'd be."

"They recognized what a sacrifice and burden it had been for you to shoulder. Who knows whether Cade would even be in the Chase if this had come out sooner."

"It still might devastate the team."

"It might, but Jamie had to be stopped. Cade wouldn't want him listed as part of their championship-winning team."

"I appreciate your support for giving them leniency. Bryan would have fired them otherwise."

They'd agreed not to fire Jamie or Laura yet. She would obviously be moved away from accounting, and Jamie would be demoted to support engineer, not traveling with the team or given any authority over the rest of the crew. If he agreed to counseling, they'd

work out a payment schedule and keep the police—
and hopefully the press—out of the arrangement.

Still, Cade was going to be devastated.

"They both have a hard road to prove their
loyalty," Parker said. "They might not."

"I know." She leaned against him, wrapping her
arm around his waist. "I thought I'd feel relieved, but
I just feel sad."

"Me, too."

She looked up at him. If she hadn't had his
support over the last several months, she didn't
know how she would have gotten through all this.
And she was still asking for more. "You sure you
don't mind being the one to tell Cade and Isabel? I
want to stick with my dad."

"I think they'll take it better from me. It makes
things more businesslike."

"You sure you're not just trying to protect me in
case they go ballistic for keeping this to myself?"

He kissed her temple. "They won't blame you."

"I'm not so sure. And watch out, Isabel has a
mean right hook."

Parker gave a mock shudder. "I've seen her at
that punching bag in the basement. Believe me, I'll
keep my distance."

She laughed, deciding that was wise when
dealing with her volatile sister-in-law, then patted his
chest for encouragement. "After we meet with Jamie
and Laura, I'm following my dad home and fixing
him dinner, okay?"

"You think he has questions about the money?"

"No, I don't think so. He has faith in you, me and Bryan. I need to talk to him about other stuff."

He searched her gaze, questions lurking in his eyes. But she wasn't ready to share yet.

Bryan's casual question about them getting married had sparked a flood of emotions. Oddly enough, the thought of lifelong commitment hadn't sent her pulse into a wild panic.

Broken marriages littered the landscape around her, and there were no guarantees about anything in life, least of all love. But whenever she looked at Parker, and her heart flipped over, she was sure everything was right.

Nearly perfect, in fact.

"You'll come by my place later?" he asked, brushing a strand of hair off her face.

She leaned into him with a smile. "Mmm. I might even bring the red shoes."

"That is an absolutely cruel thing to say to a man who has to spend the next few hours explaining to your brother why he's going to be short one crew member, one *critical* crew member, in a *critical* Saturday-night race right before the Chase begins."

She pretended to be offended. "I thought it would give you something to look forward to."

He grinned wickedly. "And now that I am, you have to deliver."

"I walked right into that trap."

"You certainly did."

She pursed her lips. "Go find Cade."

He squeezed her hand. "And break his heart?"

"Hopefully, it'll be only a bruise." Conscious of her father and brother standing a few feet away, she lightly pressed her lips to Parker's, then let him go.

There would be time later for more than a peck. There could be a lifetime of touches and smiles if they could both find the courage to reach for them.

She survived the meeting with Jamie and Laura by sitting behind her desk, her hands clenched together, trying to keep pity foremost in her mind rather than anger. The chill in Bryan's eyes, and the disappointment in her father's, communicated more than words ever could, the seriousness and depth of everyone's disappointment.

Laura cried, and Jamie bowed his head in shame, but, by the end, Rachel had hope that they could all work through the betrayal and make a new start.

AS SHE AND HER DAD rode up the speedway elevator toward his Turn One condo, she clutched the sack of groceries they'd bought and said little.

Mitch Garrison had seen a lot in NASCAR racing, both good and bad. He'd watched the sport go from a largely regional sport to an international one. He'd watched drivers get more high profile, piloting planes and helicopters, accompanied by personal assistants and PR directors to every race, sponsor commitment and autographing. He'd seen salaries and costs rise to heights never dreamed at the beginning. He'd been part of both dominant and struggling teams. He'd shifted from driver to owner. From upstart North Carolina boy to respected legend.

Through it all his charm and talent never wavered. But today he'd taken a hard blow.

Glancing at him out of the corner of her eye, knowing he was blaming himself, Rachel grasped his hand as they walked down the hall. "The team will get through this."

"Yeah." At the entrance to his condo, before he unlocked the door, he cupped her cheek. "Thanks to you."

Swallowing a lump of tears, she gripped his wrist. "Are you sure? Did I do the right thing?"

"You did." His mouth turned up in a smile. "Sometimes I think you're the strongest, and wisest, of us all."

She hugged him, relief at his approval flooding her, the doubts she'd held fading away. After a moment, she leaned back. *"Sometimes?"*

Laughing, he unlocked the door, and they headed inside. Since she was relieved to be at peace with her decisions about the embezzling, she didn't move into negative territory and roll her eyes at her father's bachelor pad. Fur rugs and slick, black leather furniture dominated the decor, and a disco ball hung over the coffee table. She'd heard a rumor from her brothers that the bed in the master suite vibrated. Rachel, cringing at the very idea, had never dared venture beyond the kitchen, living area and foyer bathroom.

Even Cade, who'd been a wildly popular and

dedicated bachelor until he'd been blindsided by Isabel, thought it was tacky.

Thankfully, the kitchen was relatively normal, with dove-gray tile and dark oak cabinets. She broiled salmon, steamed green beans and roasted new potatoes and was incredibly grateful to Parker and his sous-chef at Cardoni's, who'd taken the time to give them cooking lessons over the last few weeks.

The lessons had been a big part of the bonding between her and Parker. In his wise and subtle way, he was reminding her that racing was not all they had in common. If NASCAR's president took ballroom dancing, they could cook.

Just as John had advised months ago, taking time as a couple, making each other a priority, was important in any relationship, and only more so for anybody trying to build something meaningful in the high-pressure world of big-time auto racing.

When had her parents started to drift away from each other? Had racing been their only commonality? And when that interest waned for her mother, had their bond suffered beyond repair? Had Bryan's accident simply been an excuse to escape?

She wanted answers to those questions. As much as it might hurt and worry her, she needed to know.

Leaning back in her chair, facing her father across the kitchen table, she sipped from her glass of tea. "Are you going to marry Bambi?"

His gaze jumped to hers. "Good grief, no. What gave you that idea?"

"Beyond you two being attached at the hip for the last several months, including coziness at Cade's wedding? Racing Surfer."

Confusion pinched his face. "The racing-insider Web site?"

"Uh-huh." *He knows,* her mother had said about the Webmaster. He did. And he had a reputation for being dead-on with rumors that eventually became reality. Her father's reaction certainly made several suspicions click over to truth for her. "It seems to me his source could be only one of two people—you or Bambi. Since you deny it, that narrows the suspects pretty significantly."

Though Mitch Garrison had often been accused, among the family anyway, of being focused on racing and only racing, he was quick to pick up the direction of her thoughts. "You think Bambi's telling people we're getting married?"

"I do."

He sighed. "Hell." Rising from his chair, he grabbed a beer from the fridge. He twisted off the top of the bottle and drank. "That's not going to happen. I'm just…" As his words trailed off, he looked at the floor.

"You're just playing around."

"I can't have this conversation with my daughter."

Rachel's heart jabbed at her ribs. It wasn't a pleasant sensation, but it was necessary. And finally, *finally,* she was going to get some answers. "Too late. You are."

His eyes fired, much like Bryan's did in a fit of

temper. The move was calculated to force people to step back. "I'm a single man. I'm not allowed to date?"

She didn't move—forward or backward. "Sure you are. I just don't like seeing you get used."

"She's not—"

"Oh, please."

He turned away from her, bracing his hands on the kitchen counter.

She'd hurt him, and she hadn't meant to. The truth was often desired and not always appreciated. She'd told him opinions about his life that had lain on her heart for a while. He had to decide how to react to them. But for her to move on, to have any clarity in her own life, she had to ask even more difficult questions.

"Why did you and Mom break up?"

He turned, but he'd shut down his emotions, as if she'd pulled a shade over them. "That's between us."

As the fury of impotence, the lack of understanding and the pain rose, so did she. "I have the right to know." When he remained silent and stubborn, she walked toward him, her fists clenched. "You made me question my belief in love, in happily-ever-after. I'm afraid to take chances. I'm afraid of marriage. *I want to know why.*"

The moment hung in the air. They watched each other.

She glared; he sighed.

"Don't be afraid," he said suddenly, his voice low and rusty. He took two steps toward her, then pulled her against him. "It's my fault. It's my fault."

She held him tight. "It's okay."

"No, it isn't. You should blame me." Drawing a shuddering breath, he continued, "Blame me for the divorce."

She leaned back, cupping his cheeks between her hands. "Daddy, please. Don't."

"It's time." He tried to smile. "It's a day for revelations, isn't it?" He kissed her forehead, then backed away, as if he needed space to say what he had to say. "After Bryan's accident, I thought my life could be over any minute. Crazy, huh? Racing cars for twenty years I never even thought about the risk. But watching Bryan get hurt, lying in the hospital and not knowing if he'd ever walk again, much less race, made me miss the good old days. When I felt young and invulnerable.

"I'm trying to recapture something that's long gone. I need to accept where I am in life, to realize I'm not twenty anymore and move on. Instead, I'm stuck. I left your mother. She didn't do anything wrong. The divorce is my fault."

Walking toward him, Rachel let go of the anger she'd harbored. It rose and twisted away as if a strong breeze had rushed through the room.

You make your own life. You risk your own heart.

Her life wasn't perfect. Racing was hard. Life was hard. Neither her parents' relationship, nor the ones with her brothers, friends, employees, business associates or anybody else was always easy. But she was going to take the path less traveled, and hoped that would make all the difference.

"You can always change your mind," she said.

Her father leaned back, his gaze meeting hers. "How serious is your mother about that florist?"

Rachel smiled. "Maybe you should ask her."

THE LAPS OF THE Richmond race were winding down.

Cade was already guaranteed a spot in the Chase for the NASCAR Sprint Cup, but Parker and the rest of the team were elated to see him running fifth. Momentum was as important as quality equipment as they moved into the last ten races.

He and Rachel stood behind the pit wall with Isabel, while Sam, Mitch and Bryan sat atop the war wagon just behind them. They'd all wanted to form a circle of support. Jamie's absence was deeply felt by everyone, even though only a few people knew the real reason he wasn't around. The media and most of the team had been told he was away due to a family emergency.

The week had been stressful and a relief at the same time. Stressful to fill the job of a man who'd been such an integral part of the team, but there was relief in having an important race to focus on.

Parker's headphones exploded with news.

"Cade Garrison, in the No. 56 Huntington Hotels Chevrolet makes a move to the inside!"

Parker jumped to his feet, watching Cade flying out of Turn Four, and as he passed the fourth-place car, the momentum carried him across the start/finish line on the back bumper of the guy in third.

"Four laps to go!" the announcer called. "Can Garrison make another move, does he have enough laps to get to the front?"

Isabel paced beside them. Rachel grabbed Parker's hand, squeezing it tight. There was both excitement and trepidation in her eyes.

Cade passed two more cars and was making his move on the leader as the white flag flew. Rachel was bouncing up and down. Isabel had stopped pacing, her head turning as Cade did, racing out of Turn Two.

"Garrison's alongside the leader now. They're door to door!"

They flew into Turn Three with Cade unable to make the pass. He ducked behind the leader, following the inside groove, then jumped to the outside as they exited Turn Four.

It seemed Parker's heart was pounding as fast and as loud as the cars moved on the track.

But at the line, the leader took Cade by inches.

"What a battle to the end!" the announcer said, sounding breathless. "That was a close one, folks."

Parker pulled off his headset after he heard Sam tell Cade he'd done a great job. He hugged Isabel and Rachel to his sides, kissing each of them full on the lips. "We'll move into third in the Chase."

The women looked up at him. "How did you

figure that out so quickly?" Isabel asked, looking shocked.

"Well…" he began, feeling somewhat self-conscious.

"He has a thing for numbers," Rachel explained.

"You're weird," Isabel said.

Her arm around his waist, Rachel squeezed him. "I think he's pretty brilliant."

"Don't forget sweet," he said, smiling down at her.

"Are Cade and I this sappy?" was Isabel's question.

"Yes," Parker and Rachel said at the same time.

Cade pulled his car into the pit box seconds later. After hoisting himself out, getting a hat and a can of Go! from a team member, he kissed Isabel, then did the media interviews. He looked exhausted—four hundred miles at Richmond was no easy task—but not devastated by his defeat.

After the media moved on, Parker handed him a fresh towel and a water bottle. "Nice race."

"Yeah." Cade wiped his face. "Let's have a party."

Parker raised an eyebrow. "We're having a party to celebrate second place?"

Cade shrugged. "Everybody could use a pick-me-up."

On the flight home, Cade continued to rally and motivate the team. As of tomorrow, they were in third place and running for a NASCAR Sprint Cup Series championship. Nobody brought up that Chance Baker was second. Or that their teammate, Shawn

Stayton, was sixth. Or that their other teammate, and sentimental fan favorite, Kevin Reiner, was first.

Tonight they were all together and content. Tomorrow the pressure would crank up again, and the real battle would begin.

After phone calls to a pizza place and liquor store that both delivered on the way to Cade's, Parker found himself sitting on the sofa in the basement game room, a glass of Merlot in his hand, with Sam and Bryan sitting next to him, already plotting strategy and setups for the first Chase for the NASCAR Sprint Cup race in New Hampshire.

But he was watching Rachel, sitting between Jay and Dean, on the other side of the room, playing video games. From the looks of things, she was kicking their butts.

She glanced back at him, and their gazes met for a moment. His heart stuttered in his chest, joy swamping him.

The unexpected swell of emotion came more frequently these days, bringing happiness, then concern, then panic. The fear that she'd leave him the way his mother had, that the feelings she had for him were only temporary, was like a knife pointed at his throat.

"Excuse me, guys," he said to Sam and Bryan as he rose from the couch. Neither one of them seemed to notice he was gone. They continued to debate air pressure as he walked away, heading toward the back door.

He set his wineglass on the bar, then opened the

door and slipped outside. Wandering over to the pool deck, he noticed with relief that the chairs were deserted. He lowered himself to the end of a lounge chair and stared at the water, reflected blue by the bottom of the pool. The color was nearly identical to Rachel's eyes.

He loved her.

He'd put up a hell of a fight, for a good long time, but despite his resistance, his desperate efforts to avoid, then ignore, his feelings, he was a goner. Had his father felt this same way about his mother only to have everything fall apart? Only to wind up bitter and alone?

He was sure he did.

But here was the thing, the thing he must have known from the very beginning but was too busy making excuses to acknowledge, Rachel wasn't his mother. In fact, she wasn't *anything* like her. She was warm and genuine. She cared for and protected her family with everything in her. She was their matriarch. She'd stand for him as she stood for them. She'd love him as she did them.

And he wasn't his father. At least he didn't have to be.

He continued staring at the water, the ripples caused by the pump, the light filling the air around him with a warm glow. Rachel did that. Her belief in him continued to ripple through his life, her light replaced all the fear and darkness.

When he heard footsteps a couple of minutes later, he glanced over to see her heading toward him.

"What's wrong?" she asked, looking down at him.

"Nothing." He rose, kissing her thoroughly, with all the need and happiness running around inside him. "Everything's perfect, in fact."

"Yeah?" She angled her head. "Everybody's inside, big party going on, the team rallied, the Chase is about to begin, and you're out here, alone, staring into the water like you just lost your best friend. You kiss me like you're about to go on a month-long sabbatical. Everything is clearly not perfect."

"Well, not quite yet." He searched her gaze, waiting for the fear to overwhelm him, smiling when the optimism and confidence remained. "I've been thinking about us. About the future."

Along with surprise, something sweet and hopeful moved through her eyes. "You are?"

"You love me, don't you?"

She drew a quick, shocked breath.

"I hear you." He stroked her cheek. "When you tell me at night before we go to sleep."

She tried to take a step back, but he pulled her closer. "Every time?" she asked, looking stricken.

"From the trip to New York and afterward."

She bit her lip. "That's every time."

He was glad he hadn't missed one. Though how he'd gotten through all those nights without holding his breath, he'd never know. "Please tell me again, right here, to my face."

She searched his gaze, and though she must have

a million questions and doubts, she gave him what he needed anyway. "I love you, Parker."

He kissed her, tenderly, slowly. "I love you, too. I've loved you…forever. I know it took me a while to come around to it, to admit you're everything I want, but now that I have, it's there. Forever."

She held on tight. Her eyes were fierce with determination. "You never have to worry. I'll never leave you."

"I know." He brushed her hair off her beautiful face. "But let's get married anyway and make it official."

Rachel's heart kicked hard, once, then resumed its normal rhythm. "We—you—you're kidding."

"Definitely not." Laughing, he leaned back, and she saw an emotion so strong, so happy, she had to swallow a lump of tears. "I've thought long and hard before committing my heart to a risky project, finding just the right woman to fall for, and I'm going to work like crazy to make our relationship successful long term."

She cocked her head. "That sounds familiar."

"It should. You said the same thing to me, more or less, a few months ago."

"Okay, so…married? Really? You think we're ready?"

"Sure. I'll give you until Christmas. We'll have a grand party at the hotel."

She pursed her lips. That sounded too much like Cade and Isabel's wedding. "How about a small ceremony? Maybe here, in Cade's backyard. Or at Mom's. We could have an arbor of roses."

"Either is fine. But soon. I don't want a long, drawn-out engagement."

Rachel nodded. "I'm with you. Cade and Isabel's was way too much to deal with. Though I guess we wouldn't have to worry about your mom trying to plan every detail like my mom will want to?"

"No. But she might come for the party."

That didn't sound promising either. She was likely to smack the woman for causing Parker so much pain.

They stared at each other.

"Let's elope," he said.

"Let's go," she said at the same time.

Grinning, she grasped his hand. "Come on."

"Now?"

"Now."

"But…now?"

She tugged his hand and he followed, albeit with a stuttering step. "Should we go with the traditionally tacky and go to Vegas?"

"I have a lovely hotel on the Strip. We'll make reservations."

"Actually, I've always liked the Grove Park Inn in Asheville," she said, ignoring his panic as swiftly as she tamped down her own flutters. "We could be there in less than two hours."

"I don't think I'm familiar with that particular establishment."

"Oh yes you are. It's historic. It's close."

"I own any number of hotels…"

"You should buy this one. Maybe you can talk to the manager after the ceremony. They have a great spa, too."

"You want me to get married now, tonight, at the competition?"

"Yes."

He pulled her to a stop. "Rachel, isn't this a little impulsive? We've only been dating for a few months."

"But you've loved me forever. You just said so. Are you going to change your mind about marrying me in a couple of weeks or months?"

"Of course not."

"Then what are we waiting for?"

"I'm waiting for your sanity to return."

She scowled. "See. We've only been engaged for three minutes, and we're already arguing. I don't want to spend six months picking out bridesmaids' dresses and having anxiety attacks over what color the napkins should be. Been there, done that. No thanks."

"I agree completely. Bachelor parties in particular bring back negative memories. But…*now?*"

She angled her head. "If you have an overwhelming desire to wear a tux to the ceremony, we'll stop by your place and get yours. You probably have half a dozen of them, though, so start thinking about which one you're going to wear now."

"What are you going to wear?"

"Does it matter?"

He grinned. "No. No, it certainly doesn't."

She wrapped her arms around his neck, pressing herself tightly against his broad, firm chest, the place where she wanted to lay her head every night, the place where she wanted to cry when she was sad and laugh when she was happy. "You've become my life, Parker. Everything you are fits with me like I've found the other half of my soul. I used to be afraid of taking a chance with you. You were afraid to give in to what you felt for me. Let's not be afraid anymore."

His gaze searched hers, and the love and devotion she saw in his eyes was unwavering. "I'm not."

He kissed her, and she knew that of all the risks, chances and leaps of faith she'd ever taken in her life in racing, this one was the most important, and the one she had absolutely no fear of regretting.

Grabbing her hand, he led her around the garage, presumably toward his car, while taking his cell phone out of his pocket with the other.

"Don't call anybody," she said anxiously. "They might try to stop us."

"How about if I call Carmen's son?"

"The lawyer, the priest or the doctor?"

"I bet, my love, you can figure out who's most important at the moment."

EPILOGUE

THE END-OF-THE-SEASON celebration and belated wedding reception took place the weekend after the last race in the backyard of Rachel's mother's house.

Parker had volunteered the hotel, but since his mother-in-law of barely two months was already annoyed at him for denying her daughter a splashy wedding, he figured he ought to bow to her wishes and let her have her way on the reception. He and Rachel wanted only each other, and the event had turned out more like a homey barbecue, which seemed to suit everybody.

He certainly had no regrets, and he figured it was a husband's duty to protect his wife from her determined mother when necessary.

For Cade and the No. 56 team, the disruption with Jamie had been both a motivator and a distraction, but, in the end, two mechanical failures and one fluke wreck had left Cade fourth in points.

Teammate Kevin Reiner had won the championship—his fourth—and abruptly announced his retirement. The racing world was buzzing about who would fill the legend's driving shoes. The Garrison clan was having daily meetings and interviews to figure out what to do. Most of the quality drivers had already signed for next season. At the moment, they were hoping to lure Kevin into a partial schedule and shift one of the other GRI drivers from another series.

The plan was looking hopeful as Reiner was at the party tonight and had brought what now seemed his traditional truckload of Splash as a wedding gift. Every time Parker saw one of the crew, they grinned and asked if he'd mind doing their laundry this week.

Absently noticing the roses and ivy artfully framing the tables, the catering staff seeing to the guests' comfort, Parker wandered around the edges of the lighted tent, looking for his wife. He recalled Cade and Isabel never leaving each other's side during their reception, but he and Rachel had somehow been separated almost from the moment they'd arrived.

Seeing Isabel and Carmen stomping toward him, he wished he had a handy column to duck behind. This *couldn't* be good.

"Would you tell *her* I'm the one who got you and Rachel together?" Isabel demanded, pointing at Carmen.

"I—"

"You remember it was me, Mr. Parker, who encouraged you all those months? You even thanked me for helping you, remember?"

"You thanked *her?*" Isabel asked pointedly.

Parker scrambled for a reply. "Well…yes. She was the first to recognize—"

"*Please.*" Isabel crossed her arms over her chest, shifting her glare from him to Carmen. "I had the *hard* job. I had to deal with their issues, make a battle plan."

Parker raised his eyebrows. "*Battle* plan?"

"Custer couldn't have done a better job," Isabel insisted.

"Custer lost," Parker reminded her.

Carmen's face flushed with satisfaction. "You know your history like you know your matchmaking."

"Look here," Isabel said, jabbing her finger toward their office manager, "I'm tired of you…"

Parker used the distraction of their argument to sneak off. He *really* wanted to find his wife. But he hadn't moved more than a few feet away when he encountered Bryan.

"You and Cade are making me look like an idiot in the relationship department," he said, then scowled.

"Sorry."

Where *was* Rachel? Aside from this being their party, and simply wanting to be with her, he'd also gotten the revised drawings back from the architect that afternoon. He wanted her to see the changes. If they agreed, their house could be under construction in two months.

"I figure you owe me," Bryan said.

Parker finally gave his brother-in-law his full attention. "I do?"

Bryan looked down, then his gaze jerked up to meet Parker's. "You said you knew somebody who could help me." He paused, then added more quietly, "With my knee."

Knowing how hard it was for Bryan to ask for anything from anybody, Parker simply nodded. "I do. I'll make some calls."

"Okay. Fine."

Arms slid around Parker from behind. The scent of floral vanilla washed over him. "I missed you," Rachel said huskily in his ear.

Parker turned, framing her face with his hands, absorbing the warmth of her body. "Mmm." He kissed her. "There you are."

"I'm outta here," Bryan said, moving off.

Rachel's eyebrows drew together as she stared at Parker. "We always run him off."

"That's not always a bad thing."

She grinned. She was in an upbeat mood, one that never failed to spark his desire. Not that much *doused* his desire. "I wore your favorite color, you know."

He glanced at her jeans and red sweater. "Blue or red?"

"Underneath," she said, her eyes sparkling.

"Mr. Huntington?"

Reluctantly, Parker turned toward the waiter

bearing a tray of champagne glasses. Knowing he'd soon have his bride all to himself—though not soon enough, in his opinion—he scooped up two flutes for him and Rachel.

They'd just tapped their glasses when Rachel's mother and his grandmother appeared next to them. After a semblance at pleasant conversation, Barbara Garrison faced her daughter.

"You're not pregnant, are you, dear?"

Rachel choked on her champagne, and Parker felt his face heat as he patted his wife on the back.

"No," Rachel managed to say after a minute. "No, I'm not."

Barbara glanced around nervously. "But an elopement. Honey, people are…well, wondering."

Fingering her choker of pearls, his grandmother sniffed. "*Somebody* has to carry on the next generation of Huntingtons. You two need to get started."

Parker tried to control his astonishment. *If you people would leave us alone for two minutes…*

"The Garrison legacy is just as important, you know," Barbara said, shifting her glare to Henrietta Huntington.

"Of course it is." She leaned toward Barbara. "Don't you think he should cut his hair?"

"Well, it *is* a bit long."

As they dug into their discussion of legacies and haircuts, Parker grabbed Rachel's hand and pulled her into the crowd, hoping to disappear. After several thank-yous, handshakes and hugs, he managed to guide his wife beyond the lights of the tents, to the edge of the woods that bordered the property.

Rachel looked back at the party they'd deserted. "Parker, what—"

"I need you," he said, pulling her against him. "Only you."

She held him tight, as he had no doubt she'd do every day of their lives. Her fingers flicked away the band holding his hair, which had grown to the point that he often pulled it into a short ponytail at the nape of his neck. "Thanks for letting Mom plan this party."

"Thanks for telling my grandmother she ought to…" He leaned back and met her gaze, trying to recall the exact words. "Lighten up and let me do my job?"

"I've about had enough of her calls at 7:00 a.m. Formidable, she certainly is, but I need my sleep."

"When you're the matriarch and CEO of your families, it's hard to retreat from responsibilities."

"But we can try, can't we?"

He glanced, for just a second, at the people who cared about them, gathered in one place. Then he looked back at her, the one who mattered above them all. "It's crazy how much I love you."

She linked her hands around the back of his neck. "You think you shouldn't feel that much?"

"Not at all. I'm very glad I do."

"Then can we elope from our reception?"

LIZ ALLISON &
WENDY ETHERINGTON

77263   NO HOLDING BACK   ___ $6.99 U.S. ___ $8.50 CAN.

(limited quantities available)

TOTAL AMOUNT	$ _____
POSTAGE & HANDLING	$ _____
($1.00 FOR 1 BOOK, 50¢ for each additional)	
APPLICABLE TAXES*	$ _____
TOTAL PAYABLE	$ _____

(check or money order—please do not send cash)

To order, complete this form and send it, along with a check or money order for the total above, payable to HQN Books, to: **In the U.S.:** 3010 Walden Avenue, P.O. Box 9077, Buffalo, NY 14269-9077; **In Canada:** P.O. Box 636, Fort Erie, Ontario, L2A 5X3.

Name: _____

Address: _____ City: _____

State/Prov.: _____ Zip/Postal Code: _____

Account Number (if applicable): _____

075 CSAS

*New York residents remit applicable sales taxes.
*Canadian residents remit applicable GST and provincial taxes.

HQN™
We *are* romance™

www.HQNBooks.com   PHLAWE1008BL

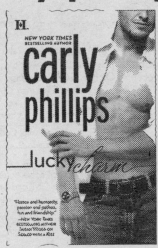

REQUEST YOUR FREE BOOKS!

2 FREE NOVELS
FROM THE ROMANCE/SUSPENSE
COLLECTION PLUS 2 FREE GIFTS!

BOB08R